D0276222

DEADLY IMPACT

LIBRARIES NI
WITHDRAWN FROM STOCK

DEADLY IMPACT

Peter Tonkin

This first world edition published 2014
in Great Britain and the USA by
SEVERN HOUSE PUBLISHERS LTD of
19 Cedar Road, Sutton, Surrey, England, SM2 5DA.

Copyright © 2014 by Peter Tonkin.

All rights reserved.
The moral right of the author has been asserted.

British Library Cataloguing in Publication Data

Tonkin, Peter
  Deadly impact. – (A Richard Mariner adventure; 28)
  1. Mariner, Richard (Fictitious character)–Fiction.
  2. Piracy–Fiction. 3. Liquefied gas carriers–Fiction.
  4. Remote control–Fiction. 5. Sea stories.
  I. Title II. Series
  823.9'2-dc23

ISBN-13: 978-0-7278-8365-0 (cased)

Except where actual historical events and characters are being
described for the storyline of this novel, all situations in this
publication are fictitious and any resemblance to living persons
is purely coincidental.

All Severn House titles are printed on acid-free paper.

Severn House Publishers support the Forest Stewardship Council™ [FSC™],
the leading international forest certification organisation. All our titles that
are printed on FSC certified paper carry the FSC logo.

Typeset by Palimpsest Book Production Ltd.,
Falkirk, Stirlingshire, Scotland.
Printed and bound in Great Britain by
TJ International, Padstow, Cornwall.

For Cham, Guy and Mark, as always.
And with thanks to Jason Prout.

100 Hours to Impact

iquified Natural Gas Transporter *Sayonara* heads out of Rat Island Pass west of Hawadax Island, through Alaska's Aleutian Island chain from the Arctic Ocean's Bering Sea south into the North Pacific. It is ten minutes before six a.m., ship's time, twelve hours adrift of London time and slightly out of synch with the Hawaii-Aleutian Daylight Time of the nearest land. In this as in so much else, the great ship is a law unto herself. But *Sayonara* is precisely on schedule.

As *Sayonara* pushes south out of one ocean into another, from a distance she seems to be like any of the other ships which follow the route from North America to the Orient. But she is not. A close observer would note her strange, bulging foredeck that looks like the hull of a second, smaller vessel secured upside down between her forepeak and her bridge house. This white steel whaleback covers the upper hemispheres of the huge spherical gas tanks containing her cargo. It stands so high that the stumpy little bridge house seems only just tall enough to peep over it. The restricted view from the command bridge is not important, for she is being guided by her on-board GPS system, not a helmsman or watch officer.

The nearest thing she has to a captain is her main command programme which governs the systems controlling her engines and rudder as well as those overseeing her cargo and her security. The only thing it does not control is the black box voyage recorder which transmits its information separately from all the other systems on board. She is as independent of humanity as she is of their terrestrial time zones. Keen eyes might note that there is no one about any of the numberless jobs which usually need doing when a vessel is at sea. But even the keenest eyes would never discern that she is being guided by computer – and by computer alone. There is not one living crewman on board her. She is, in effect, the world's largest robot.

Deep in that strange little bridge, instead of a complement

of officers and men, stands an on-board system which is even now – at six a.m. precisely according to the on-board chronometer – reporting *Sayonara*'s position to a satellite in low orbit above, confirming the information sent by the black box. She is exactly five one point five seven one degrees west and one seven eight point four four three degrees north. She is experiencing a counter-current that threatens to slow her. The satellite immediately contacts her ship's management systems. These in turn adjust the steam turbines powering her, raising the revolutions, the pitch of the propellers driving her and the angle of the rudders guiding her.

Likewise, the control systems have just reported her heading as two hundred and fifty degrees exactly – with no adjustment necessary for magnetic variation, because the GPS satellite observes with absolute accuracy precisely where on the surface of the globe she is – and knows her heading with extra-terrestrial exactness. She is as independent of the magnetic forces that affect navigators' compasses as she is of human time. The computers helm her along her pre-programmed course with complete exactitude no matter what the pressures of wind, weather, tide or current. And that course lies along the Great Circle route towards her destination at the newly constructed NIPEX floating gas storage facility and terminal off the Kashima-Nada Sea Terminal, Choshi City, Japan. She is due to arrive there in precisely one hundred hours: four days and four hours. In ship's time that will be 10 a.m. on the morning of the fifth day, but on arrival *Sayonara* will come under the control of Japan Standard Time, which will stand at 6 a.m., local.

The NIPEX terminal, still remote in time and distance from *Sayonara*, stands at the point of a promontory protecting the floating city of Kujukuri, which is currently taking shape in the bay immediately south of it, east of Tokyo City. The floating city is designed to extend the metropolis already there, to add much-needed living space to the mega-city covering the Boso Peninsula. It is a child of the Shinzo Abe administration's neo-Keynesian policy of government investment in infrastructure development – and of that overwhelming need to house people in the megalopolis of Tokyo and the suburbs closest to it.

When *Sayonara* and her sisters begin their regular LNG runs, the whole area, on land or sea, will be powered by the brand-new NIPEX gas-fired power station there. In the meantime, the power to the growing city – and to those still building it – comes from the Bashnev/Sevmash floating nuclear facility *Zemlya*, which will be tugged away from the nervously anti-nuclear islands as soon as NIPEX is fully operational. NIPEX has been co-financed by the Heritage Mariner Shipping Company, which is expanding eastwards much as BP once expanded westwards. *Sayonara* herself has been entirely financed by them, though her insurance is with a Lloyds of London syndicate. The profits promised by the overlapping projects are all-but incalculable. But so are the dangers.

Consequently, once an hour, on the hour, a zipped file of information is flashed at light-speed from the ship's management systems via the satellites monitoring *Sayonara* to a control room on the top storey of Heritage House in London. The file is also copied to Mitsubishi in Kobe, who are responsible for the engineering, and to the NIPEX facility in Choshi, where a team stands ready twenty-four seven to take remote control of the ship in case anything major goes wrong – like the USAF handlers in Creech Base, Indian Springs or their British counterparts at RAF Waddington, controlling drones in the skies above Afghanistan.

As *Sayonara* heads sedately into the North Pacific, the low sun outlines the chain of islands through which she has just passed and the vastness of the Arctic Ocean to the north behind them. It also illuminates the windswept hunk of land that has been recently rechristened with its Aleut name *Hawadax* after the rats that had caused it to be known as *Rat Island* since the 1820s were finally exterminated. The near-horizontal sunbeams also illuminate an arrow-head of fast rigid inflatable boats or RIBs racing out of the shadows on the dark side of Hawadax Island. Like a squadron of black jet fighters, they power across the calm dawn seas of Rat Island Pass towards *Sayonara*'s cliff-like stern. They bounce across the big vessel's wake, catching up with arrogant ease thanks to their big, powerful outboards capable of twice *Sayonara*'s top speed. Within a very few minutes, the RIBs are clustered around the huge vessel's stern.

Each is packed with men dressed in black cargoes and roll necks under black bulletproof vests. They wear black boots and gloves. Some of them wear black balaclavas while the rest carry them. They all wear MTM black-faced combat watches so precisely synchronized that the seconds click by in unison. The men in the bows put stubby rifles to their shoulders, aiming high. Lines soar upwards. Hooks grapple on to the aft safety rails – positioned to protect the long-departed skeleton crew and the pilot who guided *Sayonara* out of the LNG facility in Anchorage and down to the Unimak Pass. There she had joined the Great Circle Route heading north into the Bering Sea, and gone into full automatic mode. Lines allow the first few men to swing up over the stern. Once they are safely on the poop, under the shadow of the one big twenty-four-seater lifeboat that hangs there sideways behind the truncated bridge, it is only a matter of moments before they have set up winches to pull the rest of the men on board – and the bags and boxes of equipment they have brought with them.

As the RIBs cut loose and race back, the men beneath the lifeboat set to work. The bags and boxes are opened. A range of equipment is unpacked. The tallest man seems to be the leader. He opens his silver laptop and brings up a schematic of *Sayonara*'s bridge and internal sections, overlaid with her safety and security systems. As his companions finish emptying the boxes, he examines the vessel's most intimate systems with pale, cold eyes, nodding with satisfaction as everything he sees seems familiar, just as he'd expected it to be for a state-of-the-art LNG transporter. Around him, the bustle of activity slows and ceases. The others, kitted up, look expectantly at him. 'You know your points of entry,' he says in English, coloured with a Dutch accent that could come from Amsterdam or South Africa. 'You know what you have to do.'

The toe of his boot pushes the last kitbag across the deck towards them and they fall upon it silently, unzipping its top and pulling out an assortment of weapons. No more is said. They split into four teams with oft-rehearsed ease and vanish forward, past the low wings of the stubby bridge house. The leader, with his own team, lingers longest. He gestures at the other men who pack the bags and boxes out of sight. Then they too pick up their weapons and run forward.

At the starboard bulkhead door which opens into the bridge's A-Deck corridor, they pause. The leader consults his laptop, and then punches a long, complicated number into the security lock. The door swings wide open. All in all, it has taken the men less than an hour to get aboard, equip themselves and break into the unmanned vessel.

99 Hours to Impact

As soon as the bulkhead door to *Sayonara*'s A Deck swung wide open, a light on top of the receiver equipment in Heritage House started flashing red. The team keeping an eye on this new equipment went into a routine as carefully rehearsed as that of the men on board their vessel on the far side of the world. This was probably a security drill; the latest of many, but on the other hand . . .

It was seven p.m. London time and Richard and Robin Mariner were dressed and ready to attend the Old Vic Theatre for the premier of Kevin Spacey's revival of Eugene O'Neill's masterpiece *Long Day's Journey into Night*. Heritage Mariner was one of the theatre's sponsors. The Mariners were to be seated with other VIPs in the dress circle and were attired appropriately. The instant the red light flashed, however, Richard's cellphone started ringing. He put his brand-new Galaxy to his ear and a robot voice alerted him. 'It's *Sayonara*,' he said to Robin. 'Red alert.'

'Another security check?' she demanded from in front of the long mirror, settling her cocktail dress on her hips.

'It was last time. But of course, you can never tell . . .'

When in London, Richard and Robin always stayed in the company flat which shared the top floor of Heritage House with the offices where the computers were located – just beneath the mass of communications equipment on the roof. Richard strode into the huge, computer-filled room minutes later, with Robin at his side.

'That's it,' Robin said, grimly, looking at the flashing red alarm. 'Again.'

'Yup,' Richard agreed. 'Code Red as ever was. Someone unauthorized has gone aboard. What do the remote control team at NIPEX say, Indira?'

The computer operator glanced across at the monitor that linked to the NIPEX facility in Japan. 'They're locked out,' she said. 'It happened the instant the red alarm went up, before we were even sure what was going on. They can't communicate with the on-board systems let alone override them. They've lost control of *Sayonara*. Same as the last drill.'

'Looks like we'll have to send apologies to Mr Spacey and get a team of our own aboard,' Richard said grimly. 'Indira, can you get some visuals on this? It'd be good to have some idea what we're up against.'

'Visuals just coming, Richard,' promised the young computer expert, her fingers busy. She glanced up at her tall employer almost shyly. She had seen Richard and Robin under a wide range of circumstances during her time here, but never in full evening dress. Richard towered behind her now, his slim-hipped, deep-chested frame clad in black braided trousers and evening jacket with satin lapels. His waffle-patterned shirt front was held closed by onyx studs and he favoured the current fashion for Continental cross-over ties which sat neatly beneath the snowy wings of his collar.

It looked to Indira's fashion-conscious eyes as though he had taken a holiday from his usual tailor at Gieves and Hawkes. His evening dress had Alexander McQueen written all over it. A shock of his black hair fell over his forehead as he leaned forward, rapt. His lean face was angled down, the blue of his gaze fastened on the screen. The scar along his cheekbone was a straight white line against his tanned cheek – like a Prussian aristocrat's duelling trophy. Robin had told her long ago it was the result of a broken retaining clip lashing back during a typhoon in the China Sea. Which, to be fair, seemed excitingly piratical and just as romantic as a duelling scar.

Robin, too, was dressed in McQueen and her little black number complemented his outfit perfectly. It also set off her figure as it sat just on the voluptuous side of fashionably slim.

The midnight velvet seemed to add sparkle to the gold curls of her hair and depth to the still, calm grey of her eyes – and was simply made to go with the Chanel No. 5 she was also wearing. She had taken off her jewellery before coming through but Indira knew she had been wearing a long rope of black pearls, a Rolex dress watch in a silver case and bracelet earlier. Richard, as always, stuck to his steel-cased Oyster Perpetual. Individually, they were arresting enough. Together, they were simply dazzling.

Indira turned her attention back to her work, her mind ranging rapidly over the basics of what she would have to deal with. *Sayonara* had several discreet computer systems on board, all of them serving different functions, controlled in different manners and accessed in different ways. There was a system controlling propulsion and ship-handling – basically, the engines and the rudders. That system in turn was overseen by a higher system, fed with information by the ship's management systems and by the satellite systems, including GPS, all of which were programmed to assess how the ship was progressing and allow the ship-handling systems to vary their control of such matters as speed and heading to make sure the hull stayed at its programmed point on its course in spite of such variables as wind, weather and current. Zip files containing information from these systems were broadcast to Heritage Mariner and the other interested parties on an hourly basis. As well as these, the vessel had an automatic tracking device onboard like an airliner's black box flight recorder, which also recorded and broadcast the ship's position and heading on a protected channel on a regular basis. Beyond these, there were the ship's security systems designed to keep the bridge house and all other access points secure unless emergency override codes were punched into them. If that was done while the vessel was at sea, alarms were triggered and a secondary security system was also switched on, giving access to on-board cameras capable of recording what they videoed in every spectrum, from ultra-violet to infra-red. Within seconds of this occurring, unless counter-codes were entered by whoever went aboard, control of the ship was automatically passed to the remote control section at the NIPEX facility, where a twenty-four seven command and control team was ready to take over.

The computer screen abruptly cleared and Indira's attention switched back to it. 'Get me the video feed closest to the alarm that just sounded,' ordered Richard, the quiet rumble of his voice making his words sound more like a reasonable request than the orders of a tense commander.

'I have four alarms sounding,' warned Indira. 'Both port and starboard bulkhead doors of the A-Deck corridor and both aft access doors to the cargo areas forward of the bridge. That's something we've never seen before. It's quite an escalation, in fact. They seem to have all the emergency override codes needed for the drill and counter-command control codes, or some sort of malware that simply prevents us accessing the ship's command control programmes, though the monitoring programmes still seem to be online. That's why the boys at NIPEX are shut out. In fact, they've definitely got the codes: there's no sign of forced entry.'

'They have good intelligence, then,' nodded Richard thoughtfully. 'If they have access to the counter-command control codes that keep the NIPEX team out, that's worrying, though they had that access on the last drill too, if my memory serves me correctly.' He swept the hair back off his forehead thoughtlessly, frowning as his mind raced.

'What do you want me to do?' asked Indira.

'Go with any of them,' said Richard decisively.

'Going with A-Deck main corridor starboard side video feed one,' she answered briskly.

'That's just inside the A-Deck starboard door,' said Robin, sharing her husband's tension.

The screen filled with blackness. A distant glimmer of movement. A rustling whisper of sound. The squeak of a footfall, fading.

'Next one's in,' he rapped. Blackness on blackness. The merest hint of motion. Again, the whisper. Indira hit the volume and picked up steady breathing.

'Infra-red,' he snapped. Signals whipped at the speed of light from earth to a series of satellites across distances comparable to those between the earth and the moon, and back again, showing what the cameras could see at the infra-red end of the light spectrum. The picture changed as the camera adjusted its visual spectrum further. Figures moved across the screen in a range of fluorescent orange shades. Beams of strange brightness shone out of headlights ahead of them. The bodies moving purposefully forward were partially obscured by the coldness of what they were wearing and what they were carrying. They looked alien, almost robotic; different to any of the other teams that had tested the security systems in the past. More in number. More focused and purposeful. Seemingly better armed.

'Bridge?' asked Richard.

'We'll take a look . . .' said Indira at once. But when she switched feeds, the screen went blank.

'They've neutralized the bridge feeds,' observed Robin. 'That was fast.'

'Too fast and too efficient,' decided Richard. 'Time for action. Plan A.'

'So original!' teased Robin, trying to relieve some of the tension. 'Did you think that up yourself? *Plan A?*'

The edges of his wild blue eyes crinkled into a brief smile. 'No. But it'll have to do, original or not. We have to take it all very seriously, security test or not. *Especially* if not. You know what to do?'

'Of course,' answered both Robin and Indira together. Robin moved forward and sat beside the young computer operative. She kicked off her shoes – a signal that she was ready for some real work.

'OK,' he said, in motion at once. 'Usual routine. I'll hit the road. OK?'

'Aye aye, Captain,' said Robin equably as he strode across the office towards the door that led to their flat, his emergency travelling outfit, pre-packed flight bag and the lift to his Bentley Continental in the garage below. 'I'll get Audrey on to the airlines. You'll know which one you're on by the time you get to Heathrow.'

'And the assembly point for the rest of the team,' he said, pausing in the doorway, sparking with energy, clearly bursting to be off adventuring.

'Plan A says Petropavlovsk-Kamchatsky. That's Yelizovo airport, with some pick-ups on the way in Domodedovo, Moscow,' said Indira confidently, spectacularly unfazed by either the tension or the byplay – or, come to that, the lack of originality in keeping Richard's 'Plan A' label. 'Failing that, it'll have to be Yuzhno-Sakhalin, and failing that Sapporo, like last time. We'll have all three timed and factored by the time you get to Heathrow.'

'Petropavlovsk-Kamchatsky. Never heard of it,' said Richard cheerfully. 'Nor of Yelizovo. Therefore I so want to go there! Get Felix Makarov involved, just in case things in Moscow need smoothing. How soon can I be there?'

'Thirty-six hours from take-off if Audrey can get you a seat,' said Indira. 'Aboard *Sayonara* within forty. Flight with BA to Moscow and Transaero internal across Siberia. Expensive, though. Ten thousand pounds, one way. Then there'll be the chopper from Kamchatka . . .'

'Make it so, even so,' said Richard cheerfully, as though he were a captain of the Starship *Enterprise*. 'And warn the others. Including Felix. But the quicker I'm at Heathrow, the more options we'll have, by the sound of it. Sakhalin or Sapporo will have to do if push comes to shove. I'll be in touch all along the line – on the hour every hour till I get back home.'

He turned to go.

'And if you're not?' asked Robin, looking over her shoulder, her tone stopping him in his tracks. 'This lot look like they have tricks up their sleeves.' She nodded towards the computer screen, which was once again black and blank. Sinisterly silent.

'If things go quiet when we get aboard,' said Richard as he sprang into motion once more and disappeared down the corridor, 'then it's time for *Plan B*.'

'Plan B?' asked Indira in the slightly echo-like silence after he vanished. 'There's a *Plan B*?'

'There is indeed,' said Robin. 'We've never had to use it before, but there's always a first time. Plan B is Harry and the Pitman.' Which left her frowning companion none the wiser.

88 Hours to Impact

As British Airways flight 233 from London Heathrow settled on to its short finals over Moscow, Richard glanced out of the window by his side. Russia was shrouded beneath an overcast sky and there was nothing to see. He looked back at his laptop screen. The Airbus A380 was one of the new generation with on-board wifi access: he had been able to use his laptop live instead of just relying on the memory. So he was in Skype contact with Heritage Mariner's head office and aware that Plan A was falling smoothly into place. And he was fizzing with excitement as a result. It was six p.m. on *Sayonara*, six a.m. in London and nine a.m. on the ground below.

According to Robin, his team was assembling at its various points around the Pacific Rim, even though they were only eleven hours into the crisis. During that time, she had changed, returned to her computer, confirmed that *Sayonara*'s hourly zip files had stopped coming in, briefed the long-suffering Heritage Mariner executives in various time zones all over the world that their CEO was off adventuring again – and slept. She'd woken a little more than an hour ago, showered and got back online. All while he was starting out on his travels.

Now, however, Richard was just coming round from a three-hour power nap that had filled most of the flight time. It looked as though Robin was by no means the only one involved who was awake at an unusual hour – the rest of the team would all be up and about, ready to head for their final meeting place at the obscure airport of Petropavlovsk-Kamchatsky. The team's general make-up was long-decided in case of such an event, but its actual personnel was something else again.

To go with Plan A, the personnel assembling at pick-up points all over the world were, of course *The A Team*. The name amused Richard, his ready smile widening at the memory of what Robin had thought about the hackneyed *nom de guerre*.

With a gleam of her teeth and flash of her eyes, the flight attendant smoothed her skirt over her hips and swayed up the aisle towards him once again. Black-haired, blue-eyed giants with square jaws and fascinatingly theatrical scars didn't often appear in her experience. And this one had a deep, growling voice that made something profound within her seem to melt whenever she heard it. But even though the dark-haired passenger's dazzling blue eyes were precisely level with her crisply covered bust and the button straining at its cleavage, he remained disappointingly fixated on his computer with occasional glances out at the overcast skies hanging low above Moscow. So she swept past with a little moue of disappointment and he never even realized she had looked at him with anything more than purely professional interest.

But Richard had more than enough to occupy his mind. The A Team, personally identified or not, were carefully selected, fully briefed, cutting edge and at the tip top of their game. They were men who had been chosen by Richard, Felix Makarov of Sevmash and his associate, the security expert Ivan Yagula. Others, further afield, had been chosen by Nic Greenbaum of Greenbaum International and the CEOs of the Japanese consortia involved in the making and maintenance of *Sayonara* herself; the oversight, loading and unloading of her potentially explosive cargo. Comprising ex-special forces, ships engineers, liquid gas experts and computer experts, they were ready, willing and able to meet any threat of any kind to any aspect of *Sayonara*'s hull, systems, cargo, control or integrity. Their existence and constant readiness for action were two of the most important aspects of the case Heritage Mariner, Mitsubishi and NIPEX had been forced to make to the International Maritime Organization and their insurers, Lloyd's of London – not to mention to the American, Russian and Japanese governments through whose jurisdictions the revolutionary, unmanned vessel was programmed to sail. Any flaw in their emergency response and *Sayonara* would be banned from national and international waters without a second thought or any chance of appeal.

There were a couple of ships' engineers from Mitsubishi's shipyards in Kobe en route to Sapporo, briefed to come north to meet the others within the next twelve hours. With them were the computer experts who had designed the ship's systems – part of a cooperative group that had brought Mitsubishi and Fujitsu together. The Fujitsu men were headquartered at the Riken Advanced Institute for Computational Science, which was in Kobe as well. Their current focus, however, was less upon *Sayonara* than their next project – the floating city of Kujukuri which was taking shape in the bay below the NIPEX terminal.

These two teams would be met at Sapporo by the NIPEX team responsible for the oversight of the Liquified Natural Gas cargo – one of the safest cargoes currently carried at sea in its present state within the modified Moss-type spherical tanks at minus 160 degrees Celsius. Then they were booked to fly up to the meeting place at Petropavlovsk-Kamchatsky. Greenbaum International would also be flying LNG experts from Anchorage and Vancouver to Petropavlovsk-Kamchatsky by company jet as there were no scheduled flights they could use.

But the engineers, computer experts and gas men were by no means at the top of Richard's wish-list; and of course he never gave a second thought to their work on the floating city. Although in his heart of hearts he believed this to be a surprise security exercise, NIPEX's loss of control was a serious matter whichever way you looked at it, unless the men on board were all accomplished sailors with a competent captain in command. And Richard had seen all too clearly what the bright orange figures revealed by the infra-red had been wearing and carrying. They appeared to have gone aboard heavily armed – and he was among the last men on earth to get caught bringing a knife to a gun fight. If Sam Mendes, director of the play he'd missed at the Old Vic last night as well as of the most successful Bond film of all time, could ever be persuaded to make a movie of what Richard was planning instead of the next in the James Bond franchise, it wouldn't be called *Skyfall*. It would be called *Overkill*.

Richard's thoughts jumped twenty miles ahead as he felt the plane settle on to its short finals to Moscow's Domodedovo International airport. When he suggested that his Russian associate Felix Makarov might smooth things over at Domodedovo, he had only been half serious. He had documentation that would whisk him through with silken speed. But Domodedovo was more than just a stopover. It was the pick-up point for the ultimate – and perhaps the most important – section of the A Team. The most problematical one, and the only one whose details were not yet on his laptop's capacious memory.

Heritage Mariner's Russian partners in a wide range of enterprises were Bashnev/Sevmash, a consortium whose wealth and influence were based on oil, gas, electricity and nuclear power. Their various networks covered the old Soviet Union, controlling pipelines, electricity grids and road tankers, as well as the ocean-going ones they co-owned with Heritage Mariner. The two companies shared interests in oil-producing areas from the icy wastes of the Artcic to the burning heart of Africa, though the emphasis of the Russian company was on extraction while Heritage Mariner's was on transport. Within Russia, however, Bashnev/ Sevmash's fleets of trucks delivered everything in the containers Heritage Mariner shipped for them: individual machines, motor-cars, parcels and packages.

Not to mention the fact that they had enormous political and legal power. Felix Makarov was the head of Sevmash, but his friend and long-time business partner Max Asov, CEO of Bashnev Oil and Power, had been killed not long ago and replaced by his daughter, Anastasia. It was a succession in the world of Russian corporate empires that was almost unheard of. But under the joint leadership of Felix, Max and – latterly – Anastasia, the Russians had also expanded into even less traditional areas. It was Bashnev/Sevmash who supplied the ground-breaking floating power station *Zemlya* on lease to the Japanese government, powering the half-built floating city. The expansion of the business necessitated an expansion of safety measures, and so Bashnev/Sevmash's latest acquisition was a company headed by the man who was now their own head of security. It was called Risk Incorporated. And it was to Risk Incorporated that Richard turned when he needed the kind of men who knew how to counter the type of weapons the men on board *Sayonara* seemed to be armed with.

Risk Incorporated was the Blackstone of the new Russia. Staffed by ex-special forces operatives, all further trained to the highest possible level, it was a 'go anywhere, meet any crisis' organization. And it needed to be. London Centre, Heritage

Mariner's commercial intelligence arm, had briefed Richard on more than one occasion recently that it was Risk Incorporated which was watching out for Bashnev Oil and Power in particular during the dangerous days of succession in the boardroom while the new CEO settled into her late father's chair. There were rumours that the sharks were circling. And not just Russian sharks, by all accounts – everyone from the world's most powerful oil and gas corporations to the Mafia.

As the A380's wheels touched the surface of the main runway and her turbofans went into reverse thrust, Richard leaned back and hoped that whoever else was waiting in Domodedovo's VIP lounge would have the crème de la crème of Risk Incorporated's hard men with them. Although he had joked to Robin about Plan B he really did not want to have to fall back on Harry and the Pitman. But still, he thought, as the jet slowed to taxiing speed and swung in towards the terminal, it might be as well to get the pair of them lined up. And, perhaps, to let the others at Domodedovo know there was a Plan B too.

No sooner had Richard walked into the arrivals hall than a familiar figure confronted him. A huge young man stood serenely surrounded by security staff. He had a fashionably shaven head that revealed a long, muscular cranium. He was suited in single-breasted, mid-grey gabardine, shirted in white cotton, wearing a gold silk tie with a Windsor knot. All this was visible between the wings of a long black cashmere overcoat with a silk lining the colour of blood. The gold tie had no regimental crests, but there was the familiar Batman logo of the Spetsnaz special forces honourable discharge pin just visible on the lapel above his heart. The eyes were mid-blue and twinkling with good humour. The full, sensual lips quivered towards a smile as he swept forward, and the surprisingly fine nostrils flared. 'Ah, there you are. Bang on time,' he said in cut-glass Sandhurst English.

'Hello, Ivan,' said Richard, striding forward to shake the massive Russian's hand. It was the very man he had just been thinking of: Ivan Yagula, Head of Risk Incorporated, Bashnev/ Sevmash's new security chief and Anastasia's new partner – in more ways than one.

'I have people waiting to pick up your bags,' said Ivan as he swept Richard out of the customs hall with only the faintest glance towards baggage claim. 'You have a five-hour stopover, but there's a lot we need to get done. It's breakfast time here but I wouldn't bother adjusting your watch. You've a good few more time zones to cross yet. Felix Makarov is here in person, and he has a large number of people that he would like you to meet. They are, I think you'll find, just what the doctor ordered.'

'A doctor of military strategy, I hope,' countered Richard.

Ivan gave a grunt of laughter. 'Yes.' He nodded. 'Now you mention it, they are the kind of men who give doctors of medicine full employment. Doctors and undertakers . . .'

84 Hours to Impact

Richard pushed his plate away, knowing that Robin would have disapproved of the massive *obed* of steak and chips he had just consumed. He was equally well aware that he should have contacted her again – but had omitted to do so, with malice aforethought, like a schoolboy playing truant.

Felix Makarov reached for the last of the Stolichnaya *Elit* vodka that he favoured for both breakfast and lunch. 'So,' he rumbled, 'you are satisfied?' His gesture started with the remains of the steak then swept out to encompass this entire quarter of the VIP lounge's restaurant. Richard nodded as his gaze swept over the men seated around the table Richard and Felix were sharing with Ivan. Men who had assembled slowly during the time it had taken Felix to empty his vodka bottle. They were very much as Richard and Ivan had discussed. The kind who gave doctors more work than they wanted. For Richard's needs, however, they were just what the doctor ordered. They were a mixture in terms of their original training: *GRU, VDV*. Elite soldiers, the Russian equivalent to the Paras and the Green Berets. They all affected shaven heads like Felix and Ivan, and business suits, with the occasional lapel pin similar to Ivan's telling of regiment, decoration, honourable discharge. They all looked what they were – powerfully competent and extremely dangerous.

But the information downloaded from a memory stick Ivan

had given him made it clear to Richard that their expertise was as wide as he could ever require. Although they were all alike, trained to the peak and ready for anything, he had weapons men, medics, engineers and communications men. Men with backgrounds in intelligence. A sergeant, a warrant officer and a lieutenant were in overall charge. Even in their business suits it was obvious that they made a solid squad. 'They've been to Chechnya – right across the Caucasus, North and South Ossetia, and lived to tell the tale. That's taken some doing, I can tell you. If the going gets tough, you stick by them. They'll never let you down.' Ivan emphasized, 'Experienced, adaptable, trained to the top of any game in the world. Multilingual and exceptionally multitalented. They're not just the best we've got. They're simply the best there are.'

'Looks like we won't need the Pitman, then,' said Richard without thinking.

And looked up into a sudden silence; for his voice had carried across this area of the restaurant – and every eye was suddenly on the pair of them.

Felix was frowning, the only one there who did not seem to see the importance of what Richard had let slip. Even Ivan had lost some of his usual confident bonhomie. 'The *Pitman*?' he probed. Less than happily, it should be said, leaning forward.

'*Plan B*,' said Richard easily. 'If we have any trouble dealing with matters or getting our communications out, we have a back-up team. Harry Newbold and the Pitman. They work together out of Amsterdam, as I'm sure you know. They're everything we have here distilled and refined. A world-class mercenary and a world-class hacker. I've dealt with them before and, with the possible exception of your men, they are the best. I know they specialize in similar areas to those you focus on, but they're likely to cover any gaps in our defences one way or another. And I promise they'll only come if there's a problem we have trouble handling, especially as the other aspect of their reputation is that they are simply lethal.' He looked around the room, meeting each pair of eyes there. Only one strikingly grey pair held his for a moment longer than the rest, their gaze angry and suspicious.

'The Pitman,' said Ivan, recovering his accustomed bonhomie and pounding the table in loud amusement. 'That's a bit like booking a main battle tank because you're worried your limousine might break down! Well, we'll have to look to our laurels, men, and watch our backs! Only *you* would use the Pitman as fall-back, Richard,' and gave vent to a bellow of wry laughter that spread right across this section of the room. Eventually.

'Time for a briefing before we move on,' said Richard as the tense moment passed. 'I'll need my laptop for part of the proceedings, Ivan, but then I want you to hang on to it. I'm going into the kind of situation where things like laptops get broken – and insurers cut up nasty about it. Even insurers like Lloyd's of London.'

'That's fine,' rumbled Ivan. 'I'll keep it safe.'

'Good. But as I say, I still need it for a moment more. I have something to add for the first full team briefing. But who's going to give it, now that the team's all here?' He looked around. It was clear from the records on Ivan's memory stick who the top dogs were – Aleks Zaitsev, ex-GRU lieutenant, the man with the cold grey eyes. Senior Warrant Officer Konstantin Roskov. And Master Sergeant Vasily Kolchak, operations and intelligence. 'It's of no use in this particular operation,' said Ivan in a stage whisper, 'but during my initial briefing of Aleks Zaitsev, I discovered that he is an Olympic standard skier. He's master of the black piste at Mount Elbrus in the Caucasus and holds the records for the black pistes on Mount Cermis and Crevinia in Italy. Both the Matterhorn and the Zermatt runs. The Pitman would have trouble keeping up with that, eh?'

Zaitsev stood up as Ivan finished speaking and there was immediate silence. The slim, broad-shouldered young officer swivelled his shaven head as though his grey eyes were gunsights, sweeping round the room. 'We will go through,' he said in a forceful baritone. But it was Richard who led the way. Then, while the others were crowding into the conference room behind him, he put his laptop on a table beneath a white screen and connected it to the OHP system so that when Aleks eventually called them all to order, the two men were standing on either side of a screen filled with a detailed schematic of *Sayonara*.

The Russian pointed to the bow section of Richard's schematic. 'You see the whaleback on the weather deck – or main deck – begins several metres aft of the forecastle head,' he said in near-perfect English. 'There is just room for a helideck and this is our main point of access from the air. These marks in the forward wall of the whaleback immediately aft of the helideck are access points designed to allow maintenance and oversight of the Moss tanks in the interior during the various processes involved in loading and unloading LNG. The schematic makes it clear that these points, like these here and here and here' – he pointed – 'between the tanks themselves and these here at the aft, and of course these into the bridge itself – all give access to the interior of the hull.' He traced passageways and galleries that ran between the double-hull of the vessel's sides and the five perfectly spherical tanks it contained, like five beach balls in a banana boat. Inevitably, the tanks almost met at their widest points – but equally inevitably, there was much more space between them where they sat on the keel, areas where the lower halves of the ball-shaped structures curved away from each other. Areas where the strangers on board might hide themselves – or anything else they brought aboard with them. And, above the deck level where the spheres all but touched, there were equally inviting maintenance and work areas, runways and pipe sheaves under the whaleback of the bulbous deck-covering.

In the bridge house there were rudimentary accommodation and ship-handling areas as well as computer areas – no longer sealed, unfortunately. And beneath these, in the engine rooms at the lower rear of the schematic, the big steam turbines that used the LNG as fuel to power the screws that drove the thing and moved the rudders that steered her according to the dictates of those computers. That still did so, in fact, following the course as pre-programmed – unless the computers controlling her course had been hacked into, just as the rest of the vessel had been pirated, and tampered with. He explained the fundamental set up of the computer programmes, each with its own set of back-ups. One that controlled the propulsion and steering. One that communicated with the orbiting GPS and guidance systems and used their information to vary the first set as proved needful depending on wind, weather and current. One that monitored the safe disposition of the cargo. And one that oversaw the on-board security. All apparently hacked and under the control of the pirates. Only the ship's black box automatic broadcasts were still alive, allowing them to know the position of the vessel, her heading and her speed. But for how long? No one knew. She was now beyond the control of the remote command team still sitting hopefully but uselessly at the NIPEX facility in Japan, apparently yet to be given new programmed orders, and still, therefore, on course to reach Japan in a little over eighty hours from now.

The young ex-officer bounced on the balls of his feet and stared around the room. 'We have to act fast, therefore. As soon as we have deplaned, we will use these forward access points to take our various teams of experts below. Remember, our first function is to secure these points that the engineers from NIPEX, Mitsubishi and Fujitsu need to access in order to find out what the opposition has been up to, especially with regard to the ship's cargo, hull and computer systems. Then we need to keep those areas – and those personnel – safe from enemy action. Thirdly – and only *in extremis* – we may need to engage with the enemy, when we have worked out who they are, what they have done and what their overall plan is. And, indeed, whether this is the most testing exercise so far, or the real thing. Are there any questions?'

In the face of continued silence, Aleks continued, 'The point of this briefing, the fact that it is being held here and now, is that we need to be aware of elements that our Japanese and American colleagues do not need to be aware of. We are the iron fist. They are the velvet glove. We will be going in fully armed and combat ready. It is our job to get them where they need to go, to protect them while they are there and to help them reclaim control of the ship – if necessary – by *electronic* means. Not by *physical* means if it can at all be helped. We must still treat this as an exercise, not a war.' The cold grey eyes rested for a moment on Richard. 'Keep that fact at the forefront of your minds at all times, gentlemen. We are not there to start a fire fight. Quite apart from the fact that we are as yet unaware of the precise identity of whoever is onboard, or what their plans are, we can be absolutely one hundred per cent sure that they will have done their best to secure the ship against us – and that particular vessel is the last place on earth you want to start a fire fight in.'

He leaned forward, raking the room with his steely eyes.

'With the exception of a shootout on board an airliner in flight, this is the most dangerous place it is possible to imagine bullets going astray. The five Moss-type tanks are insulated, but they are not bulletproof. Each tank holds about thirty-five thousand cubic metres of gas in liquid form. And in order to remain liquid, the gas must be stored at minus one hundred and sixty degrees Celsius. There are carefully choreographed processes for getting it to and from that temperature, into and out of the tanks safely. None of which involve sending several ounces of steel-jacketed hot lead into the works. I don't know if anyone has ever tried to calculate what might happen under those circumstances . . .' He looked once more at Richard, who picked up his cue without missing a beat.

Richard stepped forward. He hit the keys on his laptop and YouTube flashed up on the screen. 'This is what happens,' he said tersely. 'It's footage taken in China back in 2012 when a road tanker carrying LNG crashed and ruptured. Five people died. As you will observe, they were lucky it was so few. You will also want to bear in mind that a standard road tanker carries about thirty thousand *litres* of LNG. As Lieutenant Zaitsev has observed, a Moss tank holds just under thirty-five thousand *cubic metres*. That's just over a thousand times as much, in each of the five Moss tanks on board. The whole cargo is just shy of one hundred and seventy thousand cubic metres, therefore.'

He looked around the room at a lot of very serious faces. He pressed PLAY and talked over the picture as it jumped into motion on the screen behind him. 'What we see first is a video shot from a bus held up by the accident . . .' A curve of highway filled the screen with a green peak in the distance. Against the distant scene was what looked like a cloud of white smoke hanging in the air. Then the smoke exploded. It turned from white gas into airborne fire instantaneously. The bus rocked. The camera fell.

Immediately another shot replaced it, far closer to the accident, showing a fuming flood of liquid pouring along the highway. Figures were fleeing ahead of it, past a neatly loaded truck. Abruptly, incredibly, the white liquid simply exploded into nothingness. And the load, the figures, everything that had been close to it, was gone. The devastation was complete. A third angle opened, from the inside of a car. The date was

6 October 2012. And then the precise time: 10:45:57. As the hundredths started running and the cars in the picture slowed to a stop, Richard looked round the room. There was silence as the men watched the plume of distant gas with a new understanding of exactly what it meant. A woman in a striped top took a coat out of the back of the car in front of the car where the filming was being done. She ran past the window. The white plume exploded. The shockwave came roaring towards them. Within the roaring there were shouts and screams.

'Sixty thousand times the force of that explosion, as near as I can calculate,' Richard emphasized quietly. 'Sixty thousand times. Enough said?'

'Enough said,' answered Ivan.

75 Hours to Impact

The Transaero A380 settled towards the newly extended runway at Yelizovo airport, thirty kilometres north of Petropavlovsk-Kamchatsky, capital city of the Kamchatka *Krai*. Richard looked out of the window at the dazzling brightness of the early morning and the breathtaking backdrop of their destination. The Pacific lay like a lapis lazuli inlay below, filling Avacha Bay and seeming to overflow into the seaport's docks and past a delta into a blue river running north. The conurbation clustered along the shoreline in regimented blocks, its rigid town planning relieved by roofs of vivid red and blue. But if the sea was flat, the land seemed to rise in great waves, rearing out of the water and heaving itself up to the snow-capped peak of a volcano.

Alex Zaitsev appeared and stooped beside Richard. 'Hell of a view.'

'Hell of a long way to come for it,' replied Richard. 'What am I? Literally halfway round the world?'

'Yes, Captain. The international dateline runs down out of the Bering Sea just east of here. Opposite Greenwich. You know what that means?'

'No. What?'

'It's breakfast time again.' The Russian lieutenant returned to his own seat on the far side of the aisle, but their conversation continued. As the plane levelled out and began its final approach, Richard got a clearer view of the runway. 'That looks like the Greenbaum International jet,' he said.

'I can't see colours or logos from here,' answered Aleks, shaking his head.

'Nor can I but there won't be many other Gulfstream G650s parked in this neck of the woods. Even for Russia, this is as close to the edge of the world as it gets, I guess. We passed the back of beyond several hours ago. But those look like what Felix and Ivan promised us. The Mil-17 chopper has a Bashnev logo, and so does that truck beside it. Are the troops up and about?'

'Keen as mustard. Straining at the leash.'

'Hmmm. Well, we have to get them kitted up and all the others briefed and out before we *Cry Havoc!* And let them slip!'

Fortunately the airport facilities at Yelizovo had been updated at the same time as the runway. Twelve billion roubles well spent as far as Richard was concerned, as although there were hotels nearby – the Eidelweis B&B in Yelizovo and the Best Eastern Avacha down in Petropavlovsk – they were too distant. No one had hours to spare for breakfast briefings and refreshment breaks. The whole team trooped up to the brand-new restaurant area for breakfast and briefing, therefore, while those in direst need tested the newly installed plumbing.

Richard used the interim to call Heritage Mariner and report in. He had left his laptop with Ivan in Moscow as he was effectively coming into a war zone now, whether this was just another drill or the real thing after all, so he contented himself with his new Galaxy instead. It was one of the new generation phones, a smartphone capable of doing almost everything his laptop or tablet were capable of . . . but on a smaller scale.

Robin was in the office, and a little worried that he had – again – been slow in contacting her. 'You know what you're risking with this foolishness,' she said snappily. 'You go outside the contact window one more time and I'll call in Harry and the Pitman!'

He looked around the hall with a start of guilt at the bell-clear repetition of their names, remembering the reaction when he had mentioned them in Moscow. But he was alone, because the rest of his men had vanished now. And everybody else on board their flight had also gone off about their various business, for this was their final destination. There was nowhere else to go but the city and the docks. People only came here if they had a reason to be here, and most of them were going to stay.

Except for Richard and his team. All in all there were twenty of them now, he thought as he joined them at last, slipping the Galaxy into his pocket. Richard and Aleks Zaitsev's men were led by Senior Warrant Officer Konstantin Roskov and Master Sergeant Vasily Kolchak, recently arrived from Moscow, the iron fist in the techies' velvet glove. The Japanese from NIPEX had flown in with the team from Osaka earlier and a couple of gas men from Anchorage had arrived in the gulfstream with executives from Greenbaum who Richard hadn't met but who, like him, were there to observe proceedings and, in their case, make sure the cargo was safe. They had been waiting with the Japanese contingent. The Japanese team were completed by Moss-trained structural engineers from Mitsubishi and computer nerds from Fujitsu.

As he surveyed the assembled faces in the airy restaurant, Alex Zaitsev unexpectedly managed to put his foot in his mouth. 'If you do call up Harry Newbold and the Pitman,' he said to Richard, 'I think we're going to need a bigger chopper to take us all home.'

The Fujitsu computer men looked at him, their eyes dark and very suspicious indeed behind twelve thick black-framed spectacle lenses. 'Excuse me,' said the nearest of them, with icy formality. 'I am Doctor Rikkitaro Sato. I lead the computer team. Did you say you were considering calling on Harry?'

'It's déjà vu,' said Richard to himself. 'Pure déjà vu.'

'Harry *Newbold*?' insisted Dr Sato frostily.

'It's an insurance policy,' explained Richard. 'Plan B. Back-up only. In case of unforeseen but insurmountable problems.'

'Such as . . .' grated Dr Sato.

'Give the guy a break, Doctor Sato,' interjected a new voice. Richard turned to find one of the Greenbaum International executives standing smiling at his shoulder. 'If he could give you a *such as*, then it would hardly be *unforeseen*. You can see the logic in that, surely.'

Dr Sato grunted, bowed and turned away.

'Domenico Giancarlo DiVito, Greenbaum's Vancouver office.' The stranger held out his hand to Richard. 'But everyone just calls me Dom. Pleasure to meet you, Captain Mariner. Rikki's a real nice guy when you get to know him.'

And you got to know him fast, thought Richard, meeting smile with open smile. *You've both only been here a couple of hours.*

'But I think you threw him a bit with the name-dropping,' the Canadian continued. 'Bit like asking Colonel Custer to take tea with Sitting Bull. See where I'm coming from? You can understand the good doctor's point. Using Harry and the Pitman as your insurance policy is not so much a safety net as mutually assured destruction. A two-guy team coupling a top mercenary with a world-class hacker. That's a bit like Arnie Schwarzenegger meets Lizbet Salander, isn't it? *The Terminator with the Dragon Tattoo*?'

Richard looked down at the open, smiling face of the young Canadian beside him. 'Nice to meet you, too, Dom,' he said after a moment longer. 'And you may have a point. But then, so may I. Tell me, what is it that you fight fire with? Especially in situations that could get explosive?'

The ingenuous brown eyes were shaded for an instant. Then another cheery voice interjected. 'Fire,' said the newcomer. 'You fight fire with fire, Dom.'

'Damned if you don't,' nodded Dom cheerfully. 'This is my opposite number from the Anchorage office, Captain Mariner – Steve Penn. Steve, Captain Mariner.'

Christened Stephano Penne, Richard remembered. Penne, like the pasta. 'Call me Richard. Nice to meet you,' said Richard, shaking their hands. 'Steve's right, Dom. Fight fire with fire. So I'll keep my *terminator with a dragon tattoo* on call until I'm sure that I'm not facing something I need that particular fire to fight.'

Again, the open countenance darkened for an instant. 'But this is just an exercise, right? A test run. In case we ever do find ourselves fighting a fire for real . . .' The two young executives exchanged glances.

'That's what we suppose,' said Richard. 'But then, my Bentley's supposed to be a safe ride and I'm supposed to be a good driver. But I still have—'

'—car insurance . . .' said Dom DiVito with a shrug. 'Sure. I get it.'

'Right, Dom. Let's get the ruffled feathers smoothed, the troops fed and watered, the briefing done and the show on the road, shall we?'

Once again, Richard was content to let Aleks Zaitsev make the running after everyone had enjoyed a peculiarly Russian breakfast of bacon, eggs, ham and blinis served with a samovar of tea and a massive jug of coffee. Richard, chatty as ever, discovered that the restaurant was well-supplied with the food thanks to another group of foreigners who had passed through a little under a week earlier, also, apparently, heading west rather than east to Yelizovo or south into the local community of Petropavlovsk.

This time there was no need for a large-scale schematic. Even the Greenbaum execs knew the basic structure and layout of a hull designed to house Moss-type LNG tanks. And *Sayonara* was not radically different in architecture from all the other LNG tankers plying the seas, except that she had that whaleback deck in front of her shortened bridge instead of four or five great hemispheres lined up ahead of an eight- or ten-deck block of flats. And neither Aleks nor any of the others except Rikki Sato and his team really needed to be aware of the differences in computer control and programming. The computers were where the officers crew would have been: between the command bridge and the engine room. So Aleks simply talked them through the basic safety procedures; where they were planning to go first; who was going to be with them to watch their backs; where they were all destined to end up and who would be there to keep the bad guys off their backs while they discovered what damage had been done and put it right. He then emphasized that this was a purely defensive exercise.

That last being an extremely important point, thought Richard as, fed, watered, rested and half-briefed, they all trooped down to the hangar with the Bashnev/Sevmash truck and chopper parked beside it. They took off their business suits, executive shirts and ties, their city shoes and so forth and pulled on cargo pants that were lined and inky black, and black wool roll necks along with black Kevlar body protectors, balaclavas, boots and gloves. Here the techies were given their laptops, their connectors and their shoulder-cases, infra-red headsets and night goggles, and open channel two-way communicators. The soldiers got their guns.

The only men going in empty-handed were Richard, Dom DiVito and Steve Penn. But Richard at least made sure he had his Galaxy at the ready. He pulled it out and looked at its flat screen, remembering Robin's frowning face and angry words the last time he had held it. She was ready and more than willing to send in the reinforcements at the slightest excuse, whether she heard from him or whether she did not. If anything hit the fan, he thought grimly, she would hear. He liked to be in control, and had no intention of causing Harry and the Pitman to be called out because of what he hadn't done as opposed to what he had done.

He looked almost fondly at the familiar, trusty Samsung Galaxy smartphone, with worldwide access to the Net.

Battery full. Pre-dial loaded.

Panic button set to press.

70 Hours to Impact

The Bashnev chopper came over *Sayonara* exactly five hours after the internal flight from Moscow touched down in Yelizovo, calculated Richard, dividing his attention between the view from the window beside him and the face of his watch which told him it was noon, local time. Accurate to the second. And, for once, local time and ship's time coincided. The vessel was proceeding at eighteen knots. A ground speed of more than twenty miles per hour, he calculated. Heading along a south-south-westerly course, following the edge of the abyssal Kuril Trench down towards Japan. He checked his Rolex again. She was exactly fourteen hundred and fifty miles from the new NIPEX facility. Seventy hours' sailing time.

Aleks Zaitsev had spent the two hours of the flight giving a
final briefing to the technicians, making sure that they were
comfortable and confident with the equipment they were wearing,
particularly the night-vision equipment they had been supplied
with on the assumption that they could well be working below
decks in a lightless environment. Richard was familiar with his
own goggles – he'd worn a similar set when he'd been involved
in night actions during a bush war in West Africa, in the days
when Felix Makarov's partner, the bellicose and dangerously
short-tempered Max Asov, had still been with them. Max had
died in that nasty little war, on the shore of a lake full of coltan
– a lake which promised to make all of their fortunes. The
search for it had taken Max from Moscow to the slopes of
Karisoke, a volcano in the dark heart of the war-torn continent,
where he had died. Max had been succeeded by his daughter
because his son and heir had died of a drugs overdose the
better part of a decade earlier. Anastasia, therefore – though
Max must be turning in his grave at the thought – and Ivan,
her chief of security and right-hand man, were the natural
Bashnev balance to Felix and his team at Sevmash shipping.

It was Anastasia, more than any requirements of business or
security, which kept Ivan in Russia now, Richard suspected.
Only Anastasia would keep the big man away from an adventure
like this one. Though, given the young woman's warlike propen-
sities, he was vaguely surprised that Nastia hadn't come along
herself. Perhaps there was trouble brewing in Moscow, St
Petersburg and Archangel, where the twin companies of Bashnev/
Sevmash had their main business concerns. Perhaps he should
ask London Centre what the word was on the street next time
he was in contact with Robin. Or rather, what the word was on
the *ulitsa*. It occurred to him that he should contact Robin pretty
soon, in fact. Perhaps as soon as they got aboard *Sayonara*.

But then the immediate requirements of the situation took
precedence for Richard. The Mil made a low pass over *Sayonara*.
They all craned to see if there was anything obvious amiss, but
there was not. The vessel swept determinedly forward, her decks
and bridge house apparently empty. There was no gesture of
greeting towards them; no declaration of war. Now it was the
turn of the techies – most of whom had worked on her or on

board her – to nod with silent wisdom while the soldiers gasped at her sheer size and the impact she made close-up, for she was a massive craft. Aleks Zaitsev, Konstantin Roskov and Vasily Kolchak were the only ones not giving vent to Russian oaths of surprise. They were focusing three pairs of electronically-enhanced binoculars upon their destination, trying to see into whatever deadly secrets lay within her.

The sides of her two hundred and eighty-eight metre hull were black and unmarked by any of the signs of age and wear that come so swiftly to working vessels. There didn't even appear to be a rust streak on the flare of the forecastle head beneath her carefully cradled anchors. Her squat bridge house sat far back at the opposite extreme of the long, lean hull, empty bridge wings stretching sixty metres from tip to tip. There was almost no poop deck and what little there was lay hidden below the hull of the lifeboat hanging from side-to-side aft of the bridge house above it. There was a glint of a safety rail in the summer sunshine then the square wall of her stern, falling towards the white heave of her propellers and the widening V of her wake.

The great whaleback of the protective cover, which stood so massively over the foredeck and the hemispheres of the Moss tanks, began immediately forward of the bridge to which it was joined. It stood more than twenty-five metres high and spread from rail to rail more than forty-five metres across the deck. Forty-eight point nine five, in fact, Richard remembered from the schematic on the laptop Ivan was guarding for him. Where the sides were pristine black, the bridge and whaleback were white, and in the midday sunshine it was as though they were flying over a snow bank so bright Richard wondered whether Aleks Zaitsev would be reminded of his Italian alpine ski runs. Pipe tops and mastheads stood in pairs above the pristine curves, like the uprights of a ski-lift long fallen out of commission. Between them, on the very top of the whale-back, there were pipes, as on a tanker, running in parallel series, fore and aft. And a little over halfway down the hull there was a cavity, with what looked for all the world like a massive balcony projecting over the side.

The shadow of the helicopter crept across the Alpine white-ness, rising and falling as the pilot sought to keep clear of the skeletal uprights. But it settled beside the starboard balcony. The lieutenant, his warrant officer right-hand man and the operations and intelligence sergeant – Aleks, Konstantin and Vasily – put their heads together, clearly debating whether this would be a good point for at least one team to gain entry, for it was a far more sizeable feature than it had appeared to be on Richard's schematic. But eventually they nodded their heads. They had a plan. This was not the moment to deviate from it. Aleks spoke into his headset, clearly ordering the pilot to proceed.

At last the Mil arrived above its destination. The triangle of the forecastle lay like a massive arrow-head below them, the circle of the helipad drawn in white on the green of the decking behind the pair of huge winches supporting the anchors, and between the slightly lesser pair controlling the hawsers by which the great ship could be moored. As the chopper pilot began to descend, Aleks was in action once again. He strode up to the cockpit, then returned with the flight engineer. Richard pulled out his cellphone, switched it on, tapped in his code and hit the predial. Robin's face filled the screen. 'We're going in,' he said tersely. 'I'll contact you again within the hour.' Then he realized it must be nearly midnight in London.

'Within the hour,' she said. 'Got it. I won't be in bed by the looks of things so don't let the hour worry you. But this time, buster, you'd better be bang on time.' And she broke contact with unexpected abruptness.

Aleks Zaitsev broke into his thoughts. Not by what he said, this time, but by what he did. As he came down the length of the Mil's cabin, Aleks patted several shoulders. The men he contacted sprang erect. The Mil's descent slowed, and as it did so, the engineer opened the sliding door in the cabin's side. Aleks and his four-man squad clipped lines to a rail above the howling vacancy of the open side and – at a nod from their leader – stepped back into thin air. Richard, on the far side, looked out and down until the four figures appeared beneath the belly and landing gear that partially blocked his view. As though they too were all controlled by *Sayonara*'s computers, they rappelled in perfect unison down towards the waiting deck, while Richard thought that skiing was by no means the only sport at which Aleks excelled. They all landed together precisely at the centre of the white circle of the helipad, unclipped and reached for their weapons. Then they fanned out, checking for anything that had been hidden from the binoculars' scrutiny – anyone concealed just inside the forward doors into the whaleback, lingering with evil intent. But soon they were signalling, and the pilots set the Mil on the landing pad so that everyone could climb out.

As Richard stepped down, the familiar sensations of being on shipboard swept over him. The throbbing of the deck as it vibrated to the movement of the engines. The subliminal feelings of movements and unsteadiness – though *Sayonara* was by no means either pitching or rolling. The stench of exhaust fumes, like the clatter of rotors, faded as soon as the Mil lifted off. Then the salt wind claimed them, with its clean tang of ozone and its gentle grumbling bluster. It was surprising how quickly it became quiet as the big chopper thrummed away towards the distant land lying invisibly below the starboard horizon. Then there was just the vastness of the ocean ahead – emphasized by the white cliff of steel standing sheer behind them. They were all turning to look at it – like tourists at the foot of an Alp.

The peaceful feeling of being at one with the great vessel and the natural world around it lasted for only the briefest of moments. 'Let's go,' said Aleks. He led one team with his intelligence man Sergeant Vasily Kolchak at his shoulder and his communications man with his back-packed radio making a third. Senior Warrant Officer Konstantin Roskov led the other. He too kept his communications man close at hand. All of the soldiers had their guns at the ready. All of the techies held their equipment carefully and safely. They each stood by a door into the whaleback while one of the techies keyed in the access code, then the soldiers led the way into the cavernous blackness beyond as Richard silently thanked God that whoever was on board hadn't thought to reset the codes. Unless of course, they had – and this was an immediate trap.

The techies and the executive observers fell into their designated squads and were following their leaders, apparently oblivious to any second thoughts or dark suspicions. Part of the briefing in the chopper had been the detailing of who was going with which team, under whose command. Steve Penn was going with Konstantin Roskov and the port-side team. Richard and Dom DiVito were with Aleks, Vasily and their men. One after another, they stepped over the raised sill of the bulkhead door into the black throat of the starboard corridor.

Richard hit the infra-red on his eyepiece and found himself surrounded by orange figures. There was a straggling line of them ahead of him, bright against the vastness of the lightless cold with which they were surrounded. But there was also a sense of cavernous immensity. He could hear the sound of the wind, muffled, against the outer shell of the whaleback at his right shoulder. He had the impression of something vast and dark reaching up and over in front to his left, but there was almost nothing to see except his companions, burning so brightly through his infra-red. There was a dull *clang* as Vasily shut the door. He shook his head, feeling a little like a pot-holer lost at the heart of some huge cave system deep beneath the earth. Vastness and enormity stood invisibly all around him, giving itself away only by the promise of echoes and distant whispers. The knowledge that he was in something superhumanly gigantic, if only he could see it.

And then he could see nothing at all as searing whiteness burned into his brain. He gasped with agony and shock, hearing all those around him doing the same. It took him an instant to realize, but then he understood.

Someone – or something – somewhere had switched on all the lights.

69 Hours to Impact

Right at the moment when Richard – on the far side of the world – was thinking he ought to call her, Robin's cellphone rang. It was the middle of the day for him, the middle of the night for her. But whenever he was away, she found herself regressing to the sort of hours her children kept as university students. At eleven p.m., therefore, she had just put the finishing touches to her late-night small board videoconference with Heritage Mariner's associates in New York where it was six p.m., Vancouver where it was three p.m. and Sydney, where it was eight a.m. tomorrow. To be fair, it had been midday in Vancouver, three p.m. in New York and eight p.m. in London when the meeting had started, long before Sydney came online, but Robin had been a lackadaisical chairwoman and timekeeper because all she had to look forward to was a big, cold, empty bed. Furthermore, she had convinced herself that she needed to refer one or two matters to their head of design, the Australian 'Doc' Weary. 'Doc' was currently Down Under, but he was an early riser and had been happy to have a chat at seven a.m. his time – ten p.m. hers. Their chat had gone on for an hour.

So Robin was still standing in the boardroom looking down at her papers when the phone rang and she answered almost automatically, her mind still on business. Very few people other than Richard and her children had access to this number, and very few indeed would ring at this time of night, but it was not in her nature to expect bad news, so she activated the handset without a second thought, actually expecting another 'catch-up' call from her errant husband. The face on her cell's screen told her who was actually trying to contact her and she paused before accepting the call with a slight frown of distaste. It was from a man she disliked, but whom she felt she had to treat civilly, if not warmly, as he was important to her company if not to her personally. His name was Tristan Folgate-Lothbury and he headed up a Lloyd's of London syndicate which insured a good deal of Heritage Mariner's fleet.

She pressed the little phone to her ear. 'Good evening, Tristan.'

'Hello, Robin. Richard about?'

'If he was, you'd be talking to him. What can I do for you?'

'Well, there's a bit of a problem, you see . . .' His oily voice drifted off without adding, *And a problem for your major insurance syndicate is a problem for you.*

'A problem, Tristan? Nothing serious, I hope?'

'Well . . . I'd have liked to have talked it over . . .'

'With Richard.'

'Precisely. But you say he's . . .'

'Unavailable. Yes.'

'. . . out of touch . . . Hmmm . . . Look, darling, how are you fixed for dinner? I know it's a bit *aprez* theatre at this hour, but I'm meeting someone who is, actually, at the theatre. Well, the opera. Verdi's *Macbeth* at the E.N.O . . .'

Robin looked around Heritage Mariner's big boardroom. She was alone in the Victorian splendour, with a mixture of paintings, prints and flat-screen televisions on the walls – except for the one on her right, where a discreet hatchway communicated with the boardroom kitchens. Beyond the little mahogany hatch was a fully-equipped kitchen where, twelve hours ago, a top-flight chef had been preparing light luncheon for the London directors. She hadn't eaten since and was ravenous now. She suddenly felt listless, lonely; as though the wind had been taken out of her sails. Many of the vessels whose models filled the display cases round the room were insured by Tristan Folgate-Lothbury's syndicate. He was a bore, but better than nothing. Better than no one.

'I'm not fixed at all, Tristan,' she said. 'And I'm famished.'

'Well, you couldn't pop across to the Intercontinental, could you? This dinner's set up at Theo's. You can join in.'

The eyebrows beneath the carefully coiffed gold curls rose into arches of surprise. Theo Randall at The Intercontinental was one of the most exclusive restaurants in Mayfair. Tristan was out to impress someone. Clearly not Robin herself – invited as something between an afterthought and an understudy. But someone Tristan wanted to impress would be someone Robin wanted to meet. And Theo Randall by all accounts cooked like an Italian angel.

Characteristically, she refocused her eyes so that instead of looking at the model of *Sayonara* she was looking at her reflection in the glass of the case that contained it. Thank heavens she had chosen to dress up for the board meeting, she thought. At least she wouldn't have to go up to the penthouse to change into an outfit worthy of the venue, though it was daywear, rather than eveningwear. But it was Alexander McQueen and it would do.

'I'll be there in half an hour, Tristan,' she said. It was during that half hour that Richard finally came through, catching her in a taxi halfway along Pall Mall, so she was unusually short with him – something she would come to regret.

Tristan Folgate-Lothbury was seated and waiting as Robin arrived. He was tucked away at an exclusive little table meant for two but set for three in a cosy alcove in the more muted, brown-on-brown section of the restaurant. He did not appear to realize that Robin was approaching his table in the wake of the maître d' until the very last moment, for he was clearly keeping an eye out for someone else entirely. But when he finally registered her existence, he leaped to his feet and gave her his most winning and welcoming smile. The crowded table heaved. The silverware chimed. A wine bottle reeled. He would have offered to shake her hand but he was too busy keeping the bottle upright. In the moment it took him to fuss the maître d' into seating her with her back to the room, she observed him. And was unimpressed by what she saw.

He had put on weight since their last meeting and would have been unhealthily corpulent even had he been a man of twice his years. For an ex-rugger blue approaching his mid-forties, he was positively portly. His blond hair was greying already and thin on top. His eyes were bagged and watery. His cheeks were flushed. Although the restaurant was perfectly air-conditioned, he was sweating – perhaps because he had been caught out by the warmth of the evening outside, for he was dressed for the day, like she was. He wore a pinstriped three-piece suit that looked to be on the tweedy side of gabardine. The buttons of the waistcoat strained alarmingly, and the gold watch-chain he affected seemed to be all that was holding the two sides of it together. His tie was slightly askew and the fact that he had tied it in a full Windsor knot was clearly a mistake, given his choice of shirt and collar. The size of his collar was, indeed, another miscalculation, given the thickness of his short neck, the number of his chins and the way his jowls were maturing.

There had been a wife somewhere in the picture the last time they had met, Robin recalled. She was clearly gone now – or as good as. No self-respecting woman would let a man she cared about go out in this state. And perhaps she had better mention that to Richard at their next contact – which should be happening soon, she thought with a frown. For the woman who so clearly no longer cared for Tristan was the source of his fortune. Daughter of a shipping magnate from . . . Greece, was it? No, from Italy; somewhere in the south. Calabria, was it . . .?

'Lovely to see you, darling,' he said, subsiding and cutting into her thoughts with a nasal drawl. He waved a hand once more and seemed surprised to discover there was an empty wine glass in it. 'Good of you to come. Mario, another bottle of this *Brunello di Montalcino*, there's a good chap. And, for the lady . . . Ah, Robin? A . . . *a pair o' teeth?*' Tristan emptied the bottle into his glass, much to Mario's disapproval, and waved the empty in the air.

It took just a moment for his meaning to register. '*Aperitif?* Yes, of course. Prosecco, please.'

'We have the *Colle del Principe*, madame . . .' the maître d' offered, without bothering to call the wine waiter or his boss the sommelier. It was hardly surprisingly – the place was packed and heaving. Patrons were dressed in everything from black ties to T-shirts; Robin and Tristan were by no means out of place.

'Perfect. A glass . . .'

'Oh, bring the *bottle*, Mario. And that's the *2004 Brunello*, d'ya hear?'

'Of course,' said Marco, in a voice that would have frozen *gellate*.

'So, Tristan,' asked Robin, her tone dangerously silky and her voice only a little warmer than Mario's. 'What's the panic?'

'Panic?' Robin's host jumped as though she had stabbed him. Wine slopped out of his glass and ran over his hands like blood. 'Oh! I see what you mean . . . No. There's no *panic*. Just a little . . . failure of communication.'

'Between whom? About what?' asked Robin as the maître d' sent the sommelier into the firing line after all with Tristan's *Brunello di Montalcino 2004* and Robin's *Colle del Principe*. 'And what has it got to do with Richard or with me?'

'Ah. Well, thereby hangs a tale, you see . . .' Tristan rumbled, frowning over the length of time it was taking to get to his bottle.

'I'm all ears, Tristan,' prompted Robin, sipping the icy Prosecco.

'Well, as one of the chaps at the centre of the insurance – and reinsurance of *Sayonara*, I was asked to arrange a little test of security . . .'

'I see,' said Robin, suspecting what was coming at once, or the start of it at any rate. Had Richard been sitting in this chair, she knew, he would have taken up the story like Sherlock Holmes. *So you asked around and someone recommended a bunch of chaps who could really test out* Sayonara*'s defences. And you arranged to send them aboard . . .*

'. . . rounded up this bunch of chaps to go aboard and test the defences out, so to speak, and sent them up to Hawadax Island, in the Aleutians. Place called Rat Island Pass. Convenient for boarding, apparently. . . .'

'That's right,' said Robin. 'They went aboard earlier.'

Tristan jumped again. More blood-red wine slopped over his hands.

'You don't say so?' Tristan sounded relieved, and looked as though he had won the lottery.

So that was what this was about, thought Robin. Tristan was under some kind of pressure – in some kind of funk – because he'd lost contact with the men he'd sent aboard *Sayonara*. And he needed Richard – or her – to bring him up to speed. But why? Why the panic?

'We lost contact, you see. Not a peep out of them in sixty hours and counting. Silent as the tomb since just after they got to Rat Island. We were expecting a call to confirm that everything was . . . ah . . . *ship-shape*, if you follow me. But they're on board after all! I had no idea! On board already? Well I'd better tell . . .'

'*Signor* Lazzaro,' announced maître d' Marco's still-chilly voice.

'Well, yes,' blustered Tristan, disorientated. 'But how did you . . .'

'Good evening,' said a new, smooth voice. Tristan looked up while Robin looked round. The regal maître d' was standing with a man by his side. A slim, vibrant man perhaps ten years Tristan's senior but less than half his weight. And yet the breadth of the shoulders and the depth of chest were there. Did they play rugby in Italy? She wondered. But, judging from the face, *Murderball* might be this man's preferred sport. Even in profile it was easy to see the sharp line of cheekbone and the way the cheek itself settled into a cavern before the equally sharp

line of his jaw. And, above the cheekbone, the deep, secret hollow
of his eye socket beneath the crag of brow and the upward
sweep of the domed forehead – hollow again at the temple,
capped with short-cropped grey hair so thick it looked like a
steel helmet. She noticed the aquiline jut of his nose down to
the thin-lipped shark's mouth, and the way his chin jutted just
where Tristan's receded. How apt, she thought. Here was a man
that looked every inch the Italian Macbeth. Or the murderous
Scarpia, perhaps, from *Tosca*.

But then *Signor* Lazzaro's profile swung towards Robin and
the eyes in those cavernous sockets proved to be a deep, melting
brown, fringed with lashes many a woman would die to possess
and surrounded by deep laugh-lines. '*Capitano* Robin Mariner,
is it not?' purred a deep voice with a frisson of nasality and
the sweet, heady Italian depth of Amaretto. 'Permit me.
Francisco Alberto Lazzaro at your service.' Robin smiled and
nodded, thinking that delicious Amaretto tasted and smelt of
almonds. As did deadly cyanide. Straightaway, Robin suspected
that Lazzaro was the source of Tristan's nervousness. But
why?

The newcomer sat in the seat that Tristan had clearly been
saving for him. Lazzaro glanced up at Mario. 'I would like San
Pellegrino to drink, and to see the menu now, please.'

Mario vanished. Lazzaro leaned forward, still without having
addressed Tristan directly, even though he was now seated at
his right hand. He was careful to keep the sleeve of his beau-
tifully-tailored beige suit jacket – Milan, Robin thought;
perhaps Gianni Campagna – clear of the puddle of wine in
front of Tristan. 'Now, I expect that Tristan here has informed
you, I have been in the fortunate position of being able to
support him and his consortium through some difficult financial
times. A *disagreement* . . .' The rich voice lingered over the
word, '. . . between poor Tristan and *Signora* Folgate, has,
shall we say, alienated the lady and her father, the *Patrizio*
Palmi. And as a result I have gained a certain amount of . . .
shall we call it . . . *influence* in the syndicate. To the tune of
a few million euros . . . As a friend of the family – of the
s*ignora's* family, true, but that should not get in the way of
business . . .'

Robin looked across at Tristan, but he was into his *Brunello di Montalcino 2004* and apparently unaware of this humiliating washing of his embarrassingly dirty laundry in public.

'And I'm afraid that it was I,' continued the smooth Italian, 'who suggested that we should test the security of *Sayonara* by sending a team of men aboard her. A little test by which I planned to assure myself of the soundness of my investment. A plan that now, however, may have gone awry.'

'No, no, Francisco,' huffed Tristan importantly, rejoining the conversation. 'It's all fine. Robin says the team went aboard in Rat Island Pass yesterday. It's all going like clockwork. Just like I planned.'

'That's where Richard is,' Robin added, her grey eyes probing the deep brown ones opposite. 'He's leading the security response team – the A Team – himself. They should have gone aboard about an hour ago if everything's running to time. And with Richard it usually does.'

'I *see*,' said Lazzaro, leaning back suddenly.

Robin too saw. More than she was supposed to see, perhaps. Something that Tristan did not – and would never have understood if he had done so. She saw a gleam in the depths of those dark Italian eyes, before those long, dark lashes came down like a visor. Tristan Folgate-Lothbury might think everything was going like clockwork, mused Robin as Mario arrived with the menus, but Francisco Alberto Lazzaro clearly thought otherwise. And if he was the new power in the Folgate-Lothbury syndicate now that *Signora* Folgate-Lothbury and her fortune had departed, it looked to her as though Tristan had better start watching his back. For the charming *Signor* Lazzaro looked as though he was up to something . . .

It was a generally accepted fact that some sections of Heritage Mariner were open and functioning on a twenty-four-hour basis. Crewfinders never closed, for instance. Captains, owners and agents could call their number at any time, night or day, from anywhere in the world – any port or any ocean – certain of a speedy reply and of a crew member of any rank or skill available to them and arriving onboard within twenty-four hours. Another section of the massive company that never slept was

London Centre – the commercial intelligence section. It would be working at full stretch even in the early hours.

All the way back east from Mayfair, Robin's mind whirled over what she had said, heard, seen and deduced during the conversation over dinner. Such had been her gathering concern that she had consumed only one glass of the divine Prosecco – with the *Cape Sante* scallops that had formed her Antipasti. Then she had joined Lazzaro with the San Pellegrino to accompany the *Taglio di Vitello* which had formed her main meal. Now, as she digested her heavenly wood-roasted veal chop, she found she had a good deal on her mind – and much of it worrying. Especially, she thought, checking the time on the screen of her doggedly silent cellphone, in the absence of any contact from Richard, who must have been on board *Sayonara* for well over an hour now.

'No,' said Robin to the taxi driver, therefore, as he slowed at the corner of Cornhill and Bishopsgate. 'Not here at Heritage House. Can you take me on into Leadenhall and down to the corner of Creechurch?'

Five minutes later, she had paid him off and was walking up towards the glass door that fronted the London Centre. The foyer was bright and an ex-army security man crossed smartly to the main entrance as she keyed in her security code, swinging it open for her and coming to attention as she entered. 'Thank you, Sergeant Stone,' she said. 'Is Mr Toomey in?'

Patrick Toomey met Robin at the lift door and ushered her down to the office as though she were visiting royalty. He was a big man, blue-eyed, red-haired and liberally freckled, as broadly Irish as his name. He was noted for his cheery bonhomie, his ready wit and a laugh that could fill a large room to the echo. He should have been the proprietor of one of London's Celtic pubs. He was actually an ex-spy, special forces trained, and perhaps second only to Jim Bourne himself in the world of commercial intelligence. He was as usual in shirtsleeves, though his heather mixture Donegal tweed jacket was hanging over the back of his chair.

'Francisco Alberto Lazzaro?' he rumbled in answer to Robin's question. 'Yes. I've heard of him, all right.'

'I'd like to know all about him, please, Pat.'

'You want a drink? It'll be a long night and you're going to need one.'

'I bet you say that to all the girls. What've you got?'

'Whisky.' He was shocked that she'd even had to ask.

'Bushmills?' she hazarded, knowing his tastes of old.

'Black Bush,' he nodded. 'And as it's yourself, I've the twenty-one-year-old malt.'

'That'll do nicely. Straight up. No ice. I'll sip.'

'That's the only way we serve it – and that's the only way to drink it,' pontificated Pat. 'Now, you'll need to shuffle round to my side of the desk while I pour the drinks. I'll show you what I've got on my laptop.'

Five minutes later, Robin was nursing a quadruple measure of one of the finest liquors in the world, with the chocolate, toffee-rich taste of it chasing bursts of mint along her tongue, paying no attention at all to the heavenly savour as she watched the pictures on Pat's laptop. A camera panned over a bullet-pocked car in which a dead driver slumped spattered with blood, and zoomed in on the first of five other corpses lying on the road partially covered with white sheets. White sheets through which more blood was leaking. 'This is Germany,' Pat was explaining. 'Duisburg, North Rhine-Westphalia. Ten kilometres north of Düsseldorf. Fifteenth of August, 2007. Six dead.'

'Who are they?' asked Robin, willing to take it as read that this was relevant – something to do with Lazzaro. 'Neo-Nazis? What?'

'Italians,' he answered. 'Calabrians, in fact. Like your Francisco Lazzaro. They were slaughtered as part of a long-running vendetta. The *San Luca* feud.'

'OK. Robin looked at the shocking pictures and took another sip of Bushmills. 'What are Italians doing in north Germany?'

'These Italians were looking to expand the family business,' said Pat weightily. 'And it seems that this particular family business involved cocaine.'

'So Lazzaro is really a drug smuggler?'

'What,' asked Pat by way of an answer, 'if there was an organi-zation that ran parallel to the Mafia? Only it was more secret? Better organized in some respects? Richer and more powerful, but most people have never heard of it?'

Pat clicked on to Wikipedia, and Robin read: '*The 'Ndrangheta is a criminal organization in Italy, centered in Calabria (near Sicily). Despite not being as famous abroad as the Sicilian Cosa Nostra, and having been considered more rural compared to the Neapolitan Camorra and the Apulian Sacra Corona Unita, the 'Ndrangheta managed to become the most-powerful crime syndicate of Italy in the late 1990s and early 2000s. While commonly lumped together with the Sicilian Mafia, the 'Ndrangheta operates independently from the Sicilians, though there is contact between the two, due to the geographical proximity, and shared culture and language of Calabria and Sicily. A US diplomat estimated that the organization's drug trafficking, extortion and money-laundering activities accounted for at least three per cent of Italy's GDP.*'

'Three per cent,' said Robin. How much is that?

'Italy's GDP is about two point two trillion dollars. Three per cent of that, off the top of my head, is in the region of sixty-six billion, give or take, if I've got my noughts in the right place . . .'

'Sixty-six *billion* dollars! It's no wonder that, as it says here, *Since the 1950s, the organization has spread towards the north of Italy and worldwide.* Yes,' Robin added thoughtfully, ''Ndrangheta. I think I've heard of them.'

She sat back, frowning. Savouring, suddenly, the sweet complexity of the whisky on her tongue. 'Heritage Mariner doesn't do a lot of container work in the Mediterranean as such, but we bring a shedload of stuff in through Suez and out past Gib. So I know a good deal about Gioia Tauro, the big new container port in Calabria – and the fact that it's supposed to be under almost total Mafia control. But clearly it's a mistake just to lump the Mafia and the 'Ndrangheta together. So that makes the 'Ndrangheta look like the biggest net importer of cocaine from the South American drug cartels. Isn't that it?'

'It is. And you're right to make the distinction: not Mafia – *'Ndrangheta*. And the 'Ndrangheta are coining it in as a result. Especially as – until 2010 – the Italian authorities were more focused on keeping the Mafia under some kind of control in Sicily . . .'

'. . . while the 'Ndrangheta grew like weeds in Calabria, just across the strait of Messina . . .'

'That,' said Pat lugubriously, 'is only the beginning. After the massacre in Germany I showed you, the Italian authorities began to go after 'Ndrangheta godfathers as well as Mafia ones. They started literally digging them out of the mountains. They had whole towns riddled with underground tunnels and hidey-holes. As a result of which, 'Ndrangheta wanted to move its money and influence abroad. It already had powerful cells in places where Italian communities exist. Taking it alphabetically . . .' he clicked back on to Wikipedia, '. . . that would be Argentina, Australia, Belgium, Canada, Colombia, Germany – as we know – the Netherlands, Mexico, South Africa and, of course, the United States. But, my point is this: they are always on the lookout for ways to expand. New associates. New markets. And they will go in via legitimate enterprises. Look.' He clicked on the link to a particular section of the page and Robin read: *Belgium: 'Ndrangheta clans purchased almost 'an entire neigh-bourhood' in Brussels with laundered money originating from drug trafficking. On 5 March 2004, forty-seven people were arrested, accused of drug trafficking and money laundering to purchase real estate in Brussels for some twenty-eight million euros. The activities extended to the Netherlands where large quantities of heroin and cocaine had been purchased . . .*

'And you're telling me that Lazzaro is a part of this?'

'No. I'm telling you that Lazzaro is the *capo* of the Gioia Tauro clan. He's among the first of the 'Ndrangheta *capi* to be moving himself outside Italy and running things internationally. He's looking to expand into markets – legitimate and illegitimate – that will glean him the most profit. He's open to suggestions and up for making contacts. With anyone. Anywhere.'

'And he seems to be the guy who's now elbowing in on the syndicate insuring *Sayonara*. The guy who sent the team aboard that Richard is facing down . . .' Robin paused and frowned, remembering the flash of irritation in those deep, dark chocolate eyes. 'Oh, shit, Pat,' she said.

'What?' Pat reached for the precious Bushmills bottle.

'Tristan Folgate-Lothbury sent the team aboard. At least, he sent them to Rat Island. And then he lost contact with them altogether . . .'

'What do you mean?' asked Pat solicitously.

'What if the team that went aboard weren't Tristan's team? Lazzaro wanted the drill. What if they were Lazzaro's men? What if they were 'Ndrangheta?'

68 Hours to Impact

R ichard tore the headset off his streaming eyes, blinking fiercely and shaking his head. His vision cleared almost at once and he saw his teammates floundering blindly all around him, their night-vision goggles overcome by the brightness. He stepped forward, fearing that this was a trick to incapacitate them before springing some kind of trap. But no. Apart from the men nearest to him – and the sounds of the second group echoing over from the port side, there was nothing. No movement. No challenge. Just the distant buzz of fluorescent strip-lighting. The sighing of the wind against the canopy. The stirring of the waves. The restless *sotto voce* rumbling of the turbines.

Richard crossed to the reeling figure of Rikki Sato and caught him by the shoulder. It took a moment to calm the jumpy computer expert, then he was able to pull off the headset and offer the blind man the glasses hooked into a breast pocket on his bulletproof vest. 'Doctor Sato, it's Richard Mariner,' he said. 'It's just the ship's lighting. Do the systems on board switch on automatically?'

'Yes! There are sensors . . .' The computer expert actually slapped himself on the forehead with frustration and anger, hard enough to send the black-framed glasses skittering down the short slope of his nose. Richard stepped back. He had never seen anyone do that before. 'The lighting system works on the motion sensors. I should have remembered,' the distraught man wailed.

'Don't beat yourself up, Doctor,' he said. 'There's more than simple slips of memory at work here. When the first team went into the bridge house thirty-one hours ago, they didn't set off any motion sensors to switch on any lights or we'd have seen it on our systems in London. This is all being done on purpose. As was that.'

'What do you mean?'

'I mean that they had the emergency override codes – the same as your guys do, and only Mitsubishi Heavy Industries and Fujitsu men have access to those. They came aboard, went into the bridge house and set off the red alert. They set off the cameras, but not the motion sensors, or the lights would have come on. They wanted to work in the dark because they wanted us to be in the dark. They wanted us to know someone was on board, perhaps, but not who. And then, when the transmissions from the on-board cameras stopped and we couldn't keep such a close eye on them any more – I'll bet that's when the motion sensors for the lights came back online; the ones we tripped just now, so they could do whatever they wanted to do without having to fuss with inconvenient headsets and infra-red night-vision equipment.'

'But if it was motion sensors that switched the lights on now,' said Sato, 'it was not a trap, or else something would be happening.'

Richard looked around as soon as Sato finished speaking and waited for the others to sort themselves out. After Sato, his next priority, of course, was Aleks. Dom would have to take care of himself. But neither needed his immediate assistance. They were all pulling off their goggles and mopping their eyes. He turned away from the group of men he had entered with and caught his breath at what he saw, losing his train of thought as the immediacy of what he was seeing simply overwhelmed him. It was even more than he had imagined in the vast, echoing darkness just before the lights went on.

True, as he had sensed, they had stepped into a long, narrow passage immediately inside the bulkhead door, for the wall of the whaleback cover rose seemingly less than a metre beyond his square shoulder, coming in over his head like the wall of a tunnel. But on the other, equally close at hand, rose a dome. A dome like the dome of St Paul's in London. And there, beyond it in the brightness, another, like the dome of St Peter's in Rome. Beyond that, St Mark's in Venice or the Church of the Saviour on Spilled Blood in St Petersburg. In fact, he thought, simply dazed, if you lined those domes up one after another, you would still have to add the great dome of Santa Sophia in Istanbul to make up the set.

Five great domes rose out of the deck before him, swelling and receding as the green nonslip decking sat around them with great circles cut out of it to accommodate them below. They differed from the greatest architectural domes fashioned by the greatest church-builders only in that they were larger than anything Palladio, Brunaleschi or Wren had ever dreamed of, and as smooth as the surfaces of gargantuan balloons, blanketed in the steel cladding of the whaleback's interior. Shrinking away from it, like breasts beneath a nightgown as they receded towards the nipples at their apexes where the pipes stood ready to conduct their liquid cargo in and out.

Each hemisphere had a radius of twenty-two metres from centre point to outer edge, and a radius of twenty-two metres from centre point to topmost curve. Five metres each way bigger than St Paul's, in fact, thought Richard, tricked into plundering his encyclopaedic general knowledge. How much bigger they were than the other great domes only Heaven knew. And, sitting in shrinking holes in the decks below, did the domes continue to make perfect spheres? He fought to remember the detail of the schematic on the laptop he had left back with Ivan. So he did what any of the techies blinking owlishly around him would have done: he pulled out his Galaxy and called up the schematic on that – the detailed one he kept in the cloud rather than the basic one stored in the memory. Or rather, he would have. But there was no signal. He checked, frowning with simple surprise. There was battery. There was memory. There was everything pre-programmed. Everything stored on the hard drive. But nothing from the cloud.

He had been talking to Robin little more than an hour ago and only a couple of hundred feet up in the air. But now there was no signal whatsoever.

The implications of the last conversation he had had with Robin hit him with breathtaking force, for the overconfident joking looked as though it would turn into a very unfunny fact very soon indeed if he couldn't get a message out. Because if he didn't find a way to stop her, she really would be sending in Harry and the Pitman. 'Aleks,' he said, his voice as always becoming deeper, slower and calmer the louder alarm bells started ringing in his head, 'how's the reception on your headset? How's the big communications centre your man over there is carrying? Any contact going out? Any external signals coming in?'

He showed the Russian his phone. 'I mean, this is the latest Galaxy smartphone. Worldwide reception guaranteed.'

Rikki Sato came over and took it. He looked at it, touching the screen gently and frowning. 'Signal's being blocked,' he decided after a while.

And Aleks nodded, tapping the equipment that filled his right ear. 'Mine too,' he said. 'I have internal comms, though, I think.' He turned to his communications man – distinguished by the size of the radio pack he carried on his shoulders and the whip antenna soaring out of it. 'Well?' he asked.

'The battlefield unit's working fine,' came the reply. 'But nothing else is. You and Senior Warrant Officer Roskov ought to be able to talk to each other fine – for the time being, at least. But we should be able to talk out to Moscow, or the moon, and we can't. We're being blocked, like Doctor Sato says. Nothing in. Nothing out. Nothing I can do about it, I'm afraid, until we find out what's responsible. Or who.'

Harry Newbold is sitting with the Pitman on the patio behind their combined house and office in Amsterdam when Robin's message comes in. Harry's fingers are shaking with cold because it is drizzling and the temperature is unseasonably low, even allowing for the time, which is a little after two a.m. And a bathing costume is the least appropriate apparel that anyone could possibly be wearing under the circumstances. In fact, Harry is fortunate not to be working stark naked. 'Come on,' snarls the Pitman. 'You can strip it faster than that!'

Harry's shaking fingers pull the little Hechler and Kock P30 apart, laying the sections neatly on the table. Harry is working blind: sight is denied for it is well after midnight and the lights are out, even though this is just another one of the Pitman's little training exercises. 'What really bugs me, Pitman, is that there's nothing equally uncomfortable I can make you do with a computer programme, a virus or a worm. I think you're begin-ning to take these exercises too far!'

'You're breaking my heart,' grates the Pitman gutturally. 'I'm not wearing any more than you are but I'm not shivering or whining. Now get a move on. Just 'cause you're the hacker doesn't guarantee you'll only get to sit on your ass and play with your laptops and tablets. And no one ever promised us we were going to have to field-strip our weapons on a sunny afternoon!'

Just as Harry snaps the final sections of the handgun back together, the Pitman's phone rings. Robin's face fills the screen, providing the only light. 'We've lost contact,' Robin says. 'Richard should've reported. He hasn't.'

'We're on our way,' promises the Pitman. 'Harry: dry off and do your magic thing. I'll look after the Hechler and get us some clothes.'

'There's more to it than that,' Robin continues as the Pitman carries the phone into the house behind the discreet little office front overlooking the canal at Jolicoeurstraat in the Zuidoost business district, flicking on the lights. 'Richard's been lackadaisical, as usual, but like I said, he swore he'd contact me the instant they went aboard.'

'OK. But you said there was more.'

'Have you heard of the 'Ndrangheta?'

'In Amsterdam, who hasn't?' answers the Pitman, frowning. 'They're supposed to be shoving shitloads of coke in through here. All through Europe – and into Russia. Europoort, St Petersburg, Archangel. Anywhere a cargo ship can dock – especially one that's come out of Gioia Tauro. Word is that a pretty high percentage of the coke they transport out of Gioia Tauro used to come into Amsterdam or Europoort for shipment and distribution through Europe. But now apparently they're opening up the Russian market. They're tough guys, the 'Ndrangheta – you don't want to mess with them. What have they got to do with this?'

Robin explained in some detail what Pat Toomey told her.

'Chill, Robin,' advises Pitman after a while. 'We're always packed and ready to hit the road. Like the flashlight batteries – *Ever-ready* . . .'

By the time Robin has finished speaking and the Pitman has broken contact, Harry is seated at the computer. Its screen is rapidly filling with flight information far more intimate and detailed than anything Flightbookers, Kayak or Expedia could offer. The Pitman is pulling out pre-packed bags and backpacks.

'Fastest way out is on a Japan airlines departing Schiphol,' calls Harry, hacking into Schiphol airport's system. 'It's operated by Finnair. Boeing 747. One stop in Helsinki, then over the Pole to Narita. I've no doubt someone can chopper us out from there. Say twenty hours in all to *Sayonara*. Twenty-two tops. Gates close at two-thirty. Lift-off at five-thirty.'

'It's fully booked,' observes the Pitman, the Dutch accent thickening towards *Voortrekker* with disappointment and disgust. 'Overbooked, in fact.'

'Not as far as we're concerned,' growls Harry. 'Two seats side by side in first class have just become available for every section of the journey. Full frequent flyer privileges. Emerald Tier.' Harry looks up and grins knowingly. 'Grab the gear, lover. I'll complete the paperwork while you get the Harley-Davidson hot. And I'll slow things down for everyone else at Schliopl with a little unscheduled security exercise, I think. Under these circumstances, twenty-four kliks in less than an hour is pushing it, even for us!'

66 Hours to Impact

It went against Richard's inclinations to begin their search in a militarily methodical manner – he was always one for unexpected inspiration, and he felt increasingly strongly that this was what was needed now. But he had put Aleks in operational command and, for once, Richard was grudgingly content to pass the authority down the line. For the time being, at least. Especially as it allowed him to watch and learn, to observe and surmise from the best in the business, which facilitated the kind of intellectual detection he normally enjoyed when he played Sherlock Holmes to Robin's ever patient Watson. He found himself thinking of Robin also because of his inability to contact her, which had to mean that Harry and the Pitman would be joining them within the next day or so, and Aleks was under added pressure to have things sorted before they dropped in and queered his pitch.

'Look, Aleks,' he said quietly at the outset, before things started going more seriously awry, 'if these people are still aboard, then they know we are here. Even if they didn't notice a bloody great chopper buzzing over the ship, they'll have seen the lights come on. They've had more than twenty-four hours to settle in and get ready for our retaliation. We'll be exploring enemy territory that they already know backwards. We have to go slowly and carefully in case they've left any surprises. They already know where everything is – whether they left it there or not. And we're out on a limb down here – with all the main computers, control and propulsion the length of the ship away up there in the bridge house. Fair enough, there are way stations where the techies can access systems, records and what-have-you if they're lucky and the opposition have been careless. But if we want to make a real difference before Harry and the Pitman show up then I suggest we make a pre-emptive strike for the bridge.'

'I'm sorry, Captain Mariner,' answered Aleks. 'We agreed that I'm in command. You and the other executives are here as observers, and to help when necessary. We do things my way.'

'Fair enough, Aleks. I signed up for this. You do your stuff and pay no attention to me.'

'Right,' said Aleks. 'Let's get on with it then.'

They stayed inside the hull to begin with as Aleks was content that the forecastle head with its winches and helipad which they had just vacated was clear. On his order, therefore, the port and starboard teams proceeded towards the stern, along the main deck, under the cover of the whaleback. The first great dome gathered and receded. The deck beneath their feet widened until it was possible to see from one side to the other, and the two teams waved to each other through the cleavage between the mountainous domes. At this point, on each side, there was a hatchway that opened at the top of a ladder leading down into the vessel's lower decks. 'Open the hatches,' ordered Aleks. 'We go down. Doctor Sato, what computer equipment is down there?'

'On the next deck down, nothing but storage. Then there's the chain lockers. In the lower decks, the engineering decks, there are lines from the sonar set and the forwards GPS in the ship's bow. Below that only the pipes that join the undersides of the Moss tanks.'

'Right. Engineer?' Aleks looked expectantly around his team.

'I am Engineer Esaki,' said a square, solid man, stepping forward. 'It is as Doctor Sato says. The decks in the forecastle head are simply arranged. As, indeed, are all the decks. This is not a complicated design by any means. Beneath the weather deck with the helicopter landing area are the storage areas, then the chain lockers. They are two decks deep and hold the anchor chains and the equipment ancillary to the winches. They are accessible at the top level but are dangerous places, particularly in heavy seas. The chains, like the cargo, will move when the hull rolls or pitches. Below these, where the flare of the cutwater itself leads down into the standard bulbous bow torpedo shape, there is a two-deck deep area that houses the sonar array. This is constantly active, of course. Lines run from this along the third deck down – the third of the four decks that go down before you reach the bilges and the double-hull where the skirts support the lower sections of the Moss tanks and the pipes that join them. These lines take information from the sonar set to the main control and propulsion computers in the bridge and the decks beneath it.' Esaki held up a schematic of *Sayonara*'s interior on his tablet. The main, or weather, deck ran along the vessel from the helideck on the bow to the stern-rail under the lifeboat. The main-deck level of the interior bridge house was A Deck. The decks in the bridge house above it mounted through B, C, and D to E, which was the main command deck where the command bridge peered over the whaleback. Then, above the command bridge was the upper weather deck, the topmost deck comprised of a large expanse of decking that stood open to the wind and rain on either side of the funnel. Beneath the main deck, the engineering decks also went down in series through B to D towards the keel. But these decks ran the length of the ship within the hull and were pierced by five huge round holes that housed the Moss tanks containing the cargo.

'Are there access points on those lines that might allow Doctor Sato's computer experts access to those computers?' demanded Richard.

'Can we link up and hack in from down there, you mean?' asked Sato, answering before Esaki could. 'It's possible, I suppose. And certainly there are access points – both where a laptop can be plugged in to examine local systems or nearby sections of the larger systems.' He gestured at the lights blazing above them. 'We clearly have power, and all my people have adapters that can handle voltages from one hundred and ten to two hundred and forty.'

'The on-board system is the standard hundred and ten volts,' added Esaki. 'This also is standard in Japan. You should not need your adapters, Doctor Sato.'

'But there are also access points built in,' Sato persisted frostily, none too pleased that Esaki was interrupting the flow of information. 'Most of these are touch-screen. It should be possible to access and perhaps regain some control over some of the systems from these points. It is what we are here to do, after all. But, of course, it is also a risk. The instant we connect, the opposition will know where we are and what we are doing.'

'Doctor Sato,' said Aleks, his voice a little weary, 'I have every reason to believe that the opposition already know exactly where we are and precisely what we are doing. But unless we do it, we will never know for certain. And we will never learn how men like these can be stopped. So let's go down.'

The problem with Aleks' methodical approach, persisted Richard's uneasy thoughts, was its predictability. They were searching for a dozen or so men in a hull whose capacity topped three hundred and fifty thousand cubic metres below decks. And that was independent of the extra capacity offered by the whaleback cover and the bridge house. Now, fair enough, most of this space was filled with anchor chains, sonar, Moss tanks, engines, alternators, computers and ancillary equipment like rudder gear and whatnot. It was right down here in the torpedo-shaped bow that the black box that recorded every change of engine and rudder setting, every variation in heading and speed, was kept. But there were still plenty of places where the opposition could hide – inside and out – while the earnest search teams sought them. If the opposition chose to, they could become like ghosts, ever present but invisible, on the deck or the deck above. Around the next corner. Or, come to that, sitting comfortably up in the bridge house with a plate of biscuits and a cup of tea, watching them on the monitors, the internal cameras, the motion sensors . . . How he itched to do what Aleks had forbidden – to strike out with a little independent commando

– running up the deck or along the top of the whaleback to avoid the cameras and sensors, hitting the bridge house from behind to see what was really going on.

'Creepy, huh?' came Dom DiVito's voice over the communications headset, unexpectedly enough to make Richard jump.

'And then some,' he admitted.

'You feel like you're being watched?' chimed in Steve Penn.

'Watched, tracked, listened to, you name it . . .' Dom chuckled mirthlessly.

'They have to control the airwaves – they're jamming out outside signals. Therefore they can probably listen to us as well,' Richard warned.

'So every time Aleks gives an order . . .' Dom observed.

'He tells them what he's up to,' affirmed Richard. 'And just because we lost transmission from the cameras and sensors back in Heritage House doesn't mean they haven't got the full array lit up like a Christmas tree on the bridge.'

'Fair enough. *But why, if this is just a drill?* Surely that's not part of the usual drill. I mean, what's the point? And who are they?' demanded Steve.

'That's for them to know and for us to find out,' concluded Richard.

This conversation, and its extension during the next hour or so, took them past the doors into the chain lockers, down as far as the first access point just behind the sonar in the bulbous bow, three decks below. By the time they arrived there, everyone was strung out, both physically and emotionally. They were increasingly aware of how far beneath the surface of the ocean they were going, and none of them would have made good submariners. The lights down here seemed dimmer. The air was staler, clammier. Even Richard was beginning to let the silences between the increasingly dark speculations he was exploring with Dom and Steve drag out longer and longer.

But at last, having completed the first survey, Aleks led them back to the access point that Dr Sato and his second in command, computer engineer Murukami, had both agreed would let them access the system. It was as they had said – two decks up from the bilge itself, on the last deck with a solid floor – the one below was made of mesh that could be raised in sections for maintenance. On the wall a couple of metres aft of the main door into the sonar area was a small screen the size of a tablet computer on the wall itself. Lines in white ducting led along the wall on either side. An access point for computer leads or a memory stick stood in a little box beneath it.

Aleks described what he could see quietly into his headset and Konstantin on the far side of the ship agreed that he could see the same. Richard and Steve agreed with their respective leaders.

Sato tapped the screen in the wall in front of him. It remained blank.

Konstantin's man did the same. With the same result.

'Give me a laptop,' ordered Sato. 'I'll see what I can access using a connection.'

Murukami passed his boss a laptop and a long connector wire. Sato plugged one end of the wire into the back of his laptop and stepped towards the wall, holding the other end, ready to make connection.

There was an explosion of sound in Richard's headset. 'STOP!' he shouted automatically, long before he knew what was going on. 'Steve! What is it? What's happened?'

'Some kind of short,' answered Steve Penn breathlessly. 'Our man plugged his laptop in and it almost exploded! Blew him right across the corridor. There's smoke coming out of the socket. He's gone down like a felled tree. I think he's dead!'

Richard just had time to register the look of sheer, stark horror on Rikki Sato's face. And then the lights went out.

63 Hours to Impact

Everyone froze except Richard, who pulled his night-vision goggles on. 'Get your goggles on,' he advised. 'And get some CPR going, Steve. If your man's not dead yet he needs help as fast as possible. Is he well clear of the shorting cable?'

'Yeah,' came Steve's shaky reply. 'But I think we might be too late for CPR. He looks really weird under the infra-red – like he's still on fire. Our medic's checking him now . . .' There followed a moment's silence, then Steve added, 'No. He's gone, I'm afraid.'

'We'll have to make arrangements to leave him somewhere safe while the rest of us proceed,' said Richard to Aleks.

'Right,' said Aleks. The Russian seemed shaken. Perhaps even shocked.

The lights flickered, luckily giving Richard enough warning to get his goggles off before they came back on. 'Have you got a volt metre?' he asked Sato, who was still standing with a laptop in one hand and the snake of the connector wavering with its head dangerously close to the wall, apparently frozen with horror. 'If the light's back on, so's the power. This one might be dangerous as well. Can you check?' Richard gently took the laptop from the stricken engineer and handed it back to Murukami. 'Has anyone got a volt metre?' he repeated. 'Anything we can check the power in this socket with? See if it's as dangerous as the other one?'

Sato pulled himself back together, took a black box out of his belt and approached the connection. There was the slightest sloshing sound. Frowning, Richard looked down and the instant he did so, he reached out and took the computer man by the shoulder. Immediately beneath the connection there was a pool of water. Anyone making a connection must be standing in it.

'Wait, please, Doctor,' he said to Sato. 'Steve, is the deck wet beneath the fused connection point?'

'Yes, it is, now you mention it. The whole passageway is damp.'

'Doctor Sato, I think we can assume that any attempt to connect to the circuits down here will be dangerous and possibly fatal. I'd leave well alone. Lieutenant Zaitsev,' he emphasized the officer's title, jerking him out of his frowning stasis, 'we need to decide what we're going to do with the casualty. Then I think we need to clear this deck level and proceed with even more caution than we have so far.'

'But it was an accident, surely!' said Aleks half an hour later as the reassembled team completed the brief Shinto service and prepared to leave the dead computer expert lying as reverently as possible at the top of the ladder beside the main hatch on the covered A Deck.

Certainly, there had been nothing to suggest otherwise at the
scene of the accident, thought Richard. The most careful examination conducted by Dr Sato and by the ship's engineers had
revealed nothing untoward. Nothing particularly unusual, in
fact, except the dampness on the deck. Which, as they all
observed, could well have come from condensation on the outer
surface of the Moss tank behind them. It wouldn't take much
in the way of a flaw in the insulation for the core of minus one
hundred and sixty degrees Celsius to cause condensation out
here where it was roughly two hundred degrees Celsius warmer.
So, yes. It looked like the kind of accident that was all too
common on working vessels, no matter how exhaustive the
health and safety regimes.

Some of the dead man's friends would observe the *Kichu
Fuda* day of intense mourning – though there was no priest to
lead the rites correctly. All of them searched in their pockets
and packs to leave obituary gifts or *Koden* beside the still corpse,
whose name in the life he had so recently departed, Richard
learned, had been Yoichi Hatta – an apt name for an engineer
of any sort. But until he was back home and the proper rituals
of immolation and *Kotsuage* could be carried out, and the
bunkotsu which would allow the founding of a family shrine,
there was nothing more they could do. 'It was more likely than
not an accident,' concluded Aleks shortly.

There was a moment of silence as Aleks looked around them
all. One by one they shrugged and dropped their eyes under
the intensity of his steely gaze until one of the younger ones,
Boris Brodski, shook his head. 'I don't see that,' he said with
quiet authority. 'In a situation like this, it's silly to assume a
death is just an accident. Fair enough, we don't want to start
panicking at every little sound and shadow. We sure as hell
don't want to get trigger happy. But, I mean, we're not on a
picnic here . . .' Something tapped on the metal outside of the
whaleback, echoing briefly, then gone so swiftly that no one
paid it any real attention.

'You both have a point,' allowed Richard. 'Loose wiring, wet
floor, a little carelessness . . . That's all it takes, I know. But
let's not jump to conclusions. We just have to take care. The
only thing we stand to lose is time. And we still have plenty

of it.' He looked at his watch. 'A little more than sixty-two hours, in fact, until we are due to dock at the NIPEX facility at Choshi.'

'Right,' said Aleks. 'Let's split up as before and proceed with the search as we agreed.'

During the next hundred minutes, they searched the midship sections between the huge spheres of the Moss tanks, from the covered weather deck down to the keel and back up again. Soon it was clear that Richard and Dom DiVito were not the only ones convinced they were being watched. On more than one occasion Aleks – or, according to Steve Penn, Konstantin – had to stop his men from destroying the security equipment they were certain was spying on their every move. They became increasingly monosyllabic, concerned – as Richard had been from the outset – that their communication and movements were being hacked into the bargain. The lighting remained on but, since Yoichi Hatta's electrocution, it seemed duller. The shadows were more numerous, more threatening; darker and closer to hand. The relentless rumbling of the motors and the alternators, the muttering of the water as it bubbled along the hull just beside them and the roaring of the wind across the whaleback just above them all seemed to cloak mocking whispers.

Both Aleks and Konstantin became the subject of increasing pressure as their men became convinced that the opposition were following their every move more and more closely. It was an unexpected consequence of the point Aleks' young associate, Boris Brodski had made. Even the more experienced began to feel that there was someone dogging their footsteps, watching and waiting to attack them. Not only on the decks they had not yet searched and those they had just searched, playing a kind of grim variation of Grandma's Footsteps, but even like spiders on the outside of the whaleback itself. And there seemed reason for this suspicion, at least, because on more than one occasion as he squeezed past the girth of a Moss tank, with his shoulder close to the whaleback's inner surface, Richard thought he heard a stealthy footstep or the tapping sound of something metallic striking the white paint of the outside. As he had, he now registered, in the silence after Aleks' observation just before they left the corpse at the top of the ladder near the hatch out on to the weather deck.

The only real relief came when they explored the midship pulpits that stood either side of the ship, open to the elements, thrusting out in little balconies that hung like bridge wings over the ocean. The atmosphere below deck had become so charged with suspicion and mistrust that it came as a simple, almost blessed, relief to stand out in the late afternoon sun, watching the great golden blaze of it westering towards the horizon as *Sayonara* sailed apparently serenely a little west of south towards distant Japan. 'You see,' called Aleks, clearly overcome by the lessening of the tense atmosphere, 'there is no one out here after all!' He gestured up at the great metal marquee of the whaleback that covered the five Moss tanks. 'No murderous mountaineers swinging on ropes along the sides to spy on us! The idea is ridiculous!' He laughed. 'Take a look for yourselves!'

At his unthinking invitation, most of the starboard team crowded across to the outer rail and leaned back dangerously, stretching their necks to see as much of the white-painted metal curve as possible. And it did, indeed, seem empty and innocent. Appearing to billow like a great metal sail stretched to the full, it curved away on either side until it vanished round the corner at the forecastle or beneath the reach of the bridge wings. Directly above, it reached up, hard edged against the evening sky, the full curve broken only by the tips of the upright pipes and tank caps that ran in series along its top.

But then Richard's keen eyes began to pick out the little inconsistencies that spoke of hand and footholds in the apparently unbroken incline and his memory clicked in, undermining the optical illusion as effectively as if a magic trick were being explained to him. The fact was that the apparently plain top was actually made up of layers as sheaf upon sheaf of pipes ran the length of the thing, coiling into and out of the tank tops as they went. Starting on the side of the pulpit they were occupying and wrapping itself round the metal sail was a metal-runged ladder that reached up to the very top of the thing, joining with a walkway that ran beside the pipes from stem to stern. And Richard was by no means the only one to remember just how many access points, walkways and ladders were in fact riveted to the outer skin of the whaleback.

'Konstantin wants to send someone up on the port side to check whether there has in fact been anyone moving around up there,' came Steve's voice in Richard's headset. 'That a good idea?'

Richard looked across at the gaggle of men grouped round Aleks. He didn't need to open Channel A on the comms to tell him what they were discussing. The gestures would have been clear enough even had they not been shouting at the tops of their voices. 'Tell him to hang fire,' he said. 'Looks like Aleks is about to send someone up anyway.' Richard immediately recognized the soldier Aleks sent up. It was Boris Brodski, the young man who had dared to disagree with him about whether or not the first death had been an accident. The lithe ex-soldier swarmed up the first few rungs with the loose-limbed confidence of an orangutan. Richard himself was just striding across the balcony with Aleks' name on his lips to advise the use of a safety line when the lieutenant stopped the young soldier, handing him a lifeline himself. Grudgingly, the young man took the line and cinched it to the thick webbing of his gun belt before snapping the carabineer at the far end of it to the hand rail that ran up the fat curve beside the iron rungs. Then he was off. Pausing only to un-cinch the clip once or twice where the hand rail was secured to the whaleback by uprights like banisters, he raced up at incredible speed. 'Take your time, Boris! This isn't a race!' warned Aleks.

'Don't worry, Lieutenant, I'll be up there before you can spit and swear,' called Boris by way of answer. And his boast seemed well-based, for he was swarming over the outer curve in record time, outlined against the hard blue sky like a mountaineer on an ice-cliff.

'Take care!' called Aleks as his soldier disappeared at last.

'*To fear death is never to be properly alive!*' called Boris's voice, beginning to sound breathless at last.

As epitaphs went, it was a fitting one – particularly for a soldier. For it seemed that no sooner had he called the mocking words than Boris was tumbling back down the side of the whaleback, face up to the hard blue heaven, etched against it in a capital X shape, arms and legs waving wildly as he fell. The safety line snaked out beside him, a solid, serpentine S against the sky. Becoming a bar-straight stripe against the white curve with terrifying speed as he reached its lower end and the carabiner clip at its upper end caught against the topmost upright of the hand rail.

Boris was still spread-eagled, facing upwards, when the line snapped taut. He had cinched it to his belt buckle. And his unbreakable webbing belt was tight across the small of his back, just above his hips, as though protecting his kidneys.

Because he fell absolutely silently, the rush of his motion and the twang of the tautening line were clearly audible to the stunned men in the pulpit beneath him. As was the *crack!* his spine made as it snapped, broken by the belt as efficiently as a neck being severed by a headsman's axe, just at the moment he came level with them all.

Boris's broken body bounced back up as his headset and goggles came tumbling down. The black line scribbled across the white metal above him, then began to straighten once again as the body fell once more – this time with sufficient force to twist the carabineer open. The line sprang clear of the handrail. Trailing the useless rope like a disconsolate tail, the broken corpse tumbled down on to the outer rail of the pulpit. The outer edge caught it across the chest. Its arms and head flung wildly inboard, as though trying to grab safe hold or call for help. But that was an illusion. Even before anyone could move, let alone try to catch the limp and broken limbs, it slammed back and outwards from the rail, throwing up its hands in surrender, and giving everybody one last glimpse of Boris's white, stricken face. And the black mark in the middle of his forehead, immediately above the bridge of his nose. Then he was gone.

Aleks and Richard led the rush to the rail and craned to see over the side in a last faint hope that he had somehow survived after all, but there was nothing to see but the eternal royal blue of the deep water stretching like an ocean of ink back towards Rat Island Pass and forward towards Japan.

It is 10 a.m. Moscow time as Ivan Yagula runs out of the Lubyanka exit of the Moscow metro and begins to stride across the square where the statue of Felix Dzerzhinsky used to stand, towards the building which housed the grandson of the secret service he had fathered. The square is bustling. Tourists wander all agog, surrounded by the jewels of Russian history. *Militsia* in police uniform and the much maligned GIA traffic cops patrol. The old KGB headquarters building towers dead ahead, but Ivan tends to the left, past the blaze of Detsky Mir, the children's emporium which is yet another example of the manner in which Russia is opening its doors to international business. The CEO of Russia's most famous toy store might be Vladimir Chirahov, but the chairman of the board of directors is still the British business tycoon Christopher Alan Baxter. *Like the old Gazprom/BP combo,* thinks Ivan; *like Bashnev/Sevmash and Heritage Mariner, though Richard's not on the Russian boards any more than Felix or Anastasia are on his.*

Ivan is not heading for Detsky Mir. He plans to pass it instead and cross the car-choked road by Kuznetsky Most metro station, to go into the new building that houses the section of the much-expanded FSB to which he has just been summoned. Without pausing or deviating, the massive man in his long black coat strides through the teeming crowd of lesser mortals all the way across to the doorway with the brass plaque which states: FEDERAL SECURITY SERVICE BUILDING. *Reception.*

Many Muscovites would be too nervous to go where Ivan is going, to talk to the men he is due to meet. But the most powerful of them, the federal prosecutor, is Ivan's father, so he feels that he has little to fear. Probably. Even if the other two are almost as powerful as his fearsome father – *otets.* Viktor Ivanov, the current head of the FSKN, the Federal Drug Control Service, and Yuri Oleshko, the FSB's Director of Investigation. So Ivan approaches the reception door on Kuznetsky Most and rings the bell, waiting impatiently to be identified and admitted.

His father lingers, massively and impatiently immediately inside and they tower, shoulder by shoulder for a moment, seeming to fill the huge room between them. 'Federal Prosecutor,' says Ivan, equably, by way of greeting.

'Hunh,' growls the federal prosecutor by way of answer.

'You're late.' He turns away and begins to walk briskly into the interior of the building.

Ivan easily overcomes the urge to consult his Poljot President chronograph. They both know he is punctual to the second. So he follows, a metre or two behind, like a crown prince in the Tsar's footsteps. Ivan the Terrible, perhaps. 'What's this all about, sir?' he asks as the federal prosecutor – whom he has never actually thought of as *otets* – reaches the stairs. 'Drugs,' Lavrenty Michaelovitch Yagula, Federal Prosecutor of the Russian Federation, says over his shoulder. 'Krokodil, heroin, cocaine, gang warfare, Afghans and Italians. Bashnev/Sevmash. Heritage Mariner.'

'Anything in particular, sir?' asks Ivan, showing none of the surprise or concern that he feels at his father's cryptic words.

'Yes!' snaps his father, going from cryptic to obscure with typical abruptness. 'Eleven bullets.'

The Yagulas come into a large meeting room side by side. Ivan's narrow eyes sweep at once over the two men at its far side and the news page enlarged on the screen between them. *FSB operatives kill 11 Afghan terrorists*, says the headline. Ivan recognizes it from yesterday's *Moscow News*. But he is damned if he could see what this has to do with Bashnev/Sevmash or with Heritage Mariner. 'That looks like a step forward,' he probes, pointing at the news report with his chin. 'Your men have done good work there, General.'

Ivanov grunts – the sound is very much like those the federal prosecutor made. '*Someone* did good work,' he growls. 'But not the FSKN. My men were led by the nose. The whole thing was a set-up.' He zooms in on the photograph that accompanies the article. Judging from the amount of blood around the shrouded figures, they had been all-but shot to pieces.

'But who . . .' asks Ivan, finding himself in the unaccustomed position of not being able to join up the dots.

Yuri Oleshko leans forward suddenly. 'The facts are these,' snaps the director of investigations, his deep voice forthright and forceful. 'We – our agencies – have been fighting the drugs war on two fronts. The Eastern Front against the Afghans and the Chechen *Mafiya* gangs who import their heroin through Uzbekistan and Kazakhstan then across the Caspian Sea into

Georgia, the Black Sea and all the way up the Volga. And the Home Front against the local gangs who hit pharmacies and pharmacy supply companies for painkillers, iodine, lighter fluid, industrial cleaning oil, with which they make—'

'Krokidil,' spits the federal prosecutor.

'The drug that eats its addicts,' nods Ivan. 'I've seen the pictures. And of the victims . . . what's left of them, once the drug rots their flesh away. From the inside.'

'Indeed,' shrugs Oleshko dismissively. 'But now we have a Western Front towards Italy and Eastern Europe with a new enemy opening up. And one cannot win a war on three fronts. Hence our reliance on espionage. A reliance that has resulted in this situation, and our request that you attend this meeting. Do you know this man?'

The newspaper on the overhead is replaced by a passport photograph. It shows a lean, dark-eyed Mediterranean face. 'Yes,' answers Ivan, surprised. 'That's Leo Gatti. He's one of our senior men at Bashnev Oil and Power . . .' He pauses, his mind racing as he fights to recall the details of Leo Gatti's position and responsibilities. 'His main job is as executive liaison up in St Petersburg. He's our man overseeing the docks, the cargoes, containers and so forth. Which makes him our chief liaison officer with Heritage Mariner Shipping up there.'

'He was also,' the federal prosecutor interrupts his son's sudden flow of information, 'working for us.'

Ivan doesn't pick up on the past tense at once. But he picks up on the rest of the words. 'For *you*?' he snarls, swinging round to lock his gaze with his father's, making full eye contact for the first time.

'He was our eyes on the Third Front,' explains Oleshko.

'Keeping us as up to date as possible on what was coming in. Especially from the Italian port of Gioia Tauro,' adds Ivanov.

'Have you heard,' demands the federal prosecutor, 'of the 'Ndrangheta?'

'Of course I have!' snaps Ivan, his mind a whirl of speculation. Were these people telling him Leo Gatti was some kind of Mafioso? No. Ivan had read his personnel file and recalled some of the details now – Leo had been a member of the anti-Mafia '*Now Kill Us All*' group. He had joined it years ago while visiting his father's parents in Calabria before the whole family settled in his mother's home town of St Petersburg.

'He was shot this afternoon,' explains Oleshko. 'Automatic weapon. Fired by a man on a motorcycle as he stopped at the lights at the intersection between Nevsky and Sadovaya.'

'Shot,' echoes Ivan, stunned.

'Eleven times,' confirms Oleshko. 'They weren't pissing about.'

'But, and this is the point,' rasps Ivan's father, 'he didn't die . . .'

Ivan's mind reels.

'Or rather, he didn't die *at once*,' the federal prosecutor continues brutally. 'He was able to say a few words to the first officer on the scene, who seems to have been sharp and reliable, in spite of being a GAI traffic cop. Gatti was able to dictate several words and phrases to him, but he was dead by the time the paramedics arrived.'

'OK.' Ivan nods. 'So what did he say?'

'He had some information. Apparently, we're not the only ones under attack. Bashnev Oil and Power is too. It's being targeted for some sort of illegal takeover. Or so the scuttlebutt in Petersburg seems to suggest.'

Ivan shrugs. 'Sharks have been circling ever since Max Asov died.'

'This is different. This is 'Ndrangheta,' the federal prosecutor whispers. 'Gatti seemed pretty certain . . .'

'But what would the Calabrian Mafia want with . . .' Ivan's voice tails off as the pieces began to fall into place.

'Precisely,' nods the federal prosecutor. 'Your distribution system. You supply oil to the entire country – in road tankers as well as pipelines. Since your arrangement with Heritage Mariner you also have a country-wide distribution network for the delivery of containers shipped in from all over the world. All coming in through St Petersburg and Archangel . . .'

'And such a system could deliver heroin as efficiently as it could deliver everything else. I see. But how is the 'Ndrangheta planning to take control?'

'We were wondering the same thing,' inserts Oleshko.

'Perhaps it will turn around the one element we can make neither head nor tail of. The one word we simply do not understand . . .'

'Unless he was trying to play Paco Araya or James Bond and die with a clever quip on his lips . . .' temporizes Ivanov.

The federal prosecutor sees the confusion on his son's face. 'Sayonara,' he rumbles. 'It's Japanese for 'goodbye'. Sayonara. It's the last thing Gatti said and we can't work out whether or not sayonara is important . . .'

60 Hours to Impact

R ichard and Aleks crouched on the top of *Sayonara*'s whaleback cover at midship. The vista of sea and sky was interrupted only by the stunted bridge house half the length of the hull distant. Other than that, there was only the horizon, beginning to draw inwards as the light failed. It was ten p.m. ship's time but they were still in high latitudes. Neither man was interested in the view. All of their attention was on the cover's top immediately beneath their feet. 'No slip-marks,' said Richard.

'No footprints of any kind,' agreed Aleks. 'But what does that tell us?'

'Nothing concrete,' Richard admitted. 'But it makes you wonder. If he didn't slip then how come he fell?'

'He was pushed, you mean?'

'Yes,' snapped Richard impatiently. 'That's exactly what I mean. Or attacked in some way, at least. I can't get the picture of his face out of my mind. That black mark on his forehead – could it have been a bullet wound?'

'I didn't hear a shot,' said Aleks.

'But there was the wind in the deck furniture down there and up here. The motors. The waves. The conversation. If someone had used a silencer . . .'

Aleks nodded grimly. 'I suppose. But then, on the other hand, he could have hit his head as he fell.' He sat back on his heels, looking around in perplexity. 'I see your point. Is it coincidence? After what happened to Yoichi Hatta . . . Two fatal accidents one after the other, so close together.'

'We need to go back down,' said Richard decisively, 'and talk this through with the others. If we don't have a plan of action before nightfall, we'll be on the back foot with a vengeance. And that is *not* where I like to be!'

'Let's go for the bridge,' Richard advised the team twenty minutes later. 'It's the closest thing to taking to high ground aboard. It's where we want to be – where we have the best chance of exercising control. It's where there's accommodation. Supplies, even. We'll get up on to the top there where Aleks and I were and charge straight up to the bridge. There's a walkway up there the entire length of the ship. Full frontal assault. Let's go for it!'

'I don't know,' temporized Aleks. 'We'd be awfully exposed running along up there.'

'The alternative could turn into a siege,' warned Richard. He had thought one of Ivan's best Risk Incorporated men would have been more decisive. But Richard was still of a mind to give him the benefit of the doubt. This was a situation that young Zaitsev had never encountered. And the fact that he was out of his depth was probably just further emphasized by the fact that the whaleback looked like the kind of Italian Alpine skislope that Aleks was the real king of. 'Especially if we have to go through the hull inside and find more unwelcome surprises waiting for us. We'll have to make up our minds quickly or we'll be doing it in the dark.'

They were all assembled on the midships balcony where Boris had died. The night was drawing on pretty quickly now and they really needed to weigh up their options and get into action, as Richard had already observed. Richard had been in situations like this before and was keenly aware of the need for level-headed balance. On the one hand they didn't want to waver and lose momentum – they needed to keep going before morale sagged further and they started fighting amongst themselves. But on the other hand, they needed to avoid recklessness. They couldn't afford to go charging ahead with no clear objective or shared purpose, or the opposition would be able to spring any number of traps on them. That would be worse than inactivity, just as the loss of life was worse than the loss of morale.

'But what's actually *going on* here?' demanded Dom, shaking his head in frustration. 'If this is an exercise to test security and anti-terrorist systems – as it was supposed to be, I thought – then it's going too far now that people are actually getting killed. Even if they are getting killed by accident! We need to call it all off, shake hands and head for home – certainly before Harry Newbold and the Pitman stick their oars in. What is the alternative? Are we actually facing a team of real terrorists who really want to kill us? If so, they're going about it in a pretty funny way!'

'That depends,' countered Aleks. 'What if it's a small team who haven't quite got full control of the ship yet? Who don't want to face us down because we're a far larger – and better armed – force. They want to fight a guerrilla campaign for a while.' He looked at Richard, frowning.

'That would make sense,' said Richard. 'It's certainly the way small terrorist cells work. But it begs several questions, doesn't it? Not least of which is *precisely what sort of opposition are we actually facing?*'

'I don't know,' answered Aleks, looking round their increasingly shadowed faces. 'I just know that I'm doing my best to play the hand we seem to have been dealt here. And, unless their deaths are genuine accidents, then we seem to be stuck in a real situation, facing some actual opposition. Not a test, but the real thing. With real dangers.'

'And in real time,' added Richard. 'With a sixty-hour time limit, unless they plan on changing course, or speed.'

'What do you mean?' asked Aleks.

Richard gestured at his Rolex. 'In sixty hours, unless we change course or slow down, *Sayonara* will arrive at the new NIPEX facility twelve hundred miles south-west of here. Six a.m. Japanese time in two and a half days. Sixty hours and counting. We'd better find some answers.'

Eight hundred miles north-east, way back in the Rat Island Pass, the long Arctic evening is stretching out all around Inuit fishing skipper Nanuq Aareak as he brings his boat *Chu the Beaver* under the cliffs of Hawadax Island on an unusually high flood tide. He slits his eyes against the low sun as it rolls along the northern horizon and silently thanks his guardian spirits for the tide. A quarter of a million ton oil tanker is pushing out of Rat Island Pass at eighteen knots, making what should have been the calm at the top of the water dangerously turbulent. Twelve hundred feet – nearly three hundred and seventy metres of her – with a wake like a tsunami. The power of her passage sets the waters all around her churning and roiling.

Nanuq yells back to his crew to make a virtue of necessity and drop some lines over the stern. The crew consists of his mate, Chulyn and his mountainous brother, Chugiak. And Nanuq's nephew, Aput, his dim sister's idiot offspring.

The sky is alive with birds, and that is usually a sign that there are big fish running. Nanuq watches the black-backed gulls, the terns, skuas and oystercatchers as they follow the trail of oil and garbage left behind the tanker which has just swept past. His wise eyes remain fixed on the columns of birds as he steers *Chu* towards the point where they meet the heaving surface like waterspouts. With luck *Chu* might hit a tuna run and pull in a haul that will keep the little crew's families fat for a month, and allow him to attract the attention of his potential third wife, Immuyak, who lives up to her name of *Butter* in almost every respect. 'Watch that line, Aput,' he bawls to his imbecile nephew. 'Don't let it snag on the weed. We're further inshore than usual. Chulyn, keep an eye on the *narpok*.'

'I'm busy,' calls Chulyn. 'Let Chugiak help him. Or do it yourself.'

Aput raises one hand to show that he has heard all this bellowed byplay, but as he does so the line is all-but jerked from his other. 'Help!' cries the boy in surprise. 'Chulyn! Chugiak!'

Nanuq throttles back and comes stumbling down off the bridge to give the boy a hand as the rest of his crew are militantly attending to their own business. 'What have you got there?' he calls. 'A whale?'

'Feels like it, Uncle Nanuq,' answers the boy cheerfully. The pair of them start pulling the line together, and Nanuq feels the dead, unmoving weight for himself.

'You've snagged some weed,' he announces in disgust. 'There's nothing alive on the end of this line.'

But as the way comes off *Chu,* the dead weight on the end of the line seems to ease and there is suddenly something floating at the surface among the hunting birds. Nanuq has fished these waters as man and boy for half a century, and he knows all too well what it is long before they drag it alongside.

'Looks like it will be a lean month after all,' he says sadly as he looks down into a bloated face, so fat, pasty and chewed over that it scarcely seems human at all. 'And a hell of a lot of paperwork and time at the police station into the bargain,' he adds grimly, as he sees the black hole of the bullet wound in the gaping cavity of the corpse's left temple.

57 Hours to Impact

They waited for absolute darkness after all, moving at one a.m. ship's time, as *Sayonara* entered yet another human time zone, eight hundred and sixty miles south-west of Rat Island Pass, according to the precise measurements of the low-orbiting satellite passing invisibly overhead. But it was another celestial body entirely that finally made them take action. Under the menace of a rising moon that threatened to be low and full, they worked their way along the whaleback, relying on their black gear to keep them invisible among the absolute darkness of the shadows and their infra-red headsets to guide them, all too well aware that their enemies were identically dressed and similarly equipped. And that the moon was rising more quickly than even Richard had anticipated.

Richard went first with Aleks' men on either side. He knew the ship most intimately and was effectively their guide and point man. Vasily Kolchak was on his right and another soldier whose name he did not know was on his left. The nameless soldier was there because he wore the comms kit and could keep the others up to speed. They were maintaining radio silence in all but the direst emergencies. Though, thought Richard, really dire emergencies tended to be self-advertising through screams and shots if nothing else. Suddenly he felt less buoyant. His concentration became fiercer. There had been no sound prior to Boris's unexpected demise and departure. No sound at all. What if their enemies were experts in the art of silent killing? Suddenly there was sweat on his upper lip that had nothing to do with the warmth of the night or the threat of the rising moon. He glanced over his shoulder nervously, relieved to see the flame-bright snake of the rest of the team reassuringly close behind him. Rikki Sato was back there, along with Dom DiVito and Steve Penn now that they were all going in together, mob-handed.

But Rikki came next behind Richard, with Aleks himself and Konstantin Roskov on either side of him. For Rikki was the man with the door codes. He had been head programmer for the entire project, and theoretically had the access codes for every programme on board. But, like his colleagues in the remote control room at NIPEX, he had been shut out by the pirates who commanded the bridge. However, if their enemies were cunning enough to have changed the codes they'd used to gain access, Rikki still had back-up emergency override codes that would open every door on board. Unfortunately he was not so confident that these codes would override whatever had been done to the main command and control programmes, but he was here to try whatever he could – if they could get him to a sufficiently central control console. The rest of them stretched out in a straggly line behind Rikki back to the pulpit halfway down the whaleback, their brightness contained by the pipework which Richard was relying on to keep them safe.

The top of the whaleback was not a smooth curve. It was a flat area a couple of metres wide where there was a kind of walkway – a crawlway, given how they were currently using it. The walkway was floored with black, non-slip paint, against which they were effectively invisible – under normal light spectrums and lingering darkness, anyway. Then on either side of this there stood walls of pipework, joining the valves standing as tall as a man on top of the Moss tanks hidden beneath them. The thickest pipes were waist-high, but there were other, lesser ones running parallel to them, making a very effective wall on either side. A wall that not only kept them safe from falling over the edge, but which, Richard calculated, also kept them safe from being shot at, even if their mysterious adversaries were watching them from the safety of the bridge. For the pipes had to be full of gas, unless they were full of liquid gas instead. And although the latter seemed unlikely, either state would mean that a stray shot would cause an explosion which would in all probability destroy *Sayonara* and everyone on board her.

But the protection of the pipes – illusory or not – lasted only as far as the final tank valve. Then the pipework all went over to the starboard side on Richard's left, where it was outlined in silver against the first rays of the moon. Dead ahead was an open space where the whaleback joined the front of the bridge. The space was large enough to allow them all to gather and to discuss their next move, but it was too temptingly open and the moon too obviously rising to allow any time for further consultation. As Richard and his escorts hesitated, however, Aleks, Rikki and Roskov joined them. Silently, the six of them crouched there, looking around while the others waited on the walkway.

On Richard's right there was a rudimentary ladder standing out from the curve of the whaleback, its proud metal rungs falling away vertically into the shadows of the port side without the added security of a hand rail. And above it the windows of the bridge wings, where, Richard was certain, inscrutable eyes were observing them. But they were here now, and this was a time for action, not for second thoughts. Richard gathered himself to move forward and down, but Aleks' hand fell gently on his shoulder. The lieutenant gestured and Roskov took point. As he moved on to the rungs, Kolchak and Aleks wormed forward as far as they dared, seeking to cover the soldier from their elevated position as he vanished into the black shadow on the ship's port side.

Richard and Rikki crouched, watching, ready to follow Roskov down the moment Aleks signalled. As they waited, so the others gathered round them, Aleks' men forming a protective square around the engineers and computer men. It didn't come as too much of a surprise when the next man signalled forward was not Richard after all, but a second soldier. Within

ten tense minutes, as the cold fingers of moonlight crept over
the starboard pipework and fell across them, making them
doubly visible to whoever was watching them, Aleks sent down
enough men to secure the section of the weather deck below
– a vital square of metal that stretched between the foot of
the ladder, the safety rail at the scuppers and the door into the
bridge house, all roofed by the floor of the bridge wing
protruding low above it.

The pause gave Richard more time to think, and as he thought
he found himself scanning the impenetrable darkness behind
the windows of the bridge wing close above them, and the
equally inscrutable eyes he was certain were watching, either
uncovered to the normal spectrums of white light or still using
the enhanced vision of the light amplifying or infra-red night-
vision goggles. He pulled off his own headset and squinted
upward through the gathering moonlight. The angle of the glass
in the clearview windows on the bridge and its wings kept the
moonbeams at bay and the whole front of the command bridge
gaped like a huge square mouth, as black as the pupil of a
god-like eye staring down at them. He glanced down at his
Rolex with a shiver. Two a.m., it told him. Fifty-six hours until
Sayonara was programmed to dock. Ten a.m. the day after
tomorrow, ship's time. Six a.m. local.

Richard glanced back up at the sinister bridge windows, his
mind racing. He found he was suddenly grateful for the *snafu*
that had called Harry and the Pitman out to them, for his straining
eyes caught the slightest glimpse of movement; there and gone
so swiftly he found himself doubting whether it had really been
real at all. He turned, catching his breath to warn Aleks, but
the Russian was gesturing him forward in any case. He scrambled forward, teeth gripped tightly together, jaws aching as
though he had just tasted the most mouth-watering delicacy. He
paused at the top of the ladder. 'I saw a movement,' he breathed.
'In the bridge wing . . .'

Aleks gave a curt, silent, nod, but he didn't move his cheek
away from the stock of the gun he was pointing down on to the
stygian abyss of the deck. And Richard swung out on to the rungs,
pausing at the point where the ladder went vertical to see Aleks
gesturing to Rikki that he was next. *Right*, he thought. *Rikki gets*

us in, then we fan out and push forward. Typically, in reaction to the unsettling thought that he was being observed by someone whose identity, motives and plans he could not yet fathom, he was suddenly excited by the thought of action. The downward scramble shortened his breath – not because of the physical effort but because of the feeling that he was dangerously exposed beneath the guns of his adversaries. Though he never slowed or hesitated, it took all of his considerable self-control not to stop every now and then to look around.

At the foot of the ladder, Richard paused just long enough to replace his night-vision goggles. Out of the velvet blackness all around him, a range of burnt-orange figures suddenly sprang into being. One of them moved forward, gesturing slowly and carefully. Although he had no idea which of the Russian special forces men this was, Richard stepped back and followed the directions. As he did so he was suddenly all too aware that infra-red vision showed him Aleks' men but did not show him who they were any more than it showed him the vessel he was standing on – or any of the crucial detail he needed to know about her. Like, for instance, where the safety rails were. He switched over to enhanced light mode and the flame-bright world around him was replaced by a dull, submarine-green one.

But at least its limits were delineated – particularly clearly where the moonlight was beginning to brighten the railings to the aft of the poop deck and the outline of the lifeboat hanging athwart-ships above them. Everything else was shrouded in fog. But at the same time the soupy green of his new vision made it clear that if Rikki was going to punch in the pass code for the A-Deck door to the bridge house, he was going to need some torchlight to let him do so. But no. As Rikki arrived in the middle of the group, the first thing he did was to pull out his laptop. With Richard at his side and a pair of guards just behind, he crossed to the door. The moment he opened the laptop, there was sufficient light to see the buttons. In the pale glimmer from the screen, Rikki punched in the access code. They all crowded forward, Richard reaching to test the handle, and the door yielded. Richard froze, calculating. If the weather deck was not the kill-zone it was so clearly suited to be, then the next most logical place with an overwhelming field of fire was immediately inside this door.

But the plan so far seemed to be to let Richard and his men come in relatively unchallenged, sucked deeper and deeper into guerrilla territory where they could continue to be picked off one by one. But whatever lay before them, Richard had read Sun Tzu's book. 'You have to believe in yourself,' he whispered. He reached up, switched his headset over to infra-red, pushed the bulkhead door to the A Deck wide open and stepped in.

55 Hours to Impact

As Richard stepped through the doorway, something made him close his eyes and jerk the night-vision headset off his face. And luckily so. For the motion sensors had switched on the lights. Even through the red curtains of his clenched lids, the brightness seemed dazzling. He opened his eyes to slits on the second step forward and was reaching for his gun instantly for there was a flicker of shadowy movement at the mid-point of the corridor ahead. Someone had dived silently into the companionway that led sternwards on his right. But it was impossible to tell whether they had gone up the stairs to the command bridge or down to the engineering decks. And as that fact registered, so did the question how had they been here and yet the sensors failed to switch the lights on for them? Then came the obvious answer – they had been standing absolutely still, waiting. It was while his mind started grappling with that conundrum that it also occurred to him to wonder why, if there had been an opposition member in the stairwell, he had not attacked the first man coming blindly and helplessly in through the bulkhead door?

Something atavistic took over and Richard found himself flattened with his back against the forward wall, his gun covering the shadowy depth of the companionway even though from this angle he could see only the narrowest possible opening. Before he could do anything more, Roskov was at his side, also jumpy with tension, his night-vision goggles dangling against his chest. Richard tensed to move forward, only to feel a restraining Russian hand resting on his shoulder. Another Russian arrived, pulling off his goggles to reveal Kolchak's square, brutal face. Within the next few moments, two more Russians escorted a wary-looking Rikki Sato into the increasingly crowded corridor.

Roskov gestured to Richard and Rikki to remain where they were and led the little block of soldiers forward. They vanished into the stairwell, and by the time they did so, Richard had moved far enough along the corridor to see that they had gone upwards. That was logical. Going for the high ground was a military strategy as old as the hills. And such controls as they could access were likely to be most easily available on the command bridge. But if Richard could work that out, so could the opposition. Had the figure he had seen gone upwards too? The bulkhead door swung open once again and Aleks led the rest of the soldiers in – except for a couple of guards whom Richard glimpsed in the bar of brightness outside watching over Dom DiVito, Steve Penn, the engineers and the technicians on the outer section of the weather deck. As soon as he arrived, Aleks broke radio silence. 'Secure, Roskov?'

'Secure,' came the reply.

Aleks nodded. 'We go up to the bridge,' he said.

'Right.' Richard set off at once with Rikki at his side, running nimbly up the companionway to the command bridge, in spite of the fact that the stairwell was in shadowy darkness. As he ran, Richard found himself trying to work out what was different in the layout of the bridge house. There seemed to be something missing that he would have expected to find. Then he realized: there was no lift system. And the simple absence once again drove home the fact that this ship was not designed for people to live in. It was for people to visit – for the harbour watch to camp out in. But that was all.

So it was almost a shock to discover a big, comfortable pilot's chair on the starboard side of the Spartan wasteland of the command bridge, just inside the door leading out on to the dark bridge wing. But other than that one touch of humanity – almost of luxury – there was nothing human about the place. He shivered, and realized abruptly that, whereas the night outside was warm, in here it was almost icily cold. The temperature, like everything else it seemed, was controlled for the convenience of the great machines that were driving and guiding the vessel, unless the men who were becoming more and more sinister by their absence were controlling the computers and their environment as easily as they seemed to be controlling everyone else on board.

It was at that moment, in an almost automatic reaction to these ominous thoughts, that Richard found a name for the leader of his mysterious foe. One that was apt if ironic, that characterized him and his abilities – defined his current game plan if nothing else, and yet at the same time reduced him. Contained him. Humanized him. Made him seem less fearsome and all-powerful. *For we have reached the scene of crime*, Richard extemporized, *and Macavity's not here* . . . He wondered whether Aleks had read *Old Possum's Book of Practical Cats*, or whether the code name Macavity might be useful to them all.

'Penny for them,' growled Dom, appearing at Richard's side.

'I was thinking about poetry,' said Richard. 'T.S. Eliot, actually . . .'

'*A cold coming we had of it*?' hazarded Dom with a shiver. He looked around the soulless vastness of the bridge house.

'Macavity's a mystery cat,' said Richard.

'I get you,' nodded Dom. 'The Leader of the Opposition. He's *not here* . . .'

'Precisely. But why?'

'They could be vanishing each time we arrive because they know they're outclassed, outnumbered and outgunned. Maybe they're running away from us. Because they're scared . . .' Dom's voice tailed off as he apparently realized he was failing to convince even himself.

'Hmmm . . .' said Richard. 'We'll learn more when the techies get to grips with the computer system – and hopefully find out what has been done to it. In the meantime . . .'

'In the meantime,' inserted Aleks as he joined the pair of them, 'my first priority is to restore communications. That way at least we stand a chance of calling off Harry and the Pitman. I've sent Kolchak and a couple of men up. If the opposition has a jamming device then logic suggests it must be up on the highest point. And there's an open deck area above the bridge house.'

'That's logical,' allowed Richard.

'And also, in the meantime,' continued Aleks, 'it is hard for a Russian to quote Napoleon, but *an army marches on its stomach*. We need to feed the troops.'

'I know where the galley is,' said Richard.

'No, Captain, we have it covered. Ship's engineer Esaki had a hand in designing the bridge house. He knows where everything is. And Ivan Karitov is our unit chef. He has the skills and the supplies to prepare something that should suit us all. Esaki says there isn't much in the way of a mess, though. The ship was designed to accommodate half-a-dozen men on harbour watch and a skeleton crew to take her out with the pilot. We'd have to eat in shifts. And the same will go for the other facilities. There's only one head, for instance. Two stalls, three urinals.'

'I hope you brought your own toilet paper, then,' said Richard. 'If there's only enough for six on board . . .' His gaze swept over the better part of twenty men crowding into the bridge around them.

'Perhaps, when Kolchak has sorted out the communications,' suggested Dom, glancing upwards as though he could see through the deck-head above to where the Russians were trying to disable whatever was blocking their signals, 'you could call up Harry and the Pitman. Tell them to bring in a roll or two.'

The idea gave Richard pause – and Aleks. He frowned, then pushed his throat microphone closer to his Adam's apple. 'Kolchak,' he said. 'Report in.'

His face assumed that vacant gaze which told he was listening to silence as he waited for a reply, Richard observed. And the vacant expression lasted longer than it should have – to be replaced by a frown, which Richard unconsciously mimicked. 'Dom,' he said quietly, 'something's happened to Kolchak. We need to go up and take a look.'

Aleks nodded agreement. 'Roskov,' he called, 'bring a couple of men here.'

Richard led the way out through the starboard bridge wing

door. Dom followed at his right shoulder. Steve Penn remained behind, crossing to watch Rikki Sato working on the main command console. The bridge wing itself stretched outward, glass-walled from waist height fore and aft, like a carriage on the London Underground or the New York Subway stripped of seats. There was a second, uncovered section further on. Immediately on their right was another door opening on to the outer companionway that led like a fire escape up to the open upper weather deck on top of the bridge house.

Richard gestured to Roskov and the Russian's tight little four-man squad took over point position. Richard, Dom and Aleks followed the soldiers as they went outward and upward, the beams of the torches beneath their short-barrelled HK 416 carbines probing forward. The moonshine made them seem weak and pallid, even as it turned the soldiers and the two men with them into silvery statues. The exterior companionway was steep and narrow. It was difficult for more than one man to squeeze in between the bridge-house wall and the safety rail. Richard had one step to himself – no one was ever going to fit in beside him. There were sixteen steep steps up from the bridge wing to the upper weather deck. Richard climbed them just behind Roskov and his team, with Dom immediately behind him and Aleks as rear-guard. They all moved with the tense and concentrated silence of men going into a battleground. Richard was all too well aware that they were under the silvery brightness of the full moon. Independently of whatever night-vision equipment Macavity and his cohorts might possess, they were utterly exposed and in full view up here, if there was anyone to observe them. For the moment Richard stepped up on to the upper weather deck it was obvious to him that the whole huge expanse of decking was empty. True, there was a funnel that stood tall, casting a sharp-edged black shadow across the open expanse of metal. There was an impressive array of guidance and communications equipment. Pieces of deck furniture that Richard recognized as storage boxes and hatch covers, varying in size from that of a coffin to a hut that looked like the housing for the upper motor on top of a lift shaft. But there was no sign of Kolchak and the men who had accompanied him up here.

Richard felt the tension tightening among Roskov's squad. Rifle-stocks tight to shoulders, bodies crouching forward, they moved as one. Torch beams swept across the deck as they walked slowly, silently forward, beginning to spread out into a carefully rehearsed search pattern. Richard slid out his Galaxy and tapped the screen. He looked across to Aleks and the Russian lieutenant joined Dom at Richard's shoulder in an instant. It took him less than a minute to call up a schematic of the bridge from the phone's memory, though Richard poignantly missed his laptop for a moment – and came close to regretting the caution which had prompted him to leave it with Ivan. They all glanced up and down, matching the features they could see so clearly in the moonlight with the 3D images on the bright screen, locating vents, hatch covers, equipment storage boxes and housings of various functions and sizes all around as Roskov's men continued to quarter the silvery deck.

Aleks moved away then, leaving Richard in a brown study listing the stunning array of communications equipment around the funnel and trying to assess the most likely place that Macavity might have chosen to place his signal-jamming equipment, and how he could have managed to jam Richard and his group's communications without interrupting the communications between the computers down below and the satellites up above. If, indeed, he had. Richard's thoughts had just come full circle when the shooting started. There were two shots in rapid succession, followed by a shouted order from Aleks immediately echoed by Roskov. One of the Russians straightened, raising his smoking carbine to point at the moon. 'In there,' he said, gesturing to the one piece of deck furniture that had raised questions in Richard's head: the hut that looked like the housing for a lift mechanism. Because, of course, there was no lift.

They crowded round the hut. It was walled with thin metal and two black pocks showed where the jumpy soldier's bullets had penetrated. The door was secured by a bolt that had a padlock through it. But the bolt was slid right back and the padlock was hanging open and useless. Roskov took it and jerked the door open. All the torch beams focused like searchlights on the black interior.

Kolchak was standing there with his feet widely straddled astride a big black box. His mouth has been sealed with silver duct tape. His fists were secured in a big round boxing glove of the same bright material. His face was white and his cheeks were wet with tears of frustration and pain. There was an ugly mark on his bulletproof vest which showed where one of the bullets, misshapen by its contact with the metal wall, had slammed into it – probably breaking a rib or two, thought Richard. The second bullet had missed his vest and smashed his shoulder to a bloody pulp.

53 Hours to Impact

Kolchak sagged forward the instant the door opened and Roskov stepped in to catch him as he fell. He was just about to step back, pulling Kolchak out on to the deck, when Richard shouted, 'Stop!' Both he and Aleks fell to their knees. Aleks shone the torch beneath his rifle barrel at Kolchak's boots and they gazed, narrow-eyed at the way the soldier's feet were positioned on either side of the big metal box. Aleks reached gingerly in on Kolchak's left and Richard echoed his movement on the right. Each man gently ran his fingers from ankle to knee, inside the calf and out, on the front of it and on the back. Only when they were certain that Kolchak was not attached to the big metal box did they straighten.

Aleks gestured to Roskov and he pulled Kolchak free, laying him gently on the deck. As the others gathered round him, the man who had shot him eased the silver duct tape off his mouth. One of the others pulled a first aid kit from his backpack and put a pressure bandage on the ruined shoulder. Kolchak groaned with agony, but his eyes remained bright. He was ex-special forces. He knew how to handle pain. And he had other priorities. 'You were right to take care,' he said. 'The box in that little shed is the signal jammer. But it has a bomb attached to it. If you try and interfere with it, switch it off even, the bomb goes off.'

'That's a bit self-defeating,' said Dom, apparently without thinking. 'I mean, we want to destroy the thing in any case . . .'

'The men who put me in there said that bomb is attached to others,' Kolchak informed him. 'I don't know how many or where . . .'

'Best leave well alone then,' decided Richard. 'Unless you have a bomb disposal expert among your men, Aleks.'

'No,' said the lieutenant shortly. 'Kolchak, where are the others?'

'In that coffin-shaped box over there,' said Kolchak, pointing with his chin. 'They came at us out of nowhere, Lieutenant. I don't know how many. But they were good. Very good indeed. We didn't stand a chance. They trussed me up and dumped my men in that box. And lieutenant?'

'Yes?'

'There's a grenade between my fists. Pin out. I'm holding the lever down but I've lost all sense of feeling in my hands. Someone is going to have to be very careful how they take the tape off them.'

'Roskov,' said Aleks, 'detail two men to take Kolchak down to the command bridge. Do the best you can with his shoulder, but don't touch his hands until I get there. Then I want you and your last man with me. We have to be very careful indeed about how we open this box.'

'Aleks,' said Richard quietly, looking at his Galaxy again and glancing across at what Kolchak had gestured towards. 'I don't think that is a box.'

They crossed to the square cover and checked for booby traps. There were none. At last, Aleks crouched own and slid his fingers under the edge. As he straightened he eased it upwards so the other soldiers pointed their guns into the widening gap, their torch beams probing the darkness.

'No. I was right,' said Richard, sadly. 'Sorry, Aleks.'

The cover was not the lid to a box. It was the top of a vertical duct which ended somewhere down in the engineering sections, six decks – the better part of thirty metres or one hundred feet – straight down beneath them. Probably in the engine room, Richard thought, reaching for his Galaxy. But then again, he thought, observing details not shown on the Galaxy's graphics, there was a ladder riveted to the nearest wall of the vertical, steel-sided shaft. Could Macavity have made Kolchak's companions climb down there as some kind of invitation? As bait? Aleks lowered the cover back into place and they all stood looking down at it for a moment, deep in thought, but none of them said anything – not even Richard – until Aleks decided, 'Well, we'd better go down into the bridge house and unwrap Kolchak's hands.'

'We'd better be quick about it too,' said Richard. 'Because the first thing your medic is likely to do is knock him out with painkillers. And you'll want him wide awake and on the ball when the duct tape comes off.'

Aleks nodded. 'You're right,' he said with a frown which showed his irritation that he had not thought this through for himself. 'Let's go down.'

The bridge house was crowded and the simple warmth given off by so many men was beginning to raise the temperature. Kolchak was sitting in the pilot's chair in the command bridge, naked to the waist with his vest and uniform top on the deck at his feet. There was a huge bruise beginning to darken on the left side of his chest, but he was breathing deeply and easily enough to assure Richard that even if there were broken ribs, none had penetrated his lung. His right shoulder was lost beneath a huge white pressure bandage. A soldier stood beside him with a bag of D5W fluid, which was passing down a catheter into his arm to keep him hydrated and keep his blood pressure up. Richard suspected there would have been a sizeable dose of morphine injected first. But the soldier's eyes were still focused. The pupils had not yet begun to dilate. Richard took a quick glance around the bridge as Aleks began to arrange for Kolchak to be moved once again. Rikki and his team were still working on the computers – either directly or via linked-in laptops. The engineers were taking it in turns to test the plumbing by the looks of things. And wisely. They would be put to work soon enough – whether the technicians managed to break into the computer control systems or not. In the meantime, Steve Penn and the LNG experts would need to keep an eye on the cargo – always assuming that whatever displays Rikki and co. could call up were accurate or reliable.

And in the meantime, Dom seemed to have attached himself to Richard.

But first and foremost there was the matter of Kolchak's hands. 'We can't risk it in here, obviously,' Aleks was saying. 'I don't even want to risk doing it on the bridge wing just outside. So we're going to have to take him right outside again. Down to the main deck or back up to the top deck we've just come down off?'

'Back up to the top deck would be quicker,' said Richard. 'And as far away as possible, just in case . . .'

'You'll need to be quick,' warned Kolchak unexpectedly. 'I'm beginning to feel all warm and fluffy.'

'Right,' decided Aleks. 'Back up to the top deck it is. Let's move. Me and the moron who shot him.'

'Ryzanoff,' growled Roskov. 'If you're certain . . .'

'I won't delegate this,' Aleks replied. 'But I will need help. Ryzanoff only needs to hold the torch steady. And keep his gun on safety.'

'I'll come too, if that's OK with you, Lieutenant,' said Roskov. 'You'll need someone to watch your back.'

'OK, if you stay well back out of the blast area,' nodded Aleks.

'Then I'll come to watch your back, Roskov,' said Richard. 'Keeping well out of the blast area too.'

'Cool,' said Dom. 'And I'll come and watch your back, Richard. I'll keep so well clear there won't be room for anyone to creep up behind my back!'

'That should just about do it, then,' said Richard, a little surprised at the Canadian's fortitude. 'But we'd better hurry. Kolchak's starting to go out on us.'

There was no time for more deliberation. Kolchak was a little unsteady, but he was in that blessed interim between the pain-killer kicking in and his brain switching off, so he was able to climb the companionway behind Aleks, with Ryzanoff, Roskov and Richard just behind him, ready to catch him if anything went wrong. And Dom just behind them, watching Richard's back.

The upper weather deck was still flooded with moonlight, though it seemed to Richard that the shadows had moved more than he would have expected. Kolchak and his two minders walked rapidly over to the outer limit of the bridge wing where the wounded soldier wedged himself in the angle of the safety rail and held the silver bundle of his fists up as high as his wounded shoulder permitted. Ryzanoff shone his torch on the ball-shaped parcel by pointing his rifle at it. Richard and Roskov were back by the coffin-shaped hatch cover, Dom was back by the funnel somewhere but they could all hear Aleks quite clearly. 'OK, Kolchak, here we go.' Moonlight caught the black blade of Aleks' knife and he began to cut the sticky tape away, layer by layer, pulling it free as gently as he could. 'What are the names of the men who went down the hatch?' Aleks asked, clearly trying to make Kolchak stay alert, but wanting to distract him for the moment from the job in hand.

'Gerdt and Kosloff,' answered Kolchak.

'I read their resumes,' nodded Aleks. 'Do you know them at all?'

'They're in my squad, so I thought I'd better . . .'

'What are your impressions?' demanded Aleks sharply as Kolchak's voice drifted off.

'Pavel Kosloff, good man, ex-GRU. Theo Gerdt, good man too. Also GRU trained. Army. Reliable. Steady . . .'

'*Steady* . . .' snapped Aleks, for Kolchak's voice was getting dreamy again. 'Either of them family men?'

'Kosloff has a wife in Minsk. He was associated with the Fifth Army Corps stationed there, but he was one of the liaison team that went with General Orlov to NATO headquarters, SACEUR and then on down to JFC facility in Naples, Italy. He's got a couple of kids, I think. Gerdt's still fancy free . . .'

'Gerdt's a cocksmith,' supplied Ryzanoff suddenly. 'Had more girls than I've had shots of vodka. Got some hot Italian he met in Moscow on the go. Met her at this *Mayfair* club. Lucrezia something. He says she'll do anything—'

Aleks called, 'Ryzanoff, come over here, I've almost got it and I need you to hold your hands over Kolchak's for a moment while I . . .'

Ryzanoff stepped forward obediently. Aleks pulled the next bit of tape back, exposing the grenade. But the moment that he did so, Kolchak's knees gave out and he slid down helplessly on to the deck. His head rolled over on to his shoulder and he was clearly out for the count. The grenade fell out of his senseless fingers and came rolling across the moon-bright metal.

'SHIT!' roared Roskov and dropped to his knees behind the hatch cover. But that only stood thirty centimetres or so high. Without thinking, Richard stooped and threw the lid up to form a solid wall in front of them as Dom joined them flat on the deck behind it. As Richard did so he saw Aleks crouch protectively over Kolchak and watched Ryzanoff fall on to the grenade. He crashed to his knees, counting. After *thirty* he picked himself up and crossed to the soldier lying huddled on the deck. He crouched beside the shivering black shape and reached a gentle hand down to take his shoulder. 'I think it's a dud, Ryzanoff,' he said. He raised his voice, calling to Aleks. 'Lieutenant! It's dud.'

Ryzanoff stirred. 'Thank God for that. But I think I've wet myself.'

And Roskov called from behind the open hatch cover, 'Hey, I think I can hear someone down at the bottom of this shaft calling out for help!'

It's 8 p.m. Moscow time. The restaurant at *Mayfair*, the fashionable new nightspot on Savvinskaya Boulevard, overlooking the river, has not yet opened to ordinary clientele. But Francisco Lazzaro is anything but an ordinary client. Neither is the man who accompanies him – for he is one of the exclusive nightspot's owners. Niccolo Rizziconi is one of the new breed of international financiers. Educated in Italy and America, he graduated from Booth Business School in Chicago, then went global. He worked in Cape Town, Canberra, Amsterdam and Vancouver before taking on a managing directorship at one of Russia's largest privately owned banks. Branches of the bank have since opened in St Petersburg, Murmansk, Archangel . . . anywhere where there are port facilities that can handle large numbers of containers. The bank's money has begun to move into shipping and insurance, among other things. Under Niccolo Rizziconi's leadership, profits have soared.

As is common in the free-market fervour of post-Soviet Moscow, Rizziconi has put his considerable and growing personal fortune into other enterprises such as *Mayfair*. He has inordinate amounts of money invested in *Ecstasy, Grozny* and *Ras-Putin*, three of Moscow's most profitable strip clubs. Although, like *Mayfair*, they are as clearly legitimate and above-board as they are fantastically popular and successful. With each new opening the local law enforcement officers have seen a sudden rise in the amount of high-grade cocaine available in the city. But the local politicians, as well as more senior government officers, have been consulted at length and with care. Blessings have been passed down from on high, like Papal dispensations. Like the blessings of a Godfather.

As the two men settle into overstuffed armchairs and look down across the Moskva River towards the apartment blocks on Brezhnev Boulevard opposite, Lazzaro comes straight to the point. 'The situation with *Sayonara* is nearly resolved,' he says in syrupy Calabrian. 'I have dispensed with Tristan Folgate-Lothbury and his Lloyd's consortium. Everything we are interested in is with the Duisberg Reinsurance Company of Vancouver now. One of your earlier masterworks, I believe. It is time to move on. How are things proceeding with Bashnev/Sevmash?'

'As discussed,' answers Rizziconi. 'If what we plan for *Sayonara* works as we hope, then the stock in both Heritage Mariner and Bashnev/Sevmash will crash. The potential which that could offer puts even the profit we can make on the loss of the hull into the shade.'

'The potential for growth seems limitless,' nods Lazzaro. 'At one stroke we gain control of one of the largest commercial entities in Russia – one of the few countries that has remained less open to us than we would like.'

'And, of course,' adds Rizziconi, 'we also get our own private shipping company. Everything from passenger ferries to container vessels. Our own private shipping company to go with our own private port of Gioia Tauro. The other families will regret building bunkers beneath the *Aspromonte* when they should have been building businesses abroad instead.'

'We will show them,' agrees Lazzaro, suddenly consumed with terrifying anger. 'We will show them that it is not just those old men down in Sicily or the historic buffoons up in Rome – the Corleones and the Caesars – who know how to conquer the world! We Calabrians will do it better. The 'Ndrangheta holds the *testicoli*, the *balls* of the world here!' He cups his taloned hands as though holding the members in question. Then he grips his fingers into a shaking, emasculating fist.

'Just so,' agrees Niccolo Rizziconi smoothly. 'We will have Beluga and Dom Perignon with dinner to celebrate. But in the meantime, Don Francisco, would you like a little distraction? We have a young lady called Lucrezia who, I assure you, will do anything you desire. Anything.'

50 Hours to Impact

R obin's phone started ringing at eight the next evening and she grabbed it, hoping that it might be Richard. But it was Patrick Toomey. 'I'm at the Lloyd's building,' he said. 'Can you come over? It's important.'

'Where are you exactly? Number One Lime Street is a big place.'

'I'm with Sir Gerald Overbury. We're in the Old Library.'

Robin frowned. Sir Gerald Overbury was a big wheel. A very big wheel indeed. Apart from that, he was the opposite of Tristan Folgate-Lothbury in almost every way. And she wasn't surprised he was talking to Pat. If Lloyd's could be said to have their own London Centre intelligence section, then Gerry Overbury was the head of it. And here he was, in the office at a time most of his co-workers would consider dinnertime. Pat had obviously been talking to him about Tristan and Francisco Lazzaro – and now they wanted to talk to her. She looked across the dressing room at her reflection in a wardrobe mirror in the flat atop Heritage House. She assumed a Chanel cocktail outfit would not offend Lloyd's strict dress code, for there would be no time to change. She speed dialled her old friend and hostess. 'I'm going to be a little late for drinks I'm afraid, Annabelle,' she said shortly. 'Something's come up.'

Twenty minutes after she broke contact with Annabelle, a security guard ushered Robin into the Old Library and both

Patrick and Sir Gerald rose to greet her. 'You look lovely, Robin,' said Sir Gerald. 'As always.'

'Thank you, Gerry. You're looking well yourself. Now, what's this all about?'

Sir Gerald threw his bantamweight frame back into one of the priceless Hepplewhite chairs that looked to have been purloined from the nearby Adam Room. His blue eyes sparked with urgent energy and his clipped moustache seemed to bristle. 'Young Toomey here came to me asking about the Folgate-Lothbury set-up. Concerned that there might be a Mafia connection or some such thing . . .'

''Ndrangheta,' said Pat helpfully.

'Just so. Not at all the sort of situation we would dream of countenancing, of course. But while we were looking into the possibility, we began to wonder why the Mafia would bother.'

'Well?' demanded Robin. 'Why would they?'

'You don't insure your own bottoms, do you?' asked Gerry, apparently inconsequentially. 'Not even a percentage of the worth?'

'No. Heritage Mariner policy is to lay off all the insurance on our hulls to other insurers, mostly here at Lloyd's. It's expensive, but if anything goes wrong it's far safer. I mean, look at the *TK Bremen*; look at *Deepwater Horizon* . . .' She shuddered.

'And Folgate-Lothbury's syndicate carries insurance risks for *Sayonara*?'

'You should know, Gerry. But, unless they've laid it off in turn, then yes . . .'

'And the cargo?' Gerry probed.

'The LNG is Greenbaum International's. But that's insured in Canada.'

'The Duisberg Reinsurance Company of Vancouver. Yes.' Gerry nodded as he spoke. He and Pat were both frowning.

'What are you saying?' Robin demanded. 'Where is this leading?'

'How much did *Sayonara* cost to build?' asked Gerry, and Robin began to see where this was heading after all.

'Seventy-five million dollars, give or take. And, before you ask, I have no idea how much the cargo's worth.'

The two men exchanged glances. 'In excess of fifty million dollars at current rates,' said Gerry.

'So the whole package is worth, what, one hundred and twenty-five million dollars, just for the hull and cargo?' calculated Robin.

The two men nodded thoughtfully.

'There you have it, then,' said Pat.

'What?' demanded Robin. 'There we have *what*, precisely?'

'Going through the Folgate-Lothbury records – in ways we will not discuss, none of which would ever stand up in court – we have come to suspect that since this man Lazzaro became involved with the Folgate-Lothbury syndicate, all of the reinsurance for hull and cargo has been laid off.' Gerry Oldbury leaned forward, eyes sparkling, moustache bristling. There was the faintest whiff of Imperial Leather soap and Bay Rum cologne. 'None of the other insurance – collateral damage, environmental impact, loss of business arising, et cetera – has been laid off at all as far as we can ascertain. Folgate-Lothbury still carries all that. But *Sayonara*'s hull and cargo have apparently been laid off quite recently and are now with this Canadian company, Duisberg Reinsurance.'

Robin went cold. 'And Duisberg Reinsurance is Francisco Lazzaro,' she hazarded, knowing in her bones that this was the truth of the matter.

'Or at least it is owned by one of his associates,' confirmed Gerry grimly. 'So it's not likely to be completely legitimate. Not only that, but Duisberg seems to be laying it all off again to other insurers all over the world – some of it back to other Lloyd's syndicates, which is how we can be fairly accurate. It's a variation of the sub-prime mortgage market scam so popular in the nineties. Brokers bought bad debts and then sold them off to other brokers who sold them off in turn, all collecting a fat fee for the business in the knowledge that if anything went wrong – if the borrower failed to keep up the mortgage payments, say – the debt itself would actually be owned by some poor bugger in the Caymans or the Turks and Caicos. It worked like clockwork. Until the sub-prime market crashed and even the banks started going belly-up.

'But this set-up with Duisberg seems to have one other, potentially lucrative little twist – one that's far more familiar to us at Lloyd's, though traditionally it's owners rather than insurers who try to pull it off. And it's this: the total value for *Sayonara* and her cargo being insured to date seems to be in the region of *two hundred and fifty* million dollars.'

'But that makes no sense . . .' said Robin without thinking. 'Why insure something for twice what it's worth?'

'If anything were to happen to *Sayonara*,' said Pat gravely, 'then Duisberg Reinsurance stands to make a hell of a lot of money. One hundred and fifty million dollars clear profit, as near as we can estimate. They've effectively set *Sayonara* up to be a coffin ship. They *want* her to sink so that they can collect huge returns on her loss.'

'Can you prove any of this?' demanded Robin.

'No,' said Gerry. 'None of it at all.'

'But we know a man who can,' added Pat. 'Your old mate, Tristan. We're trying to contact him.'

And just as he did so, Gerry's phone began to ring discreetly. 'Excuse me,' he said, rising. 'This must be important. My people have orders to contact me only in the event of an emergency.'

He rose, pulling the cellphone from his pocket, and crossed to the far side of the room. Robin sat silent, her mind racing round in circles, trying to get a grip on what seemed to be happening here. Of what it might mean for Heritage Mariner. For Greenbaum International. For Richard, the *bloody man*. If only he knew. If only there was a way to warn him. But Gerry was only away for a moment. 'We have a problem,' he said as he limped back across the room at top speed. 'The police are here. Tristan Folgate-Lothbury has just been found floating under Blackfriars Bridge.'

'Floating . . .' Robin had a vision of Tristan like an inflatable dinghy drifting down the Thames.

'Floating,' said Gerry brutally. 'Face down. He's been there for some time, apparently.'

'*Tristan!*' she gasped. 'But I had dinner with him yesterday evening.' Her stomach fluttered. Her ears rang.

'You'll maybe want to tell the police about that,' warned Pat. 'I'd better get your solicitor down here post haste, just in case.'

Robin saw the familiar shape of solicitor Andrew Atherton Balfour's Bentley swing in behind them as the police car turned off Newgate Street into Snow Hill. Even though she had been treated with reassuring courtesy and was seated between a female constable and the comforting bulk of Pat Toomey, it was still something of a relief to see the personalized number plate AAB1 beneath the grille of the Arnage. Pat saw it too and also seemed to relax. 'Cavalry's arrived,' he growled.

They assembled in interview room number one of the Snow Hill police station. Or rather, Robin, Pat and Andrew did. The sergeant who had first appeared at the main door of Lloyd's waited there with Gerry Oldbury as the members of Tristan's syndicate were called.

'This is not official,' said the young detective inspector who seemed to be running things. 'We may want formal witness statement later, but for the time being I would be grateful if Captain Mariner could just tell us what she remembers about last night. Anything about Mr Folgate-Lothbury's demeanour. What he talked about. What sort of frame of mind he seemed to be in . . .'

'I'm fine with that,' said Robin. 'Andrew? Any problems?'

'Not as far as I can see,' answered her solicitor briskly. 'This is just a preliminary enquiry, Inspector?' he confirmed.

'Absolutely,' said the inspector, nodding her long, dark head decisively. 'We're just gathering impressions at this stage. It's what we refer to as a *soft* interview.' She glanced across at Robin with a smile. 'Now, Captain Mariner, you and Mr Folgate-Lothbury dined together at Theo Randall's restaurant at the Intercontinental Hotel, Park Lane yesterday evening. You arrived at eleven-thirty and left just after one. Mr Folgate-Lothbury left with you. Well, at the same time as you. There is no implication—'

'I should think not,' snapped Andrew.

'That's OK, Andrew,' Robin soothed her overprotective friend, and caught Pat's outraged eye as well. 'That's not quite accurate, Inspector. When I left, *Signor* Lazzaro was still there. He was the one who was most closely involved in conversation with Tristan.'

'*Signor* Lazzaro.' The inspector's eyes were full on Robin now. 'I don't have any record of a *Signor* Lazzaro being there. The maître d' and the sommelier only mentioned Mr Folgate-Lothbury and yourself. You were deeply engaged in conversation, apparently. We know what you had to eat and we know that he had two bottles of red wine and you had a bottle of Prosecco which you did not finish. But there is no mention of a *Signor* Lazzaro.'

'There must be some mistake,' said Robin, glancing across at Andrew, her forehead creasing into a frown of simple surprise.

'The maître d' and the sommelier both saw *Signor* Lazzaro arrive and talk to Mr Folgate-Lothbury. He arrived at about a quarter to midnight and was still there when I left.'

'Perhaps he was staying at the hotel,' suggested Andrew.

'I'll get my people to check with hotel reception,' said the inspector, and phoned through the orders at once.

'Now,' she said a moment later as she broke contact. 'Returning to the subject of your conversation, Captain Mariner . . .'

Robin went over the main topics she had discussed with Tristan, adding Lazzaro's input without mentioning his name again. The inspector nodded and made the occasional note on a pad.

'We'll want copies of those notes,' observed Andrew.

'Of course,' promised the inspector.

After about twenty minutes, a constable came in and whispered to the inspector. Robin had more or less finished with what she remembered anyway, so she was happy to sit back as the constable left and the inspector frowned thoughtfully. 'No, Captain,' she said after a moment. 'There is no record of a *Signor* Lazzaro staying at the Intercontinental. Not that that proves anything, of course – neither you nor Mr Folgate-Lothbury were staying there either. But the maître d' and the sommelier are certain that no one else was at your table.'

Pat leaned forward suddenly. 'Inspector,' he said, 'have you any idea where the maître d' and sommelier originate from?'

'Yes. They're both on work visas. We have place of birth and so forth as part of their statements. They are cousins, as a matter of fact. And they both come from a place called Seminara. It's a little village in the hills . . .'

'In the hills of Calabria,' Patrick finished her sentence for her. 'Just up the road from Gioia Taura. 'Ndrangheta country.'

In spite of the fact that it has come over the Pole and is therefore approaching Tokyo from the north, Japan Airlines flight 7080 from Schiphol via Helsinki swings east and south of Narita as it settles into its short finals. The Pitman, seated next to the window in first class, is therefore given a clear view of the facility that *Sayonara* is fifty hours away from and the bay to the south of it. 'Hey, look at that, Harry. That's really something!'

'What?' demands Harry sleepily.

'Those huge honeycomb sections being tugged out into the bay. Each one big enough to hold houses, gardens, roadways, infrastructure . . . They've already begun clamping them together. That's where they're starting to build the floating city you were reading about online. Kujukuri. They're extending it from the mainland. And that cool-looking white and blue barge all covered in Russian writing must be the floating nuclear power station. What did Richard call it?'

'*Zemlya*,' answers Harry, beginning to waken up, an elegant Boston accent coming and going. 'It's one of only two afloat at the moment but there are more in the pipeline according to the IAEA PRIS.'

'The what?' The Pitman's Dutch intonation is thick enough to sound almost Afrikaans again and matches the blonde crewcut and hard blue eyes.

'International Atomic Energy Agency's Power Reactor Information System,' Harry explains, brown eyes blinking owlishly. 'It's all online.' One hand thoughtlessly tries to tidy a mop of brown curls while the other straightens a severely cut grey suit jacket and open-necked shirt.

Their conversation is interrupted by an immaculate air hostess who comes to explain in person that they should prepare for landing now. It's a message repeated immediately by the captain in Japanese, Russian, American-accented English, Finnish and Dutch. All of which languages Harry and the Pitman speak with varying degrees of fluency.

Their luggage is checked through automatically for the internal connection to Asahikawa so, after they have performed the necessary procedures, Harry and the Pitman wander into *Café de Crie* to wait for their flight to be called. Although it goes against character and flint-hard reputation, the Pitman has an achingly sweet tooth and so they order their waffles American style with crisp-grilled bacon and syrup. Harry asks for the closest they can get to bacon, eggs over easy and wholewheat toast. And the blackest, bitterest coffee the café can come up with. Then the two of them settle to their long-awaited breakfast – and are for once focused on what they're eating rather than where they are and who might be coming close to them.

So it comes as more of a shock than a surprise when an enormous man wearing a single-breasted, elegantly tailored, mid-grey gabardine suit, a white cotton shirt and a gold silk tie sits down beside them unannounced and uninvited. Harry looks across at his smiling face and frowns with amazement.

But when the Pitman looks up, squinting a little to see beyond the massive stranger, there behind him, standing tall in a black business suit that looks like Chanel, with a sable wrap carelessly open over the top of it, stands a woman whose simple beauty takes the Pitman's breath away. It is a moment before the Dutch mercenary registers the identity of the stunning vision. Then the little half-smile, familiar from hundreds of news clips and photographs gives it away. That and the ID badge beneath the sable and the rope upon rope of black pearls: *Mme Anastasia Asov, Chief Executive Officer, Bashnev Oil and Power.*

The seated giant runs his hand over his shaven scalp as he leans forward. 'We have some bad news and some good news. What do you want first?'

'The bad news,' says Pitman through a mouthful of waffles and syrup.

'The bad news is that Richard's in deeper shit than he realizes,' Ivan announces. 'I've just received word that some Eskimo fisherman has pulled half-a-dozen dead bodies out of Rat Island Pass. It seems that the recently deceased are a team hired by Tristan Folgate-Lothbury of Lloyd's of London to test the security systems on board *Sayonara*. The Folgate-Lothbury syndicate apparently gave them all the access codes and whatnot in order to make this as severe a test as possible. But precisely what they were given is hard to be certain of because this Tristan Folgate-Lothbury has apparently been found floating face-down under a bridge in London. And it may be that he was pushed rather than that he jumped. The news services are going wild. And it is only reasonable to assume . . .'

'To assume that whoever killed the men have taken the codes

and gone aboard in their place; and may, indeed, be associated with whoever pushed Tristan Folgate-Lothbury,' continues Anastasia Asov smoothly as she eases herself into the fourth and last seat at the table and signals a hovering attendant. 'The dead men's kit has been found on Hawadax Island. All their dummy guns and so forth. It seems only reasonable to assume that the men who have replaced them do not have dummy guns.'

'They have the real thing,' Pitman calculates.

'And then some, in all probability,' adds Harry thoughtfully. 'They certainly seem to have state-of-the-art signal jammers.'

'Coffee,' Nastia orders as the waitress approaches. 'The same as they have. Two cups. No sugar. No cream.' She rejoins the conversation, locking her eyes with the Pitman's. 'We assume they have state of the art everything. We don't yet know for sure what their overall plan is, but Robin Mariner's been in touch. The 'Ndrangheta connection you already know about may have widened into setting *Sayonara* up to sink as part of an insurance fraud. All we know for certain, though, is that their men seem to have gone aboard at Rat Island Pass fifty hours ago and *Sayonara* is due at the NIPEX facility in fifty hours' time – unless they have managed to reprogramme the control computers. Which is, of course, a strong possibility because they've shut the remote control team at NIPEX out and seem to have screwed the communications system communicating with NIPEX and HM altogether, though I understand there are still locator signals coming through from the automatic black box system. That's only supposed to stop if the ship goes down.'

The coffee arrives and a short silence falls as Nastia and Ivan pour themselves a cup each and sip thoughtfully. 'Could these pirate guys have done that?' Ivan asks Harry. 'Reprogrammed the engine and navigation computers so that they have control of the ship then blocked almost everything else so we only know where the ship is and where she's heading but not what's happening on board?'

'Hard to say,' Harry shrugs. 'Robin sent me everything available about the systems the last time we were in contact and I have it all on my Apple's hard drive. I went through some of it last night as we were coming over the Pole. The systems are so complex, with so many checks and balances, information streams and cut-outs that it would be a tough job to re-programme the whole lot. But I guess if they were careful, they could tinker with the edges. Maybe vary the speed and heading. Fool the engine monitoring system and even the GPS. I mean, I know GPS has come on leaps and bounds since the early days, but we all remember stories about cars being sent the wrong way down one-way streets, trucks being guided into municipal parks instead of car parks, or being trapped at the end of dead-end streets they couldn't turn round in or reverse out of. It's still got built-in room for error. And on top of everything else, there are GPS jammers easily available over the internet.'

'OK,' interrupts the Pitman impatiently. 'So we can assume these guys have the ability to mess with the ship's management systems and if they haven't done so yet then that'll be part of a larger plan. One that will probably involve *Sayonara* coming to a violent end, involving at least some of the people currently on board her. Or those planning to go aboard her – *us*. Unless we can stop what they're up to and screw up their plan instead. That's the bad news. Now what's the good news?'

'The good news,' says Ivan expansively, 'is that we're here to help.'

The Pitman gives a shout of derisive laughter. 'Thanks! But I have to tell you, Ivan, that *we're* all the help we need.'

'Not so fast, Sergeant Van Der Piet!' snaps Anastasia, leaning forward. 'Hear us out. You've come all this way relying on Heritage Mariner to get you the last few miles. We at Bashnev can do that faster and more efficiently. You can't have brought much in the way of weaponry halfway round the world with you. We can put that right. There's no way you would be able to get aboard *Sayonara* without alerting friend and foe alike. We can get aboard so quietly that even the alarm systems will probably not notice. And, although we look like corporate amateurs, I have to tell you that we can hold our own even in your company. *More* than hold our own.'

Something taps against the top of the Pitman's thigh. And there, on the black cotton of the cargo pants is the tip of a metre-long blade as wide as Ivan's palm, curving wickedly, steel-bright and razor sharp.

'It's a matchet,' explains Nastia. 'The blade they use in the jungles of Congo, Rwanda and Benin La Bas. It's what the Interahamwe, Boko Haram and the Lord's Resistance Army cut off your hands with. And your feet if you piss them off. The only difference is that this one's made of composite. It doesn't show up on airport scanners. But it still does the job. I'm an expert in its use. You didn't know I was carrying it. You didn't see me get it out. And if I wasn't on your side, your guts would be lying on the floor now.'

'Not really a match for my plastic and polymer Glock, though,' observes the Pitman conversationally. 'I know it's only partially composite but quite clearly the guys at Schiphol, Helsinki and Narita haven't had the latest up-to-date training on how to recognize it. And it's now pointing at the bits of you that you and your boyfriend here would least like to have damaged. Good though you may be, Ms Asov, I'm afraid you just brought a knife to a gunfight.'

'My God,' laughs Ivan, throwing himself back theatrically in his chair and knocking Anastasia out of the line of fire, apparently by accident. 'This is *fun*! In fact, Madame Asov will not be joining us on board – she has quite enough to keep her occupied here. But I will, with your permission – and I have brought one other less lethal sweetener with me – I have Richard's laptop, which contains all the information available about everyone that he put on board. And a memory stick with further information, and a remote hard drive courtesy of my father and one or two associates of his, which contains everything that the FSB will release to me from their records on organized crime – especially the Mafia and the 'Ndrangheta.'

In the infinitesimal moment of silence while all four of them exchange glances, Harry Newbold gives a secret smile. They are all so out of date. Harry can send an email anywhere in the world containing the specifications of a gun. A 3D printer like the one flat-packed in the case with the Apple laptop will print it out. Then all that's needed to make a weapon as powerful as the Pitman's Glock is a firing pin the size of a biro nib and a little ammunition. Harry, still smiling, gives an infinitesimal nod and the Pitman rasps. 'OK, Ivan, you're in. Just don't get under foot, that's all!'

Ivan gives a bellow of laughter that turns heads right across the cafe. 'Fair enough!' he agrees. 'I am so going to enjoy playing with you people!'

48 Hours to Impact

'Of course it's a trap,' Richard agreed. 'But I still think there's a way round it.' He gestured at the screen of his Galaxy. They were still relying on that because the techies had so far failed to break into the ship's own computers. And, while the Japanese experts tried in vain to undo Rikki Sato's original good work and find ways around the barriers they themselves had designed and erected, their laptops were all spoken for. Besides, the seven-inch screen showed what Richard meant as clearly as anything stored on the larger laptops.

The hours had flown by in a mixture of argument and frustration as they had tried to work out a way of helping the missing men – any way short of going down there themselves. Ship's time was ten a.m. – but that was well adrift of terrestrial time now – or of lunar and solar time. According to the moon – the sun being somewhere below the horizon – it was not quite dawn. Like the chronometers, the computers had proved to be of little help. 'It is the system's automatic override,' Dr Sato had explained apologetically on behalf of his increasingly helpless colleagues. 'We programmed every fail-safe and protective device we could into the control and command system when we set it up. They come on automatically if an outsider tries to tamper with it. Clearly one of two things has happened. Either the men who came aboard before us tripped these by accident when they tried to access the system . . .'

'But they had all the other codes,' probed Richard. 'Why would they not have the emergency override codes for these devices?'

'That is my second supposition,' said Sato. 'They may have used the codes, changed or damaged the programmes, then tripped the cut-outs on purpose to frustrate anyone seeking to find and fix what they had done. The effect at the moment is the same.' He looked around, trying to think of an analogy that would make his predicament clear to all of them at once. 'It is as though you have misremembered your online password,' he said at last. 'You have tried three times erroneously. And everything is closed against you until you contact the service provider and get a new password.'

'So why . . .' began Steve Penn.

Dr Sato raised his hand and the American fell silent. 'We cannot contact the provider in this instance, of course, because we have no external communications. And even if we did, we could not reset the password in mid-voyage. The back-up emergency override codes are no use now; we would have to wait until the ship prepares to dock and the GPS alerts the relevant satellite to send the master unlock codes so the skeleton crew and pilot can come aboard and take control.'

'And you can't even hack it?' asked Richard, frowning.

'My engineers are not hackers, Captain Mariner,' answered Sato severely. 'And even if they were, it would take a genius-level hacker to break into our system. Someone such as the Chinese government apparently employs to worm their way into Western systems.'

Richard nodded, silently praying that Harry Newbold was as good a hacker as gossip, reputation and research led him to believe. And that Harry and the Pitman would be here soon. He shrugged and reached for his Galaxy. 'OK,' he said. 'Keep trying, though, while we attempt to work out the more immediate matter of getting our men out of the engine room.' Aleks squinted a little as Richard turned towards him and continued, tapping the Galaxy's screen gently to enlarge a section of the diagram it was showing, 'Look, Aleks. There are two shafts reaching from the upper weather deck down into the engine room. The one we opened and this other one here. They'll both be covered by groups of Macavity's men waiting for us to make a move and try and rescue our friends. And I would suggest that Macavity is sufficiently on the ball to have the main doors in from the engineering decks covered too – always assuming he hasn't booby-trapped them. But here – you see it? – *here* there is a ventilation shaft. It's not the sort of thing you'd expect even Macavity to notice or know about. I only saw it on this schematic because I was looking for it. But it's over a metre square. And it leads from the engine room up into the funnel system. We could get into it up there and worm our way down and round behind him. There's only a grille covering it at the engine room end and that should be easy enough to kick out.'

'It's all a bit *Die Hard*,' observed Dom DiVito sceptically, and Steve Penn nodded. 'I mean, what would you *do* once you're down there?'

But Aleks took the idea more seriously. 'If we timed it so that Macavity and his men were watching someone coming down the main shafts, then you could get the drop on them. Then we could do quite a lot. You wouldn't be able to take much kit, though. Not if you're crawling along a tunnel one metre square.'

'I couldn't in any case,' Richard answered. 'Those things aren't designed to carry much weight. We should really be looking for the slimmest and lightest people here.' He glanced round the bridge as he spoke. The slimmest and lightest were Steve and Dom. After them, a couple of Japanese technicians; an engineer or two. The people they could actually trust to do the work – Aleks's men – were all built like brick outhouses.

'Hey,' said Dom suddenly, 'if you're serious, I'm up for it. I'll tag along. I should be able to go anywhere Richard goes.'

Aleks looked at the young Canadian executive speculatively. 'But will you be able to do what Richard can do when you get there?' he asked.

'Probably not. Sure as hell not, if everything in his Greenbaum International file is true. But I can carry a gun and I'm a real good shot.'

'Even so,' said Aleks, 'we'll need to send at least two of my men with you.'

Dawn was just beginning to threaten as they came back on to the topmost deck. There was just enough light to see the door on the side of the funnel that allowed access to its inner workings. Like the funnels, it was a bundle of shafts of various widths, shapes and sizes, heading off in various directions at various angles to various depths of the vessel. Once again, Richard's Galaxy gave them enough detail to ease their way in through the maintenance door and to the hollow funnel itself. There was a toolbox secured beside the doorway and that contained the spanners needed to unbolt a section of the shaft they were planning to crawl along. Then it was simply a matter of Richard and Dom easing themselves into the steeply angled duct. And then Aleks' men following them.

As they prepared to climb in, Richard gave them all a short course which was a combination of wide experience and prescient imagination. 'It's not the most elegant of positions,' he said tersely. 'But when you're crawling along the ducting, try and keep hands and knees out in the angles of the corners. Don't put your weight on the centre of the panels. They'll bend and make a noise. If push comes to shove, lie on your belly and pull yourself forward by pushing your hands against the walls on either side. If the duct becomes steep, we'll have to go that way and use our hands as brakes in any case. I've gone over the schematic and it doesn't have any vertical sections of more than a metre or two, so we should be able to negotiate those. And it's a constant airflow system that operates without fans to assist it, so there'll be no problems there. OK?'

'As OK as I'll ever be,' said Dom. Like Richard and the Russians, he was dressed in black roll neck, bulletproof vest, black cargoes and boots. Neither man wore a balaclava, though both had one rolled in a cargo-pants pocket. Both men wore thin black gloves. All four carried Glock nine-millimetre handguns with red-dot sights in side holsters and carbines with torches under the barrels and stocks folded shut slung across their backs.

'Give us plenty of time,' said Richard to Aleks, as he settled everything into place. 'Then start down the main hatch.'

'I'll be there,' said Aleks. He glanced at his watch. 'In an hour.'

'You'd better be,' answered Dom as Richard looked at his Rolex and made a mental note. 'Because this is a one-way trip for all of us if you're not.'

The ducting was slightly larger than Richard had calculated but the metal-sided tunnel became claustrophobically lightless once they turned the first downward corner. Without the Galaxy to light and guide them, the whole enterprise would have been every bit as foolhardy as Dom's original *Die Hard* thoughts had made it seem. But the seven-inch screen not only gave them illumination, the diagram on it guided them along the intricacies of the pipework down level after level towards the engine room where the grille was set in the wall just below the deck head, in a section well away from the main work areas and equally clear of the lower ends of the maintenance shafts that led up to the hatchways that Aleks and his men were due to come down.

Richard checked his watch on a regular basis, assessing the speed of their progress down the levels as shown on the Galaxy against the time they had left to complete their mission. But he and Aleks had calculated the timing flawlessly. And so, as the minute hand ticked round, it became clear to Richard that they would reach the grille five minutes ahead of schedule. More than enough time, he thought, to allow the final section of his plan to fall into place.

The structure of the tunnel system leading to the engine room itself was quite complicated. There were shafts leading off to either side, designed to ventilate the alternator room and the pump room as well as the main engineering area. Richard stopped at the last of these, then crawled carefully forward until the beak of his nose was pressed against the grille over the tunnel mouth. The lights in the engine room were on. It was hard to see much detail, but it seemed pretty clear to him that one of the Russians was lying on the deck beneath the shaft up to the upper weather deck. The man was bound with cable ties and duct tape. He was moving. All around him stood a group of black-clad figures wearing more or less what Richard and Dom were wearing.

Apart from the enormous bulk of the ship's engine standing like a metal cathedral away on his left, there was little else that Richard could make out. He took as much time as he dared to look around the panorama in front of him. He was in an off-shoot of the huge, three-deck deep enormity of the engine room. The section of the engineering area he was preparing to enter was blessedly smaller in scale. The duct grille was only three metres up from the deck itself – an easy drop if he was careful. He switched off the Galaxy and slipped it into his cargo-pants pocket. Then he slid his fingers gingerly through the wire lattice of the grille and tested it. It flexed promisingly – but there was obviously no way he would be able to pull or push it free. And there was no way his fingers could get at the butterfly screws holding it in place from this angle. He checked his watch one last time and began to reverse back up the tunnel to where Dom and the Russians were waiting.

As he came back to the last side tunnel, Richard pushed his head and shoulders into it, and carefully rolled over and slid the carbine on to his chest before reversing out again and swinging round so his head was in the tunnel and his feet towards the grille. He was then able to move back along the final section of the torturous route on his back, looking up at the tunnel roof. And it was his feet, not his face that came to the grille. He hoped that Dom and the others had the wit to copy his actions – though it wouldn't matter too much once Richard was out what way they followed him. He bunched himself up as much as possible with the soles of his boots just behind the grille and his knees brushing the tunnel roof. He looked at his watch just as the minute hand completed the circle of an hour. There was an echoing noise and an audible stir of action. The hatch cover was open and Aleks' men were coming down the main shafts. Macavity and his people started moving too, their boots squeaking against the metal of the deck.

Richard kicked with all his might at the grille. The top screws gave and it fell open like a flap. Richard wriggled forward as quickly as he could, turning over again with the carbine at his side so that he was able to ease his legs out and follow them until almost six full feet of him were out of the opening before he let himself drop. He landed easily and turned at once. Macavity's men were all looking up at the Russians coming down the shafts. Or, rather, pretending to come down, making enough noise to distract the pirates and give Richard and his men a window of opportunity.

Well aware of the movement of Dom and the Russians coming out of the system behind him and jumping down on to the deck, Richard began to move forward. He swung the carbine into position as he moved and sucked in breath to call out. But then there came a blinding explosion of pain across the back of his head. He first saw a blinding light, especially around the edges of his vision. Then the brightness almost instantly became darkness, which began to gather across everything he could see.

And what he could see, suddenly, was a line of men in balaclavas who seemed very tall indeed. He had no sensation of having sunk to his knees. The shock of pain in his head was repeated and the dazzling lights came and went once more before his sight began to fail. But his ears worked well enough for a moment longer.

'Welcome, Mr DiVito,' said a rough voice in that almost Afrikaans accent. 'And well done. All we need to do is close the trap on the others and the ship is ours!'

42 Hours to Impact

The FORMOSAT-7 satellite sees the danger the instant it comes over the North Pole into the eastern hemisphere, heading south in low orbit along the 180-degree line of longitude, at 4 p.m. ship's time. The celestial time, however, beneath which *Sayonara* is actually positioned is a good deal later than that and is heading towards sunset. FORMOSAT-7 sails through space, above Hawadax Island precisely fifty-eight hours after *Sayonara* passed through Rat Island Pass. The equipment on board the British-made weather-sat measures every aspect of the atmosphere ahead and below and broadcasts its observations to the big weather-prediction computers in Tokyo, Taiwan, Washington and London, assessing the effects of minuscule variations in atmospheric conditions that have massive outcomes in the weather factory.

The critical elements in the observations that FORMOSAT-7 transmits are measurements of the heat and humidity immediately above a particularly warm outcrop of the Kuroshio current flowing north out of equatorial waters towards the North Pacific. A stream of water heated further by the sweltering weather in the west Pacific and the Sea of Japan. This torrent of hot, unstable atmosphere is being forced to rise over a great wedge of unusually cold air flowing off eastern China where the central province of Wuhan has been unseasonably chilly.

The forces unleashed by this meteorological conflict are

causing the warm air to twist and writhe along the edge of the lower layer as it is pushed inexorably upwards over it towards the icy stratosphere, as though over an invisible mountain range above the Philippine Sea. This destabilizing movement is further exacerbated by the relentless eastward rolling of the globe itself and the Coriolis effect that it generates, which in turn is aggravated by the insistent westward rushing of the jet streams high above. The forces are all running counter to each other, twisting, turning, sucking and blowing the unstable air mass until the pressure gradients within it go wild.

And, even as FORMOSAT-7 watches with scientific detachment, a swirl of the humidly stormy air tears free, seeming to form a whirlpool defined by cloud. From the Olympian height where the satellite sits above the turning earth, it looks as flat as a swirl of cream on a cup of coffee. But it actually reaches from wave-top to troposphere like an enormous tornado. And a vicious super typhoon is being born within it. FORMOSAT-7 observes the tightening swirl of cloud moving relentlessly across the surface of the earth far beneath and relays its information to the men who programmed the great weather forecasting computers but, as the storm appears to be following the current on its eastern edge, well out in the Pacific, no one raises any alarms in the Philippines, Taiwan or Tokyo.

However, the watch officer on every vessel ploughing the seas between Alaska and Formosa receives a warning, for the computers predict that as the storm tracks north into ever-warmer and more unstable conditions, it will gather force. They prophesy devastating winds and massive seas. Watch officers begin to alert their captains and vessels of every size and shape, type and tonnage start to run for safe haven. But, of course, *Sayonara* has no watch officer. And what has been done to her computers and communications equipment means that the warnings beamed to the weather prediction systems and then broadcast more generally across the North Pacific do not reach her after all. So, blissfully unaware, she pushes relentlessly along her programmed route, precisely on a collision course with the meteorological monster heading north towards her. And, ironically, the only real sailor on board – the only man capable of reading the danger signals in the sea and sky ahead – lies secured below. Along with most of the men he brought aboard, in fact, because Macavity has sprung a very effective counter-trap.

The pilot of the Sevmash AW 139 helicopter sees the approaching storm, however. Coming down from the cruising altitude of fifteen thousand feet, the chopper remains in the sunshine at a similar altitude to some of the middle-ranking storm clouds. Those on board, therefore, have a far clearer view of the weather system than anyone down at sea level would. 'That looks nasty,' the pilot growls. 'I'd try and stay clear of that if you can.'

'The ship or the storm?' asks Ivan Yagula, whose massive frame is wedged in the co-pilot's seat, just allowing room for the Pitman, Harry Newbold, their weapons, equipment and the RIB in the cabin behind. The co-pilot is back there too, getting ready to help them all off. The chopper has been in the air since noon and they are all getting near the end of their tolerance. The AW 139 passed the point of no return more than an hour ago, though flying back to the little airport at Yuzhno Sakhalinsk was never an option. The plan is simple – the chopper will stay clear enough of *Sayonara* to remain unobserved. It will settle low above the water while the RIB goes out and the co-pilot holds it secure until the three of them and their equipment are all safely in it. Then they will power up, get in close behind the ship and go aboard over the stern – as silently as possible and, hopefully, unsuspected. The chopper will head north to the nearest Sevmash freighter *Fydor Litke*, which is currently running for shelter in the little port of Severo Kurilsk, only just below the northern horizon.

'Both the ship and the storm,' answers the pilot, who has overheard enough of their planning to know that they are headed into a situation that's probably somewhere between dangerous and deadly. 'But the storm for certain. That's going to be a total *mudak*, by all accounts.'

Ivan eases himself round to look south. Even though the AW 139 is still well above the ocean, the cloud wall stretching across the evening sky down there towers astonishingly high. Its base is black and its top purple. *Sayonara* glitters unnaturally, like a splinter of glass gleaming on a grey granite pavement. From here it looks as though the storm front will gulp her down at any moment – and the huge Russian fervently hopes that this is an optical illusion. They have to get aboard before the two come together or they are dead. 'Can we get there any quicker?' he asks the pilot.

'No, sir. But we're nearly there. I'm just about to take her down.'

Things look even worse at sea level, but they feel better. There is a dead calm, disturbed only by the down-draft of the chopper's rotors. The sea is oily and flat, except for the circle torn away by the engines. But the wall of cloud to the south now appears to have its foundations in the sea itself, and there is no blue sky above it. The co-pilot holds the RIB steady as Harry and the Pitman lower their precious equipment down into it, then Harry eases out and down while the Pitman unloads their guns before Ivan gives the Pitman a hand down then eases out and down himself. By the time the huge Russian settles into the RIB, the Pitman is at the tiller, powering the inflatable southwards while Harry sorts through the equipment again and the AW 139 lifts off above them, thundering away to the north.

The Pitman brings the RIB round in the tightest curve possible, driving towards the high stern at full speed, as well aware as any of them of how threatening the sky beyond their target is looking. The battering downdraught of the chopper is replaced at once by the wind of their passage, even though the air through which they are hurling is as still as the sea beneath it – and almost as humid. By the time *Sayonara*'s stern is sitting like a steel cliff up above them, the three in the RIB are all drenched in sweat, the gathering heat and humidity worsened by the protective vests they are all wearing. Then Harry raises a short gun loaded with hooks and ropes, firing unerringly upward. As soon as the ropes are anchored on to the aft rail beneath the shadow of the big lifeboat, the Pitman joins Ivan in the bow and they swarm upwards, laden with kit. As soon as they are standing shoulder to shoulder at the aft rail, it takes only moments for Harry to send up the rest of the RIB's cargo and then come upwards, hand over hand. The last thing Harry does before swinging up on to the rope is to pull a toggle on the RIB's blunt bow. There is a flat *pop* and a lingering *hiss*. The sturdy vessel's sides deflate and the weight of the motor pulls the solid base of the thing beneath the heave of *Sayonara*'s wake. None of them gives it a second glance as it begins its long voyage down to the bottom of the ocean nearly eight thousand metres below. They are too busy checking their kit and weapons, and making sure that all signs of their arrival are packed away out of sight – or following their RIB to the bottom of the sea. 'Think anyone saw us come aboard?' asks Harry as they cross to the bridge-house doorway.

'Doubt it,' answers Ivan. 'With that cloud dead ahead, who's going to be looking back astern?'

'A cloud as big and black as that has to have one hell of a silver lining,' says the Pitman. 'Harry, you hacked that door mechanism yet?'

'Piece of cake,' says Harry cheerfully. 'I thought you said this system was top of the line, Ivan.'

'That's what I was told.'

'Hmmm. Anyway . . .' The bulkhead door to the A Deck swings wide open, just as it did for the pirates and Richard's men. They hesitate for that one second which allows them to be sure that their name tags and Sevmash ID logos are clear. That way they are less likely to receive any friendly fire. So they hope. And in that second, the sun sets and darkness comes.

Then the Pitman and Ivan step over the raised sill of the bulkhead door side by side. After a heartbeat, Harry follows them, as they change from cheery companions to special operations soldiers as though a switch within them has clicked over, from *peace* to *war*.

39 Hours to Impact

Heritage Mariner has an arrangement with the restaurant called *Gem* at 145 Lothbury. Once a week, the small board of the huge company meets there at eight a.m. for a business breakfast. The restaurant reserves a table in a private room for Heritage Mariner and supplies those board members who attend, offering them the full range of food and beverages served in the more public areas nearer the street. Everything from green tea and skinny lattes to a full English breakfast is available, with more than a nod towards ethnic tastes which suits the increasing diversity among those that make up the Heritage Mariner board. There is also more than a nod towards the twenty-first century in that the private room has unlimited hi-speed wifi access and a range of booths round the walls suited to laptops and tablets – in contrast to the ancient refectory table which dominates the centre and seats twelve with ease.

Which was just as well, thought Robin: there would be at least nine more executives joining her here within the hour. And they, like her, would bring a range of laptops, tablets and smart-phone devices. This morning she was there first, in spite of the fact that she had slept for little more than six hours, stepping out of the humidity still lingering after an almost tropical night into the air-conditioned, fragrant freshness of the place just after the doors opened. Within five minutes she sat solitarily sipping Earl Grey with lemon and thanking God that she had over half an hour to plan how she wanted the meeting to go.

The small board of Heritage Mariner Shipping consisted of personnel director Rupert Bligh, ex-Royal Navy, whose grandparents emigrated from Grenada; financial director, Stanford-trained Hong Kong Chinese Anthony Ho and Crewfinders director Audrey Gunnel. Then there was Richard's back-up, Will Cochrane, director of shipping, as often as not accompanied by his number two, captain Morgan Hand – his 'right-hand man', according to the company in-joke, which turned not only upon Morgan's surname but the fact that the captain, like Robin, was one of the most senior female officers to command the Heritage Mariner ships. LSE and SOAS-trained company secretary Jada Newton completed the list of board members. Alex Garner, Robin's PA, would also be there to record the minutes, and was due any second now with his laptop and printer to produce the order of business – when she had finally settled on precisely what it was going to be. This morning, the board would be augmented by company solicitor Andrew Atherton Balfour, intelligence man Pat Toomey and Lloyd's representative Gerry Overbury, for they all had direct input to make.

While she waited, Robin slipped out her tablet and scrolled through her online news apps as she began to assess her priorities and consolidate her plans, but found herself distracted when her email icon lit up with an incoming message. The London *Daily Telegraph* sent her its front page packed with top stories every day at seven a.m. and five p.m. She rarely, if ever, saw the seven a.m. edition arrive, for she was by no means a morning person. Frowning, she opened the message and the familiar masthead came up. She swiftly scrolled down the page, pausing only to smile at today's wryly cutting cartoon. There was a follow-up in the news section to yesterday's story about Tristan's mysterious drowning, which at first glance offered nothing new. The financial section speculated about his assets and commitments, promising a list of those involved in his Lloyd's syndicate, whose names Robin already knew. Their names and a hell of a lot more. The social section speculated about his marriage. There might be something there, Robin thought; she'd check later.

Robin did not click on any of these. Instead, she found herself distracted by the most-viewed videos section. Here there was a click-through entitled: CLIMATE: *The Storm of the Century?* With a note promising *video footage from the North Pacific showing the effect of Tropical Cyclone FUJIN on the seas east of Japan.* Robin clicked on the link and her screen filled with a clip from a news report. At the top of the picture was the logo TV Japan 24/7. Yesterday's date stood beside it. The bows of what seemed to be a deep-sea fishing vessel plunged into a wall of white water. It was a marvel that the Japanese fishing boat climbed up it and broke through the foaming crest. The picture shook as the cameraman staggered. The clearview, through which the pictures were shot, went white with spray. It seemed almost miraculous that the water did not smash through the glass and flood the bridge. Instead, the spray washed downwards to reveal wall after wall of white-topped water. The vessel was running with her stern to the storm, trying to sail just a little faster than the huge swells which surrounded her. It was the safest way to proceed in seas as dangerous as these. The caption scrolling across the bottom of the screen read: *Fishing vessel* Etsu Maru *runs through the outskirts of typhoon Fujin.*

'Penny for them?' growled a familiar voice. Robin glanced

up and met the bright blue gaze of her PA. Once again, she was struck by how much Alex resembled the thrusting, youthful Richard Mariner she had first fallen in love with. Physically, at any rate, but he lacked Richard's simple commanding power. The only thing the two men shared, apart from physical similarities and a warm regard for Robin herself, seemed to be an excruciating sense of humour. And, to be fair, she could certainly do with a laugh at the moment. But when she simply, wordlessly turned the tablet round and let Alex see a re-run of the Japanese footage by way of an answer to his greeting, the last of the humour drained out of the young man's angular face. 'That looks very nasty indeed,' he observed. 'Speaking as an inveterate landlubber, that is. Or should that be "*invertebrate*"? Spineless, certainly. You know I get seasick just looking at a muddy rugger pitch if the puddles are big enough.'

'Be that as it may,' she said, 'it's what Richard seems to be heading into the middle of. Or rather, it's heading straight for him. Unless,' she glanced at her watch with a worried frown, 'he's already in the middle of it.'

Alex immediately changed the subject and got down to business, pulling his laptop and collapsible printer out of the carry-case and getting ready to process and reproduce. A huge mug of cappuccino arrived at his elbow as he settled to work. 'Now, what do you want me to put on this morning's agenda?'

'Insurance scams, organized crime, murder, mayhem . . .' she answered.

'Right,' he said. 'Business as usual. Where d'you want to start?'

'With your breakfast,' she replied, coming over all motherly. 'Full English?'

Pat Toomey was the next arrival and both Robin and Alex watched with a mixture of awe and envy as he settled into the Full Irish, which seemed to be the Full English with extra fried potato bread and pancakes, wheaten toast, soda bread and lashings of butter and marmalade. Pat was still partway through this when the others turned up and, like Robin, settled for a start to the day that would do less for waistlines and more for cardiovascular health.

The most pressing order of business was *Sayonara*. Gerry

and Pat brought the others up to speed about the current situation. Pat added his suspicions about the links between Diusberg Reinsurance of Vancouver and the 'Ndrangheta. 'The long and short of the matter,' concluded Andrew Atherton Balfour, 'is that *Sayonara* is sailing effectively uninsured. The Duisberg Insurance Company seems to be less than legitimate so we can't rely on them paying out. So is her cargo. The paperwork is all in place and everything seems to be above board. But it is clear that if anything should happen to her, Heritage Mariner and Greenbaum International would be locked into years of litigation before one penny could be claimed.'

'If anything significant could in fact be claimed,' added Gerry Overbury. 'Because we at Lloyd's are planning to close Duisberg down and put most of its employees in jail. With the help of The Combined Special Enforcement Unit of British Columbia; the Mounties' anti-organized crime people.'

'In the meantime, what do you suggest?' asked Anthony Ho, the finance director. 'We can't risk *Sayonara* proceeding uninsured. What can we do?'

'I suggest,' said Gerry, leaning forward in turn to stare the stony-faced Hong Kong accountant down, 'and I've been thinking this through quite carefully – I suggest that you take out another, entirely legitimate insurance with a copper-bottomed, one hundred per cent reliable syndicate . . .'

'What's that going to *cost*?' demanded Anthony, throwing himself back in his chair so forcefully that his salmon sushi skittered across the table, slopping soy sauce.

'In the short-term, certainly, I can guarantee preferential rates. Under the circumstances, I can promise that,' answered Gerry and Pat nodded.

Robin's tablet lit up as a Skype message came in. The screen which had made Alex almost seasick earlier was suddenly filled with a face familiar to Robin if not to the others. 'Robin,' said Anastasia Asov. 'Robin, are you there?'

Robin picked up the tablet without thinking. 'Yes, Anastasia. What is it?'

'I think you'd better get out here as fast as you can, Robin. The Japanese media are reporting that *Sayonara*'s vanished. She went into the cyclone Fujin late yesterday and even the automatic ship-tracking systems in contact with the black box seem to have lost all sight of her.'

Robin was on the Austrian Airlines flight OS452 out of Heathrow just under two hours later. She had her laptop with her and the Airbus A320 was set for wifi so she was able to keep on top of what the board discussed and then decided via Alex's Skypes and emails. It all seemed academic to her now, for if *Sayonara* had been swallowed by the storm they were too late to change anything in any case. But then, as she was passing through Vienna airport, hurrying purposefully from European Arrivals to International Departures as she found herself fighting the almost overwhelming temptation of apple strudel piled high in Strock bakery, her cellphone rang. In spite of the fact that she was already late for the connecting flight that would get her to Naruto just after seven-thirty a.m. tomorrow – twenty-two-and-a-half hours before *Sayonara* was due to dock at the NIPEX facility, she stopped and pulled the slim machine out.

It was a text from Indira, who was back in position at her computer in the huge room at the top of Heritage House, waiting for a zip file update as she and her team had been for the sixty-eight silent hours of the crisis so far. The text simply said: *New zip from* Sayonara. *12.00 noon BST. No info re: position, speed, disposition or situation. Automatic distress call, repeated three times, then all silent again.*

36 Hours to Impact

They came for Richard a little after ten p.m. ship's time and by then it was already too late. He had spent some of the intervening hours in dazed sleep, having nightmares about the men he had led aboard and what was happening to them. Some others were in partial wakefulness, cursing Dom DiVito and probing the tender back of his skull where there was a large matted lump. But he had also a good number of them in full wakefulness, during which he had disregarded his discomfort and explored his surroundings and his situation with increasing insight and success. He might be unable to escape and uncertain as to the fate of his team – trusty and turncoats alike – but he could prepare to take action when the chance arose.

When he came to, clear-headed, some uncounted time after Dom laid him out, he sat up, heart racing and eyes wide. He had a dream-like half-memory of feeling the back of his head in brief moments of painful wakefulness and he did so again without thinking. Thus he discovered that he was not tied up or taped. The lump on his skull was large, tender and crusted with dry blood. He had no idea how long it took for blood to dry, but he assumed he had been out of things for several hours. He brought his left wrist in front of his eyes to check the time and two other facts he had known but not yet really registered became obvious: he was in utter darkness and his Rolex had gone; where the luminous face should have revealed the time, there was nothing. Where there should have been a forearm, there was blackness so absolute it seemed to have been painted on the backs of his eyes. His right hand closed round the wrist. Bare flesh. For the first time in how many years?

Richard was not a man who panicked easily. He wasted no time in worry or recrimination, therefore. At this stage he didn't regret the loss of his watch any more than the loss of contact with Aleks and the others. Nor did it occur to him that Dom's blow had somehow caused him to go blind. He put the most positive interpretation on things that he could – he would get his Rolex back, he was not blind and he would escape from this lightless prison. If his men were captive, he would release them. He accepted the position in which he found himself and began to try to work out how to escape from it. His first order of business was to establish what exactly *was* the position in which he found himself. He was immediately in a quandary. Should he search himself to discover what else was missing? Should he explore his surroundings to determine how – and perhaps where – he was being imprisoned? Either course of action might furnish the first chance to start planning his escape. Both alternatives seemed to require that he stand up and so he pulled himself to his feet and stood, swaying a little at the heart of an immense darkness. But the act of coming erect triggered another series of impressions which formed distracting multitudes of thought. Because he could not see, he found himself relying on his hearing and his sense of smell. One deep breath gave him an array of odours which he catalogued almost subconsciously as he thought of other things. Metal, paint, a faint but piercing chemical stench.

But what he could smell abruptly seemed much less important than what he could hear. And he realized immediately that the loudest noise in the soundscape surrounding him was the rhythmic pounding of the engines. He frowned. He had spent much of his adult life on board vessels like this one, powered either by diesel motors or by steam engines. The vast majority of those vessels had proceeded for almost their entire voyage at eighteen knots. He knew the rhythm as well as he knew his own heartbeat. And *Sayonara*'s engines were running too fast. Just a shade. So little that he hadn't noticed until now. But now that he had, he frowned as his mind whirled off into new areas of speculation and suspicion.

As Richard began to assess the implications of his suspicions, he began to sort through his clothes to see what had joined his Rolex in the possession of his captors. The Galaxy was gone, of course. His pockets were empty, but he was still wearing everything he had been when he crawled into the ducting, except for the protective vest. His laces still secured his boots so, whatever else they thought he might be, they didn't consider him a suicide risk. And, he suspected, they could be confident enough that he wouldn't be able to use the laces to garrotte anyone either. He had taken it for granted that his communications equipment would be gone. And he had also taken it for granted that his guns would also be gone. Laces were one thing. Carbines and nine-millimetre Glocks were something else entirely.

But he could only be certain of what was missing if he checked the deck beside his feet. And that in turn led him to explore the room he was being held in. The darkness was strangely disorientating and it took him much longer than he would ever have imagined to establish that he was in a small, square, four-sided space whose height was taller than he could reach either standing or jumping. Four increasingly confident and forceful jumps into the air with his hands above his head established that the deck head was far above him – something confirmed by the slightly cavernous echoes as he landed. Four careful paces forward, arms out, fingers spread, brought him to a wall. The fingers discovered that the wall was featureless in all the areas that they explored. It was cool but gently throbbing to the power of the engines. When Richard sniffed his fingertips, they smelt of metal and paint. He was not surprised. But he decided he was more likely to be in the engineering areas where he had been captured rather than up in the bridge. He wasn't sure whether the strange, half-familiar chemical smell made engineering more or less likely. So he put that on the back-burner for the moment.

Being right-handed, Richard moved right and after six sideways steps the fingers discovered a corner, which he checked with his elbow, then his shoulder and knee. Richard turned right and after three sideways paces the fingers discovered on the wall a vertical seam which he assumed to be the frame of a door. The door was one and a half paces wide. He could not reach the top of it but the bottom stood on a lintel a couple of hands-breadths above the deck. Even before he found the big lever handles, he knew this was a bulkhead door, therefore. It would be secured from the outside. It would be metal – probably steel. There was no way through it unless someone opened it first. Three paces to the right of the door there was another wall. He followed that to the corner he assumed must be at the inner end of his prison cell.

Six sideways steps led Richard across the back wall but demonstrated a flaw in his method of proceeding. Made increasingly confident by the predictable smoothness beneath his fingers, he moved sideways more briskly – until, hands still spread on smooth paint-covered metal, he barked his right shin painfully on something that seemed to be sticking out of the wall just below knee-height. He crouched, cursing silently, hoping that the pain in his leg would distract him from the pain in his head, and discovered that there was a metal-sided chemical latrine in the rear corner of his cell, which explained the half-familiar smell. And the fact of its existence brought to the forefront of all his physical sensations the overpowering need to use it. He just had the good sense to confirm that whoever had placed the latrine here had also supplied toilet paper to go with it.

As Richard sat there with the walls that met in a corner behind him pressed against his back and shoulders, his mind cleared by the immediacy of physical relief, he noticed the next thing that seemed important to him. During the time he had been focused on exploring his invisible environment, the way the ship was moving had changed. That change was emphasized now not only by the disposition of the deck beneath his feet but by the constant need he felt to adjust the position of his torso because of the way the walls were moving. If he listened carefully, he realized, he could hear the gentle slopping of the restless contents of the latrine to which he had just added. And, if he closed his eyes and really concentrated, he realized he could hear the vastly larger liquid body of the Pacific Ocean moving equally restlessly just outside *Sayonara*'s hull.

Frowning with increasingly disturbing thoughts, Richard closed the lid of the latrine and secured it as firmly as he could. He then followed the wall down to the corner by the door and sat, his back in the angle of the walls, his legs spread on the deck and his hands spread flat beside his hips. He closed his eyes once more and listened. In this position, it was the throbbing of the engines that dominated. Every now and then he thought he could hear footsteps and voices. But the sounds were so faint and dream-like that he could not be certain he was not imagining them. His mind drifted into speculation as to what was actually going on here – extrapolating the things he was certain of, adding in the things he suspected, seeking a wider pattern so that he could begin to formulate a plan of action; a plan to be implemented when he got out of here. And, oddly enough, perhaps, he never doubted that he would get out of here.

After some time, Richard pulled himself to his feet and moved to the inner corner of the cell, opposite the latrine. Here the throbbing of the engines was slightly fainter – though still strong enough to make all the surfaces around him vibrate in sympathy.

The sound of the increasingly restless ocean was louder and, he now realized, the sounds of wind and spray. As logic dictated, therefore, the wall with the door was facing midships while the wall with the latrine and the corner he was sitting in now was closest to the outer wall of the ship's hull, probably a deck or two below the waterline. But the waterline was becoming increasingly restless. He nodded without thinking and bashed his tender skull against the wall. *Sayonara* was heading into a storm.

At first this fact did not seem to be particularly important. Storms were not uncommon in the waters the great ship was programmed to cross. She would be able to handle anything up to a strong typhoon. And if anything more severe than that were predicted, the vessel was programmed to receive early warnings from the FORMOSAT-7 weather satellites in constant polar orbit. A typhoon prediction from the weather satellite should automatically cause an alert at the NIPEX centre where it would be decided whether to guide the ship to temporary safety remotely or whether to send a crew out to her. But that was the system under normal circumstances; circumstances that no longer remained. Even if the guys at NIPEX knew that a storm was coming, they had no way of alerting the ship's systems if communications were blocked by that thing up by the bridge. No way of moving the ship to safety by remote control. No way, now he thought of it, of getting anyone out here and aboard her, unless Macavity and co. were willing to allow it. However, there was no reason to think that *Sayonara* was unlucky enough to be heading into anything too dangerous at this point in time. He returned to his brown study, trying to work out what Macavity and whoever had sent him aboard was really up to – and how to frustrate their plans.

But after a while longer, Richard found that the increasingly acute sensations his body was experiencing pulled his mind back into the present. The conditions through which the vessel was sailing were coming to him almost subliminally from the deck through the nerves of his palms, fingertips, calves and buttocks; from the walls by his back, shoulders, spine and cranium; from the whole hull's disposition and movement through the six degrees of freedom was transmitted to the delicate mechanisms of his inner ear. The semi-circular canals of the vestibular system inside his skull, just above the hinges of his jaw, were capable of the most minute discrimination. Normally this system served to keep Richard's massive body balanced. Now, as he rested his head gingerly into the corner of the wall behind him, they transmitted not his own movements but those of the ship as she began with increasing liveliness to heave, sway and surge back and forth, pitch, yaw and roll up and down.

Long before the first hesitation in forward movement – speaking to Richard of *Sayonara*'s bows hitting an incoming roller like a car colliding with a house and smacking his head against the wall once more – he had realized that his earlier, almost careless, speculation had been correct: Macavity's interference with the computer systems meant that any warnings sent out by the weather satellite had not come aboard after all. Even if NIPEX had been alerted, the ship was almost certainly proceeding as programmed – into the heart of a severe typhoon. And he'd realized that he was likely to be the only man on board with the slightest idea what to do about it. Once he was certain of all this, all he had to do was to sit and wait for the big steel bulkhead door to open and for someone to get him up on to the bridge before *Sayonara* sank into the abyss, taking all hands on board down with her.

35 Hours to Impact

Alerted by the sound of the handles turning, Richard was standing ready, eyes half-closed, when the door opened and the lights came on. The instant these things happened, *Sayonara* lurched again, hard enough to make even Richard stagger, then she tossed her head up, heaving and hesitating before surging forward and pitching almost sideways. The way she yawed and rolled allowed Richard to begin the conversation even before he was certain he was talking to Macavity. 'You have big seas coming in on the port forward quarter,' he said, spreading his legs and standing fore-square. 'From the *ten o'clock* position in military parlance. This means, unless you have changed course since you put me in here, you are sailing southwards along the Great Circle route as programmed into the leading edge of a large tropical depression which is in turn heading north. Depending on the composition of the depression and the eyewalls around it, you can expect stronger winds and much rougher seas from that quarter, swinging round to broadside-on from the port side until we get to the central eye. Then the weather will reverse and probably intensify even further. Not that we're likely to still be afloat by then if this is anything like a serious storm, because even a ship this size will roll over or break up under those conditions. I don't know how much worse you're expecting things to become,' he continued after a heartbeat, 'but unless someone starts employing some elementary ship-handling immediately, we're going to find ourselves swimming.'

'*Not waving but drowning*, eh?' quipped a familiar voice with a new, sneering tone.

Richard opened his eyes fully. Dom DiVito was standing at Macavity's shoulder, his face wearing a lop-sided grin. Richard's head twinged. 'Hi, Dom,' he said, coolly, still uncertain of the best way to deal with this turncoat employee of one of his oldest and best friends. 'I'll talk to you later.' Then he switched his gaze to meet Macavity's. 'You won't get a chance to wave. You'll all go down so fast.' As though in support of his words, *Sayonara* gave another lumpy heave, swaying, pitching and rolling all at once. Richard staggered again.

'Come,' said Macavity in his flat Dutch/Afrikaans-accented English. He gestured with a gun that Richard recognized. It looked very much like his own nine-millimetre Glock. He wondered briefly whether his watch and his Galaxy were close at hand as well. And, come to that, his men. Then he crossed the little room and stepped over the raised lintel into the main engine area. Macavity's men crowded round him and he immediately smelt the stomach-turning bitterness of vomit. At least some of the pirates were seasick, then. *Good. Serves them right.* On a less childish note, he thought, *That will make them less efficient. Maybe make them lower their guard. Give me an edge.*

He looked around the engine area. There was no sign of anyone except Macavity's men and Dom.

Macavity took the lead and ran them forward out of engineering into the lower decks beneath the stubby bridge house until they reached the lateral corridor bisected by the stairwell. Then, staggering every time *Sayonara* heaved over a wave punching in on her left shoulder, he ran them up the companionway. The little squad moved with such speed and confidence that Richard had realized before they were two decks up – coming level with the weather deck itself – that his worst fears must be true: Macavity and his men must now be in total command. He paused for a moment, his mind racing. But his thoughts were immediately overwhelmed by another howling assault from the gale outside, strong enough to make the air in the companionway stir despite the fact that the bridge-house doors and windows all seemed to be tightly secured. Macavity and his men paused when Richard did, stopping dead in their tracks by the threatening roar of the storm. Richard looked at Dom, but for once neither of them had a clever quote or quip to offer. There was a serpentine hiss leading to a watery explosion of sound as a big wave washed across the weather deck outside and broke against the door at the end of the passage like surf on a reef. Richard felt the whole hull shudder and try to swing to starboard under the weight of the pounding sea. The throbbing of the engines reached almost cardiac intensity for an instant and the engineering sections below seemed filled with groans and whines as the automatic steering system fought to bring the ship back on to her pre-programmed course. A course that was likely to kill her unless the motors gave out or the computers were overridden.

If this weather continued or worsened, then it really didn't matter who controlled the bridge, Richard decided, turning to pound upwards once more. Just as long as they were willing to allow the computer engineers to disable the programmes – if such a thing was possible – and give him control of the vessel before it was too late. And so it proved. For as the squad ran him on to the command bridge four decks further up, Richard saw masked guards at the doors and at the corners of the wide, cold command space. A glance told him that this had been the situation for some time. There was no evidence of Aleks and his men. Presumably they were somewhere down in the dark depths of the engine room too, listening to the labouring engines spinning the thrashing turbines and the protesting servos swinging the battered rudders, puking and praying in equal measure. Rikki Sato and some of his men were working on the computers under the guns of the pirates exactly as they had done under the command of the Risk Incorporated men. And they needed to work fast, by the looks of things. Unless they wrested control back off the recalcitrant computer programme soon it would be too late – if it wasn't too late already. But, very worryingly indeed, they had been trying non-stop for twelve solid hours since they got on to the bridge here, thought Richard, frowning up at the ship's chronometer. Trying off and on for thirty-five hours since they came aboard, with absolutely no success.

Macavity crossed to the pilot's chair and threw himself in it, looking morosely out through the clearview windows down the length of the foredeck. Dom stood behind him, holding on to the chair's back. Richard went forward and came to stand beside Rikki Sato where the main computer access was immediately beside the helm and movement controls – the engine room telegraph on old-fashioned vessels. He steadied himself with his left hand on the rally-sized steering wheel of the helm. His gaze flicked down to the screens that automatically monitored all the systems on board – whether computers or people controlled them. He noted the engine revolutions coming up to the top of the green and the servos controlling the massive rudders already well into the red. His eyes flicked up to the monitor on the deck head above him that showed the rudders' disposition. It was shaking as though it were made of jelly as the great fins battered this way and that under the turbulent waters of the wake. He glanced down again but before he could check on the pitch of the propellers something made him glance up through the clearview windows angling in from the top towards the control console immediately in front of him.

All the ship's lights were fully on outside, giving Richard a rather clearer view than he would have liked. The great white whaleback stretched forward into a maw of blackness; a huge, gaping, cavernous mouth fanged with lighting. Huge white bolts struck almost in series from port to starboard, giving the jaws of the storm ahead some kind of depth. Sheet lightning illuminated a roiling insanity of storm clouds seeming to stretch away forever ahead, starting just above the top of the bridge itself. There was a second eyewall out there, a ring of thunderstorms standing immediately across their course an hour or so ahead. That was where the really big winds would be. And, of course, the really tall seas.

Not that those they were sailing through at the moment were much less dangerous. Especially, thought Richard, given the dynamics released by that great whaleback standing along the foredeck. As the winds whipped across it, they seemed to be clawing at it as though it were a sail, pushing *Sayonara*'s head relentlessly round to starboard. And, in the face of the counter-pressure caused by her rudders, programmed to turn her back on course, the wind and weather was threatening to roll her over. The foam, spray, rain and spindrift lashed across it from left to right with a speed that made it hard to focus. And beyond, as *Sayonara* slid off the top of another great incoming comber, there was an immense, white-fanged wilderness revealed by the lights as they struck out ahead.

The sound was incredible – howling, whining and keening through the upper registers to levels that only bats could bear, while at the same time booming and thundering through bass registers that Paul Robeson and Fyodor Chaliapin could only dream of. And the volume was more than overpowering. It was like being in the middle of a battlefield. Disorientating. Terrifying. Unless you were used to it, thought Richard. He was battle-hardened in ways these soldiers could never conceive of. Like the sea-sickness, the disorientation and naked terror might serve to give him an edge. If he survived for long enough to need one, that is.

'. . . do anything?' came Macavity's voice like a distant whisper. Richard turned and was surprised to observe that what he could see of the soldier's face was red with strain. Macavity had been bellowing at the top of his lungs.

'Not unless Doctor Sato can find some way to give us back control,' he answered, pitching his voice to ride over the cacophony with practised ease. 'Come to think of it, you guys seem to have done the damage – can't you undo it? Or tell Doctor Sato how to undo it?

'No need. I will have control in ten minutes,' promised Sato suddenly. 'Perhaps less.' Richard swung round, shocked, then suspicious. Paranoid, perhaps. After all this time trying with no success . . . The moment the going really got tough, suddenly Rikki got going. That made him wonder about the Japanese computer expert. Especially, now he thought of it, after what Sato had said about the master codes . . .

'Ten minutes?' He probed. 'You can override the programmes in ten minutes?'

'As I said, perhaps less . . .' Rikki Sato nodded, his black hair falling over the dome of his forehead, glasses slipping towards the end of his nose.

'Absolute override? Complete control?' Richard could hardly believe it.

Another huge wave came in from the ten o'clock position, jerking his attention away from the suddenly shifty-looking computer programmer. It smashed into the whaleback, threatening to tear the whole thing off. Spray exploded up and thrashed away down the wind so fast that Richard was able to see the way the incoming water seemed to split, a wall running back along the pathway he and Aleks had followed on top of the whaleback to get into the bridge before moonrise. It rushed along the flat top between the pipe walls to rear up against the clearview and blot out everything for a lingering moment with a wash of foam that seemed glued to the glass.

The whole hull shuddered. Heeled to starboard. The port-side bridge wing made some very strange sounds indeed and Richard reckoned the foam from the incoming wave crest must be beating against the overhanging underside almost hard enough to tear it off. The bulkhead door out on to the bridge wing rattled in its frame as though an invisible giant were beating at it. And suddenly Macavity was out of the chair beside it and standing at Richard's shoulder, Dom DiVito just beside him. Looking, with Richard, through the slowly-clearing glass as though they understood the full importance of what they could see. 'Ten minutes, then, Rikki,' said Richard, keeping his tone conversational even though he had to bellow to be heard. 'Less would be good.' Then a thought struck him. 'All the controls?' he repeated. 'Did you say *all*?'

'Yes. I will close down all computer controls . . .'

Richard glanced over his shoulder. 'When those controls come off,' he bellowed at Macavity, 'there will need to be men who know what they're doing in the cargo control room. God knows what this is doing to the cargo. It'll certainly be slopping about in these Moss tanks as wildly as the waves outside. The NIPEX men. Steve Penn from Anchorage, maybe. If there isn't an experienced hand at the cargo control, the inertia of the liquid in the tanks will just become another force trying to roll us over or tear us apart.'

Macavity nodded, then began to turn.

'*But* even more important than that, I need guys who know what they're doing down in engine control. Someone from Mitsubishi Heavy Industries who knows how the engine control system works, who can back up on my signal. I'm not convinced that the engine room telegraph will communicate directly to the engines if the computer systems are all down. But I can rely on the old-fashioned way, I think. What I set those levers to will come up in the engine control room and they can control the engines from down there.' He gestured to the telegraph as he spoke, and Macavity looked wide-eyed at the levers with the timeless commands written beneath them. FULL AHEAD, HALF AHEAD, SLOW AHEAD, DEAD SLOW, STOP ALL, FINISHED WITH ENGINES . . .

'It's now set up for skeleton crew,' insisted Rikki defensively. 'Good control from here when all online.' He too gestured at the helm, the engine room telegraph levers and the movement control systems.

'A skeleton crew was supposed to dock her,' emphasized Richard. 'A skeleton crew with half the programmes still keeping watch on the cargo and governing the engine movements, the rudder settings, headings and so forth. A skeleton crew who were supposed to just put her into a facility pre-programmed to receive her,' insisted Richard. 'A skeleton crew was never supposed to bring her home through a typhoon with every support system on board shut down!'

He rounded fully on the hesitating Macavity and met him face-to-face, staring down those cold, pale eyes. 'And even if they were,' he snarled, 'I'm a *slim captain*. I'm not a bloody *skeleton crew*! I need Engineer Esaki, maybe Murukami – they know their stuff.' Macavity got the message. He turned, gestured to Dom and one of the men by the door. The three of them vanished through the doorway in the middle of the aft bridge wall running down into the well of the companionway. Richard swung back to confront Rikki Sato. 'How long?' he grated.

'Five minutes, Captain,' muttered Sato, suddenly seeming to be nervous now that Macavity was away.

But Richard had no time for speculation or confrontation – though he really wanted to tear apart the tissue of lies Rikki Sato seemed to be spinning. They were coming closer to the outer eye wall now and, ahead of the line of thunderstorms, the typhoon suddenly started throwing waterspouts at them. As Rikki wrestled with the last of the cut-outs preventing him from closing down his own programme, Richard began to wrestle with an increasingly responsive helm, trying to remember from what he had studied of the ship's management systems how independent of the computer circuitry the command and control systems actually were. Out of the darkness at the ten o'clock position where the winds were coming from, he saw a tall, pale spout of spray-filled whirlwind suddenly join the heaving water to the roiling clouds.

As sinuous as a snake dancing to a charmer's flute, the waterspout writhed out of the wilderness towards *Sayonara* – a snake more than a hundred feet high. A snake whose tail in the water kicked up a circular wall maybe thirty metres across. Richard had never seen anything quite like it and found himself just for the briefest moment trying to work out what peculiar set of physical circumstances could have led to such a thing appearing under these conditions in this place. But then Rikki Sato said, *'Hokay,'* and the helm sprang fully to life beneath his grasp and immediately set about trying to rip his arms off. Richard had planned for this moment. He knew what he was going to do – what he had to do if he was going to save the vessel. He was going to maintain the engines on full ahead and use all the power at his command to ease the helm over to starboard. Perhaps play with the fact that *Sayonara* had twin propellers that could turn independently of each other. Vary the thrust from each to help with the manoeuvre. Look for help also from the conditions he was sailing through. He was planning to allow those big seas to help turn *Sayonara*'s head round until the weather was coming in from her stern, and then he would adjust the engine settings until he was running just a little faster than the wave-sets. He had enough sea room to run due west for the better part of a day if he wanted to. Though, judging by the speed with which the typhoon seemed to be moving, *Sayonara* would be past the eye within a day and able to reverse her heading to ride the counter-winds eastwards back on to her original course. It looked as though he would be at the helm himself for the next thirty-five hours or so, if they could even get back on schedule. But what he had called *an exercise in simple ship-handling*, let alone anything else, would have to wait until he had dealt with the waterspout.

Richard pushed the right-hand lever of the engine room telegraph hard into the full ahead position, therefore, and pulled the left-hand lever to full astern, treating the sedate LNG transporter as though she were a frigate able to turn on a penny. He hauled the helm hard over to port and pushed *Sayonara*'s bows straight into the spray-wall at the foot of the waterspout. 'Attack is the best form of defence,' he said to himself. And so it seemed. At first. The spraywall swept across the deck, seeming to ooze up on to the whaleback before the veil of wildly whirling spray swept back towards the clearview. Through it, Richard was able to see the central column of the spout writhing on to the helideck at the forecastle head. It seemed to linger there for an instant, then it stepped sedately down on to the water to the starboard of the bow.

But just as it did so, the largest wave so far came thundering in from the port side. *Sayonara* gave that strange, unsteady swoop again. Her forecastle slid down and to the left into the trough in front of the oncoming giant. The whole hull yawed and rolled to the left, then heaved off the back of the last wave and surged down after the forecastle head. Rikki Sato, completely thrown off balance, came crashing across the deck and cannoned into Richard. The collision was so unexpected, coming at a time when Richard was so focused on handling the ship, that he was knocked sideways. He lost his grip on the helm and was bizarrely replaced there by the sagging, winded body of the Japanese computer expert. He fell heavily and went skidding and rolling painfully across the non-slip surface of the bridge's deck. But he pulled himself to his feet the instant he stopped rolling and turned, staggering, just inside the bulkhead door that opened on to the port bridge wing. So he was able to see what happened, even though he was unable to do anything about it.

Still turning hard to port, driven by the push of one engine full ahead against the suck of the other full astern, helm held hard over, wedged by Rikki's considerable paunch, *Sayonara* turned into the oncoming wall of water. Her forecastle tried sluggishly to ride up the near-vertical green cliff, but almost immediately there was white water boiling on to the forecastle head so recently occupied by the waterspout. Then, as the bows dug deeper into the oncoming wave, green water thundered on to the forecastle and the whaleback above it. White water was largely foam. Green water was much more substantial. Moving at this speed, it was effectively as solid as ice, and nearly as deadly. As though channelled by the pipewalls secured along the top of the tall white metal construction, the topmost five metres of the wave surged back towards the bridge like a battering ram.

Richard took a step towards the helm, thinking that there might be something he could do. But an explosion of sound behind him made him look back. Behind and below, oddly. The bridge wing seemed to leap upward as though a giant was trying to kick it into touch. The door to the bridge wing twisted in its frame. Jets of water sprayed in as though the most powerful of fire hoses was playing on the outside. Richard slipped in a puddle that seemed to have formed out of nowhere and in no time at all. He went down on one knee.

And the wave came in through the clearview. It smashed the thick glass panes and hurled them inwards as though some huge bomb had exploded on the foredeck. Solid green water came in so hard that it swept everything and everyone to the back of the bridge. Because he was on his knees already, Richard escaped the worst of it, but he was still tumbled helplessly against the bridge's aft wall, and was all-but drowned as the water surged over him, minute after minute, and nearly deafened as the pressure flexed his eardrums as though he were deep under water. He was lucky, in fact, not to be swept into the deadly waterfall that the companionway had become as hundreds of tons of water went roaring down on to the lower decks.

But then, after some uncounted time, he found he was able to move – to pull himself across the dripping wilderness that had been an orderly command bridge, into the howling gale that burst in through the gape of the smashed bridge windows. He wiped the water from his eyes and grasped the helm, thanking God that it still seemed to be alive. Thanking whoever had designed *Sayonara* that they had made sure the propulsion and conning systems were more robust than the computer systems, at least, for they were still working. He still had command and control of the ship. But he had realized the moment he staggered erect and began to push through the howling darkness towards the helm that all of the computer equipment was dead. As far as he could see, the water had shorted out every electrical circuit on board.

32 Hours to Impact

The next hours passed in a kind of blur for Richard. It seemed brutal, but his one focus was to save the ship. Nothing else mattered to him. Not who was where, or how they were. Not who was captive and who was free. Not who was sick and who was getting their sea-legs. Not who had survived the destruction of the bridge unscathed and who had not; who was alive or who was dead. Had they been his crew it might have been different. But even those he had brought aboard with him were the responsibility of other companies and corporations – of other countries. As long as the helm was responsive, and the engine room answered the telegraph and gave him power as and when demanded, he was content. What was going on around him was of very secondary importance and he hardly allowed it to impinge upon his thoughts and calculations at all. He was not a man given to second guessing himself, and even had he been tempted by the alternative to his plan – to try and face the storm head-on – the state of the glass-strewn bridge around him showed the mortal danger of heading into the wind. So he settled to the business of turning *Sayonara* so that she could run before the storm.

To begin with, as he planned how best to get the weather on his aft port quarter and full on his stern, it seemed to Richard that he was alone on the bridge. But the whole windswept wreck was now in darkness, alleviated only by the lights of the basic emergency control systems, which did not at this stage include radar, sonar, or other communications – merely the helm and engine controls, which gave almost no illumination. Apart from the power to move and to steer, the vessel seemed, for the moment, dark and dead. The shadows were occasionally brightened by bolts of brilliant white pouncing down from cloud base to wave top, or by flickers of sheet lightning that lit the madness above in neon. But the brightness was too brief for him to make out any details even had he been willing to look around. Which he was not; he was far too busy.

Nor was he able to judge who was there from the sounds they were making. All he could hear was the raving of the mad wind, the thunderous roaring of the seas and the occasional cataclysmic detonations of the thunder. And yet even these slowly sank into the back of his consciousness as he tried to nurse his ship on to the safe course he had planned for her. This was particularly true because the first part of the manoeuvre he proposed to undertake was the most dangerous. And yet it could not be put off, for conditions would only worsen – the wind would get stronger and the waves would grow higher the nearer *Sayonara* came to the eyewall defined by that line of thunderstorms dead ahead. In order to move from her present heading, leading into the waves with her port forequarter, to her optimum position, stern-on to wind and sea, she would have to turn broadside-on to the storm. And that was the position in which the brunt wind and the relentless waves were most likely to roll her over altogether.

Richard's first action, therefore, was to ease the port-side engine room telegraph up from full astern. He then eased the starboard down from full ahead. Little by little, as he began to swing the helm over towards dead ahead and then starboard, he juggled the two levers, feeling the speed at which the ship responded, judging how far he could rely on the reactions of the men in the safety of the engine control room far below – and how fast they could answer his commands. And, when they did react, how swiftly their reaction resulted in a response from the engines and, in turn, from the propellers thrashing the heaving waters in her wake. Ensuring as best he could that, no matter where the levers of the telegraph stood, *Sayonara* never lost her way. To slow and lose one iota of steerage way would kill her as quickly as rolling her over or running her on to a reef.

As soon as he resumed control of the helm, even as he eased the icy engine room telegraph handles forward and back a little while he kept as much way on her as he could, Richard felt *Sayonara*'s head begin to come round, bashed sideways to starboard by the huge seas, blown sideways by the pressure of the typhoon winds on the whaleback and, no doubt, by the sloshing of the cargo in those mercifully spherical Moss tanks. The motion of the hull changed surprisingly rapidly. The swooping heaves were replaced by a more regular rolling motion that Richard calculated would add to the misery of anyone on board who was seasick. It was at this point that he wondered for the first time who else was on the bridge. He glanced over his shoulder, searching the shadows for an instant. Then turned back to the job in hand.

He was tempted to just think, *Sod it!* Reverse the telegraph handles at a stroke, wrench the helm over as hard as he could and swing *Sayonara*'s long hull round as hard and fast as she would let him. But that meant passing the ultimate control over to the vagaries of chance and the whims of the storm. And Richard was not a man who gave control away lightly. All his adult life he had taken command of situations, some of them almost as dangerous as this one – and he had come through them because of what he did, not what he gave up doing. He simply could not find it in his nature to close his eyes and hope for the best. Live or die, he would do it by keeping command and by exercising control from one second to the next. Or, as it turned out, from one minute to the next. In the final analysis, from one hour to the next.

The moment he completed his initial series of actions, the navigation lights instantly came back on. Richard felt a growing awareness that even if he were alone on the bridge, there were others on board as committed to the survival of the vessel as he was. He had his teams in the engine control and cargo control rooms, the latter led by Steve Penn, who was hopefully more trustworthy than Dom DiVito. The electricians, probably led by engineers Esaki and Murukami, were also clearly hard at work, and he hoped that more circuits would soon be restored. And, he assumed, Rikki Sato would be fighting to get the computer systems up online again, though what state the programmes would be in he hesitated to guess. Just as he also hesitated to guess whether Macavity and his pirates were allowing complete freedom to the men fighting to restore as much power and control to the vessel as possible.

While these thoughts flickered through his head the deck lights switched on and he continued to reverse the disposition of the engines – an exercise complicated by the fact that he wanted one to go from full ahead to full astern while the other did the opposite, without ever allowing them both to reach 'stop' at the same time. The speed with which he was able to achieve this delicate operation was further dictated by his attempts to read the state of the seas coming in from the port side as they swung slowly and inevitably from port forequarter towards broadside-on. It was crucial that *Sayonara* remained at right angles to the wind and sea for the shortest time possible; that she was moving forward at optimum speed to allow the fullest manoeuvrability, so that she was ready to emulate the agile frigate she most certainly was not – and change her heading the instant Richard asked her to.

Richard went into himself – into feeling the very fabric of the ship, just as he had when he was sitting in the darkness down in engineering, feeling her disposition and movement through the nerves of his hands, legs, shoulders and spine. Most of all he felt the sway of his ship as she slowly swung round to full broadside-on to the storm. He had timed it so that the instant she arrived in this situation, *Sayonara* was tilting steeply to port as she slid down the back of a long surf and into the trough of the next one coming in. The moment he felt the deck tilt to his left, Richard completed the setting of his telegraph so that the starboard screw was in full reverse while the port was full ahead, the combination of thrust and drag swinging the long hull to starboard. He already had the helm hard over, feeling his nerve ends seeming to run into the fabric of the vessel as the physics he had committed her to fell into place.

It was impossible that the pounding engines would push *Sayonara* up the wave's rear slope from this angle, but the way he had positioned the rudders meant that the stern offered less resistance to the water than the bulbous, equipment-packed bow. The weight of the stern helped too, while the bridge became less of a sail as it dropped into the wind shadow of the oncoming second wave. And so, even as she slid down the back of the first wave, *Sayonara*'s stern was moving faster than her bow and gathering momentum. The rear of the vessel reached the trough of the wave first, therefore. Because of the new angle of the hull, the weight and the momentum, it sank deepest, giving most purchase to the racing screws – allowing them to react most powerfully against the angle of the huge rudder fins which were also plunged deep beneath the surface where they too could find most purchase and do the most good. Spume boiled in over the poop, foaming up to thunder against the keel of the lifeboat suspended there. Then the oncoming face of the second wave took her. She was already coming round from broadside-on, so that the thrust of the rising water came under her aft starboard quarter and pushed her up while the deeply buried propellers thrust her forward and round. For a moment she behaved almost like a surfboard, riding the big wave forward, still turning, coming up by the stern until the wind took the top of the bridge house like a sail once again. But now it was blowing from behind, pushing against the starboard aft quarter.

This was the moment of crisis, Richard knew. *Sayonara* was still almost broadside-on to the power of the storm. She had heeled over to starboard during the manoeuvre, but now she was heeling to port once again as the angle of the wave was enhanced by the power of the wind against that long, dangerous whaleback. She heeled further over to port as the wave rose under her, coming closer and closer to sitting on her beam ends. That would be the last thing she would do before she rolled over, turned turtle and headed for the bottom of the Kuril Trench. Or the Japan Trench, Richard realized. For she had come so far south that she had passed the point where the one abyss led into the other.

But there was one last element that Richard had calculated on. On which, in the final analysis, he had gambled the life of the ship. As the stern came up on to the crest of the wave, albeit at a crazy angle, tilted so far over that Richard no longer dared look at the clinometers, so the stern burst out of the water first, propellers whirling madly in the air. He had been watching for the moment and pulled both levers back to 'stop engines' an instant before they tore themselves to pieces, racing madly without any water resistance. The long hull balanced on the crest of the wave. But 'balanced' was the wrong word. For the weight of that bulbous, equipment-laden bow was still in the grip of the wave-front downhill. And all the weight of the cargo in the five spherical tanks surged forward as though the big seas were passing through them. And that great burden twisted the hull right round as though an elephant had jumped on one end of a see-saw.

By the time the wave was passing beneath the forward section of the ship, the bow was pointing uphill but downwind and the stern was swinging upwind in a counter-movement while it buried itself deep beneath the water once again. As the poop deck settled into the trough behind the passing wave, Richard pushed both levers to full ahead and brought the helm back to midships. The wind stopped blowing rain and spray in through the gape of the clearview as though someone had somehow managed to close all the windows. *Sayonara* surged forward obediently, slowly settling on to her new course as the waves continued to come in under her poop. But the crests pushed her forward now and even the wind helped her gather way as it blew on to the rear sections of the bridge house, using the square metal construct as though it were a sail. The LNG tanker settled into a see-saw motion, throwing up her heels instead of her head, but the motion eased quite quickly as she continued to speed up, beginning to catch up with the waves; her rocking motion growing slower and slower until she was moving just a little more swiftly than the seas, under full control and safe at last.

Richard suddenly realized that Macavity was standing behind him with one of the pirates at his shoulder. 'I've never seen anything like that,' he said.

'Thanks,' said Richard. 'I think she's safe for the moment. We have enough sea room to run west for more than a day. Now what about my men? We still need them to keep the ship safe. If Esaki or Murukami and the engineers can get power to the collision alarm radar it would be good. We won't need the sonar; we're over one of the deepest trenches in the Pacific. I don't know how far south we are at the moment. GPS would be good as well. Tell Rikki Sato . . .'

Macavity broke in then. 'You can tell him yourself for all the good it'll do. He wants to see you and I said OK. He's in the mess.' Something about the word 'mess' seemed to give Macavity grim amusement.

'What about all this?' Richard's expression and gesture took in the storm, the state of the bridge, the helm and the necessity of keeping it under control.

'Verrazzano here can take over,' insisted Macavity. 'He's a US-registered Able Seaman Unlimited. I can stand watch. There isn't much navigating to be done. And between us I guess we can keep just ahead of the following seas. That was your plan?'

'Yes. You have the papers?' demanded Richard without thinking.

'I had my naval lieutenant's papers before I took the Ultimate Challenge,' said Macavity. 'I served on the *Warriors*. I was specially selected to come aboard and I personally selected the men who came with me. We know what we're doing, Captain. More than the *poesdom* crew you brought with you! And now I have all the guns and you need to do what I fucking say, man.'

Richard hesitated for an instant. That settled the question of accent, he thought. *Warrior Class* were fast-attack craft used in the South African navy. *Poesdom*, as far as he knew, was Afrikaans for 'dumb pussy'. And only South African citizens were allowed to take the Ultimate Challenge and join the special forces. Very few passed the challenge and most of them were soldiers. That made Macavity either a liar or a superman. But this was not the moment to push matters further. Normally, in any vessel Richard actually commanded, he would briefly discuss with the officer relieving him on watch such matters as the ship's position, the set of the sea, weather and visibility, course and speed, compass heading and errors, if any, navigational equipment, communications and traffic in the immediate area. All of which, under the circumstances, were almost utterly redundant. 'Very well, Lieutenant, you have the bridge,' he said formally. *And you're welcome to it*, he thought. He suddenly registered that he needed to empty some parts of himself quite urgently. And he needed to fill others – preferably with something substantial, hot and savoury. But apparently he had to see Rikki Sato first. It didn't occur to him to wonder why, which was a measure of how exhausted he was finally becoming. Leaving American-registered Able Seaman Verrazzano holding the helm and South African Naval Lieutenant Macavity in charge of the bridge, therefore, Richard walked carefully back across the drenched upper weather deck, crunching broken glass underfoot and registering for the first time that there was blood as well as water in pools among the sheets and shards.

If the upper weather deck was a mess, the companionway was a disaster and, as he walked down it, treading carefully on warped and twisted steps, holding on to slack and serpentine handrails, Richard began to register the scale of what must have happened here. He remembered the strange sensation of being alone on the bridge when he took the helm – how long ago was that? And then he began to try and recall how many other men had been on the bridge when the clearviews smashed in with several tons of water behind them. And to speculate what might have happened to the water, the glass and the men.

Richard walked thoughtfully back into the areas that the skeleton crew or harbour watch would occupy when they were on board. The largest of the rooms there was the mess, where Macavity said Rikki Sato was waiting for him. And the instant he walked through the door he understood Macavity's grim amusement. For a mess it was, thought Richard sadly. Half-a-dozen men in varying states of disrepair were laid out on the floor. Clearly someone had rifled the cabins on the decks above to get sheets for makeshift bandages and blankets to make up beds on the deck. There was some basic first aid equipment on show but no real medical equipment. Aleks's stores had been confiscated, clearly, as well as his guns, for there were pressure bandages and the sort of drips that had been used to tend to Kolchak after he had been shot in the shoulder. And Kolchak himself lay in a corner, comatose. But there was no sign of Aleks; there was hardly anyone who seemed familiar at all, in fact. Even the stony faces of the men working as medical orderlies were unfamiliar, though Richard felt he should have known some of them from Aleks's command.

Rikki Sato lay on the floor beneath a blanket that was piled worryingly high, as though the body beneath it was thickly bandaged, and suspiciously stained with what at first glance looked like melted chocolate. His face was bandaged but recognizable, even though his glasses were gone. As Richard walked in, his eyes seemed to light up and he began to writhe like a butterfly trying to escape from a chrysalis. Richard knelt beside the wounded computer programmer. 'I'm sorry,' said Rikki earnestly. 'I apologize. It was madness. *Madness*. All those lies . . . All this damage . . . I never meant . . . Tell Yukio . . . Tell Yukio . . .'

But the effort of movement and speaking seemed to tear something deep within him. Halfway through what he was saying, he began to cough and choke. His mouth filled with blood and his eyes rolled up. Richard stood up and stepped back, shocked and distressed. One of the orderlies crossed to him and shook his head, gesturing to him to back off as he knelt beside the choking man. Feeling oddly as though he was trapped inside some hospital drama, Richard straightened again. 'I'll come back later,' he said.

'Maybe you'll get the full skinny then – if he's in any condition to give it.' Richard turned and found Dom DiVito standing at his shoulder.

'What happened?' asked Richard as they left the sick bay. That question seemed at the moment to be more important than any other – and more likely to get answered truthfully.

'Glass from the clearview cut him open and then the water

washed him down three flights of stairs,' said Dom. 'His guts are held in with duct tape and his neck is probably broken. Yukio is his daughter.'

'I remember that much, even without my laptop records,' said Richard, his eyes narrowing and mind racing as he formulated the questions he was burning to ask the supercilious young Canadian traitor.

'OK,' temporized Dom. There was a short silence. 'So what next?'

'Food and the head,' said Richard. 'I need something to eat and somewhere to piss. It's been a long day. Then I have some questions.'

'Right this way,' said Dom, and led him out into the crew's quarters. 'Food and facilities I can supply. But don't count on getting any answers from me.' The heads were at the end of a long corridor whose lights, like a good number of others, Richard now registered, were not working properly. Dom stood back and let him walk urgently alone down the corridor to the door marked FACILITIES in big, bold letters. 'See you up in the new mess,' he said and walked away. Richard pushed open the door and stepped into a surprisingly large room, thinking that Dom could afford to be so apparently overconfident. Richard was in no position to insist on confessions. And he sure as hell wasn't going to escape. Where in God's name would he go? Three stainless-steel urinals were suspended waist high along one wall. Two cubicles stood open beside them on the left. A sizeable shower stall stood at an angle on the right, its curtain closed and opaque because the light in the shower was another one out of commission for the moment. Between the urinals and the shower there was a pair of moulded steel basins with soap dispensers above them, paper towel dispensers beside them and bevel-edged mirrors screwed to the wall above them.

Richard crossed to a urinal and made copious use of it. Then he turned to the basins and began to wash his hands. As he did so, there was a strange whispering sound behind him and to his right. He looked up into the mirror and saw a square face reflecting over his shoulder; a broad forehead topped with short-cropped blonde hair. Straight, honey-coloured eyebrows that almost met in the middle above the blade-straight thrust of nose.

Cold blue eyes a shade or two darker than his own and clouded like opals regarded him expressionlessly. 'Hello, Angela,' he said, secure in the knowledge that he was one of the few men alive who could call Angela van der Piet, the Pitman, by her given name. 'Welcome aboard *Sayonara*. And how is Harriet?'

30 Hours to Impact

'**H**arry's fine,' answered the Pitman. 'But what about you? You look like shit.'

'A bit tired, maybe. And a bit stressed,' Richard admitted.

'I'm not surprised,' snapped the Pitman. 'Either the computer programme has screwed up big time because of this typhoon or there's been some total asshole driving the boat for the last couple of hours. What do you think?'

'I'd go with the asshole driving,' admitted Richard. 'But didn't the computers all go down when the windows came in and the power went off?'

'Windows came in, hunh? That would short out a shitload of stuff.' The Pitman shrugged. 'All I know is that everything on board shut off all of a sudden, then all the computer programmes went back to the equivalent of factory settings as the power began to come back on and an emergency file was sent out thanks to the black box. Harry went into the programmes like a pig into a truffle mine. I know some things came back online at midnight when we got full power on for the first time. There was a distress beacon. They've shut it down now, though. But you need to talk to Harry about all that.'

'Will do,' nodded Richard. 'But . . .' he hesitated, swaying thoughtfully as the hull pitched lazily up and down while she calmly overtook a storm wave. The watch and the helm were doing well, he thought.

'But what?' demanded the Pitman impatiently, sounding very much like Macavity up on the bridge.

'Well, thanks for rescuing me and all,' said Richard, 'but I'm

not sure I should vanish quite yet. I could do more good staying
where I am. There are things I still want to find out, and under
the current circumstances I'm in a pretty good position to do
some detective work. And the storm's still pretty dangerous. I
feel responsible for the people I brought aboard.'

'Up to you.' The Pitman shrugged her broad shoulders again.
'But don't flatter yourself. I wasn't after you. I was trying to
liberate Doctor Sato. Harry wants to talk to him. Something
about the programmes.'

'It would be,' nodded Richard. 'But you're too late to talk
to Rikki Sato, I'm afraid. He was chopped up pretty badly when
the windows came in and may have broken his neck when he
was washed down the companionway.'

'That's a bummer.' The Pitman frowned, looking worried for
the first time. 'Harry'll be pissed if she doesn't get her own
way.'

'Well, I'd better get back, I suppose,' said Richard. 'I really
don't want them to come looking for me and find you hiding
in the shower.'

'No skin off my nose whether they come or not,' said the
Pitman easily. She didn't need to stroke the Heckler and Koch
G36C short-barrelled rifle she had cradled across her breast,
nor to ease the nine-millimetre Sig in her holster or even to
fondle the Fairbairn and Sykes black-bladed special forces knife
she carried strapped to her thigh. Richard got the message.

'No, I know,' he said. 'But let's leave the mayhem for later,
shall we? Until I've worked out precisely what's going on.'

'You know it's the 'Ndrangheta, right? Ivan's brought a shitload of stuff on organized crime from the FSB.'

'*Ivan?* Ivan's on board?'

'Couldn't keep him away.' The Pitman shrugged. But her
eyes sparkled a little and there was the ghost of a smile at the
corners of her mouth. She didn't dislike Ivan, thought Richard.
High praise indeed. 'His father the federal prosecutor and some
other high-ups gave him an external hard drive with about a
terabyte of information on it. He's got your computer too, which
is compatible with the drive by some kind of miracle . . .'

'Where is he?' asked Richard. 'Is he close enough for me to
have a quick word and still get back before they notice?'

'Well, I guess so. If they thought you were doing a little more than popping it out then zipping it up . . .' She nodded to the cubicle, then frowned. 'Or if they're not too worried about keeping a close eye. What's so important all of a sudden?'

'Yukio,' he answered.

'Well, fuck,' said the Pitman, her voice dripping with irony. 'That explains *everything*! Let's go, big fella.'

As they crept down the corridor, Richard breathed, 'Angela, do you know where they've put the new mess?'

'One deck up, then follow your nose.'

'Good. I'll have a quick word with Ivan, check something on my computer, then go there. It was where I was going next. They might think I . . . ah . . . *zipped up*, washed up and went straight up for something to eat.'

'If they're tired or seasick enough it might work. Or if whoever you're trying to convince is easy to fool.'

Richard, Aleks and the rest had had no real opportunity to explore the decks in and immediately below the bridge house itself, and he was surprised by how many unexpected little stock cupboards and store rooms there were down there. Harry Newbold and Angela had obviously set up camp in one of those least likely to be visited, and had given a little extra room to Ivan Yagula as well. It was an electrical equipment storeroom, doubling as some kind of back-up to at least part of the computer system. On one side of the room there were piles of cardboard boxes that Ivan had arranged into a makeshift work bench. By the look of the labels on the side they contained wiring, relays, hoses, manifolds, cooling banks, air-conditioning spares and back-ups. On the opposite wall stood tall banks of old-fashioned-looking computers. There were flat screens with touch controls, serial ports and all sorts of stuff Richard didn't recognize. Harry was going through it. She had her laptop plugged into one of the ports and had taken the front off one of the other machines nearby.

'Hi, Ivan, Harriet,' Richard said easily. 'Nice to have you on board. I'm sorry to say Rikki Sato's not likely to be well enough to talk to you. Can you do without him?'

'If I have to.' Harry shrugged philosophically. 'It'll just take longer to sort this stuff out and make sure I've broken in to everywhere I want to. Then, I believe, with luck, I can take full control of most of the computer systems on board . . .' She didn't look at either of them as she talked, her fingers too busy with circuit boards and brightly coloured wires.

'What's all that stuff?' Richard just had to ask.

'Back-ups and spares,' she answered. 'Mirrors the main system up on the bridge. MC4510-C23 marine computer system with the MD 220 display integrated with the MPC-220W-C23 marine panel . . .'

'You had to ask,' Ivan said wearily. 'Harry's only just finished explaining it all to me.'

'Good,' said Richard brutally. 'You can talk me through it all later, then. In the meantime, Angela says you brought my laptop aboard.'

'I did. Seemed like a good idea . . .' Ivan began defensively.

'It was,' interrupted Richard. 'There's stuff on there I really need and couldn't access on my Galaxy before I lost it.'

'You lost your Galaxy? That's tough.'

'That's not the half of it. But we don't have time to go through all my adventures now. I want you to access Rikki Sato's personnel file for me. I want to know about Yukio. His wife's name is Seiko.'

'Like the watch,' said the Pitman.

Richard looked down at his wrist. 'Let's not talk about watches,' he said.

'Got her,' said Ivan suddenly. 'Yukio. She's Sato's daughter. Born, let's see, twenty-three years ago. Attended Seitoko Elementary School. Top of her class in everything. Went to Kobetokiwa Girls' High. Top of her class again. Prizes galore. Special commendation from the principal. Speaks several languages pretty fluently, including Mandarin, English, French, Spanish and Italian. Graduated from Kobe University, Rokkodai Campus Number One with First Class Honours in Applied Economics. That was eighteen months ago. She went back into the graduate school just over a year ago to start her first post-grad degree. Invited back by the faculty, apparently. Joined the European Erasmus Mundus programme. Special recommendation once again. Currently halfway through her Master of Applied Economics course . . .'

'At Rokkodai?' asked Richard. 'Her father works at Kobe. The family lives there.'

'No. The Erasmus Mundus programme has allowed her to do an exchange year. She's partway through it, according to this.'

'If she's not in Kobe at the Rokkodai campus, then where is she?'

'She's in Cosenza, Italy,' answered Ivan. 'At the University of Calabria.'

28 Hours to Impact

When Dom DiVito caught up with him a little while later, Richard was alone in the makeshift mess, using a box labelled Air Conditioning as a seat and a slightly larger one as a table. He was consuming something that had been called all-day breakfast on the tin. Though where it had come from God alone knew. The brightly printed 'contents' section boasted that it consisted of baked beans, button mushrooms, sausages, bacon slices and pork bites filled with scrambled egg. It tasted of nothing in particular, and was more slimy than chewy. The only strong flavour seemed to be coming from the plastic plate and fork he was using. And that was of fish. But Richard didn't care. The food was steaming hot, filling, and of all the assorted tins and packets piled between the microwave and the kettle, it was one of the few whose label was in English and which did not consist largely of seafood with rice or noodles.

In any case, Richard could have been eating anything between sirloin steak and sewage and he would hardly have noticed, for his mind was simply not focused on the here and now. It was hardly, in fact, on board at all. Such was the depth of his brown study that he noticed nothing of the food, of Dom's hurried entrance and first question, or of the new, uneasy motion of the ship.

'WHERE. DID. YOU. GET. TO?' repeated Dom suspiciously, slowly and loudly – as though speaking to a deaf man.

'What? Oh. Hi, Dom. After I tested the plumbing, I came up here. Got a bit lost on the way, but ended up following my nose.' Richard wrinkled the organ in question and Dom looked around as though suddenly becoming aware of the strong briny stench which Richard's all-day breakfast stood no chance of overcoming. Not, frankly, that it actually smelt any better.

Dom nodded once, clearly unconvinced, and Richard kept his vague but innocent expression in place as he finished his meal in two hasty forkfuls and plonked his plate in a bowl full of lukewarm water, scum and fish bits. 'Coffee?' he asked, reaching for the kettle and shaking it to establish that it was half full. As he did so, the deck stirred again and he rode the movement with all the ease that came from his years at sea. 'Tea? No milk or sugar, I'm afraid.'

'No time,' answered Dom. 'You're wanted back up on the bridge. The lieutenant started calling for you some time ago.'

Richard put down the kettle and followed. 'Speaking of which, does our beloved leader have a name, or shall I just call him *Leutnant* for the duration?' he demanded as the pair of them strode out into the corridor. He used the German for lieutenant on purpose. 'Or, considering he's Afrikaans, *Kapitanleutnant*, perhaps. What do you think? And, now that we're asking questions . . .'

Dom threw him a questioning look over his shoulder, as though he was wondering how far Richard was going to push his schoolboy confrontation. Whether, perhaps, he was planning on playing this game with the lieutenant himself. 'Are you going to push him like that? Needle him all the time? I mean, it's getting nowhere with me. With him it might get you a broken nose . . .'

'I'm considering it, though. He doesn't seem exhausted or seasick. The next best thing is to make him angry. Angry people don't think straight.'

'That why you haven't come after me for hitting you in the head?'

'Could be. Anyway, my nose has been broken before and I've survived. Or it could be that I have a cunning plan and I'm just biding my time. You never can tell.'

'I'll be able to tell soon enough if you start winding up the lieutenant,' answered Dom.

'Maybe you will and maybe you won't,' Richard needled cheerfully. 'What I may or may not have planned is for me to know and for you to find out.'

Dom opened his mouth, about to ask a question in turn. But then he registered how Richard had turned the tables on him and closed it again. 'For us to know, and for you to find out,' was all he said in the end.

Richard soon found out. Or thought he did. 'What can I do for you, Lieutenant?' he asked, as though butter wouldn't melt in his mouth the moment that Dom led him on to the bridge. He used the English form of lieutenant, as they do in the South African Navy. 'I notice you seem to be having a little difficulty keeping the hull stern-on to the weather. Is that what you want to see me about so urgently?'

'Very smart!' snarled Macavity. 'How did you know?'

'Let's just say I felt it in my bones. Now, what can I do for you?'

'For me? Nothing,' answered Macavity. 'But you can help the ship out. Help those on board who are still alive, especially those who have started puking their guts up once again. And see about getting back on course and schedule into the bargain.' The flat, South African tones were raised almost to a shout. But this time the noise they were riding over did not come entirely from the storm. The bridge was bustling with teams of men – led, Richard noted, by the engineers he had brought aboard – purloined from the engine control room, clearly. Two teams of them, under close guard by Macavity's men. The most obvious difference between them being that one set had all sorts of tools while the others had all sorts of weapons. Though not quite as many, Richard observed happily, as the Pitman.

But, Richard realized at once, the fact that the engineers were here meant that Macavity and his men had managed to restore a good deal more of the basic control system, if nothing much of the higher systems as yet. Clearly, the engineers could only be spared for bridge maintenance if the engine and rudder-control computer system could be relied upon to transmit the helmsman's orders on the telegraph directly to the engines and the steering gear. So the systems were coming back online, even without Rikki Sato's help, and despite whatever Harry was up to in secret down below. One team led by an engineer was clearing up the broken glass. Another was working on replacing it. And, with the typhoon still squarely astern, Richard reckoned, they should not be having too much trouble positioning the big squares of glass in the bridge's wind shadow. But they were. Those on the starboard especially, caught by sudden, unexpected side drafts. And the way the ship had been riding since he left Angela checking her armaments, Harry working on her computers and Ivan searching through the personnel files looking for other unexpected Italian connections, also alerted him to changes in the conditions through which *Sayonara* was sailing. 'You got the weather predictor up yet?' he asked.

'Partially,' answered Macavity guardedly. 'The GPS is still offline.'

Richard walked across to the digital display and glanced down at its blank screen. Then he looked out at the sea and the sky, his eyes narrow and his expression thoughtful. Everything confirmed what he had been calculating deep in his subconscious since he first felt the new movement of the hull at the start of his all-day breakfast. 'As I'm sure you remember from your meteorological training, Lieutenant, a northern hemisphere depression is basically a whirlpool of winds and water running in a circle anti-clockwise round the eye,' said Richard quietly, but with such authority that even Macavity stood and listened. All around him the noise of the work stilled as even the engineers waited to hear his explanation of what he had saved them from already – and what he needed to do next. Soon the only sound was the wind through the half-fixed clearview. 'They all work in roughly the same way. The eye is the low-pressure centre sucking air up into the troposphere and the Coriolis effect makes the winds rushing in to replace it spin, while the pressure gradient pulls warm, wet water vapour up into high, cold air and causes the precipitation. And the only real variable – as in our case – is that the tighter the whirlpool, the lower the pressure at the centre, the steeper the pressure gradient, the stronger the winds, the more powerful the rain and storms and the higher the seas.'

Richard walked to the gaping clearview and peered out into the drizzling darkness above the watery glow of the deck lights.

'The way *Sayonara* was programmed meant that we sailed south straight into the northern edge of a very tight depression – a typhoon, in fact – as it in turn ran north to meet us. This meant that the wind and the seas came in from our port quarter. Strongly enough to threaten the ship, even before the bridge windows came in and the electrics all went down. So we turned and ran west with the weather behind us, best to keep out of the wind and keep on top of the waves – in every sense. Now we've come far enough west to be running out of the leading edge at last, so the airflow is swinging round again. And, I suspect, the typhoon itself may have turned quite sharply east. Meanwhile, the eyewall of thunderstorms that nearly swamped us has probably choked off the central eye and closed the whole system down. It happens sometimes. In any case, our new position relative to the depression means we have winds swinging round to the north, and fairly large swells beginning to run in from the west – moderating, thank God.'

Richard turned to Macavity and his helmsman. 'If you continue to keep the wind to your back, you will slowly circle southwards and, although things will get a little uncomfortable again as we start taking sea coming in from starboard, they won't be big enough to roll us over. And we should be back on course – perhaps even on schedule – within twelve hours or so. I can't give you our precise course or headings until the electronic navigation chart system comes back up. Until then, you'll just have to do it by feel.'

'No!' snapped Macavity. '*You'll* do it by feel. And *I'll* feel much happier with you at the helm, Captain. At the very least, I'll have a fair idea of where you are and what you're up to!'

'Better than the brig, or wherever it was you had me locked up,' allowed Richard. 'But, as someone's already remarked, I look like shit because I'm exhausted and strung out. I'm feeling a bit better since I've had something hot to eat, but you'll need to relieve me at some stage. Someone else will need to take over the watch and let me get some rest.' He moved the helmsman away from the wheel and took it over. 'In the meantime, unless you want me asleep at the wheel, I need coffee. Jamaican Blue Mountain High Roast Arabica for preference, but anything hot, black and full of caffeine will do.'

Macavity gave a curt nod and one of the men guarding the engineers fixing the windows turned smartly and doubled down the companionway. The South African stood for a moment, looking calculatingly at Richard as he eased himself into a comfortable position towering over the helm, resting his right hand on the engine room telegraph, adjusting the levers slightly and feeling the engines' response. He remained there until after the coffee arrived, and even then he lingered suspiciously as Richard began to ease *Sayonara*'s head southwards until the wind stopped thundering across the window frames and the hull, which had been pitching like a see-saw, began to roll like a cradle.

Richard looked up at the ship's chronometer, the only piece of equipment which had been unaffected by the flooding of the bridge. 'Oh six hundred ship's time,' he said. 'Captain Mariner takes the wheel halfway through the morning watch. State of sea westerly, five on the Beaufort Scale but moderating. State of wind northerly, gale force but also moderating. Sky one hundred per cent occluded. Ship's heading just south of due west, swinging towards south-west and planning to be due south by the end of the watch. It should almost be dawn, but dawn's a long way off.' He paused, then added, as though the thought had just occurred to him: 'We're due at the NIPEX facility at oh six hundred hours tomorrow. But that's Japanese time. We'll be four hours adrift of that. So we don't have exactly twenty-four hours left – we have precisely twenty-eight.'

25 Hours to Impact

Richard was as good as his word. By the time the watch ended *Sayonara* was heading a few degrees west of south with the wind behind her pushing her along through the moderating westerly seas. The watch ended, but no one appeared to relieve the lonely watch-keeper. He hadn't actually expected anyone to turn up, so he wasn't really surprised. In the nearest time zone – Japanese Standard Time – it was still four a.m. and

the night remained overcast and utterly dark, although the chronometer read oh eight hundred. There was nothing to see outside
the newly repaired clearview windows except the ship's lights,
and precious little to see inside them except the illumination of
the control systems and the increasing number of computer
display screens that kept flickering into life quite unexpectedly
– apparently with no rhyme or reason at all. And Richard's own
reflection, looking haggard, gaunt and strung out. Hollow-
cheeked, with dark rings under his eyes and thick black stubble
around his chin. Looking, as the Pitman had observed, *like shit*.

Rather than bemoaning his appearance or trying to work out
who must be fixing what down in the back-up computer areas,
Richard concentrated on keeping a lookout for other ships. So,
while the nerves of his body seemed to be part of the fabric of
his temporary command, his eyes stayed fixed on the far
horizons. He had no collision alarm radar yet and no communications to warn of impending crises. In spite of the fact that he
had managed to turn *Sayonara* pretty handily in the emergency
of the typhoon, she was by no means a nimble vessel. She
wasn't quite the legendary super tanker which is so difficult to
stop or turn according to the popular saying, but nevertheless,
he didn't want to find himself on a collision course with
anything. It would take a miracle to swing her off line in anything
short of a mile. And it would take maybe five miles to stop her,
assuming the computers allowed him full and immediate access
to the engines. So Richard did his best to keep watch and prayed
that *Sayonara* was big enough and brightly lit enough to keep
anyone sharing these waters well clear of her. But although the
typhoon might have eased, all the shipping nearby seemed to
be staying in safe haven, just in case. So *Sayonara* sailed on
through the black night utterly alone. And, given the frenetic
activity of the last few hours, on top of the excitement of the
voyage so far, Richard remained wearily unsurprised to find
himself also alone on the bridge, hour after hour.

In the dream-like state of gathering exhaustion – not to
mention mild concussion, though it was a good many hours
now since Dom had cold-cocked him – Richard felt utterly at
one with the ship. Indeed, through the vessel's movements along
her course and through the six degrees of freedom, he felt at

ease with the huge forces that made up the vast, invisible night that surrounded her. He knew from the slightly elevated throbbing of her engines that she was running at that unsettling twenty knots again, instead of the optimum eighteen knots, and that the rhythm no longer varied, no matter what he did to the engine room telegraph levers. Little by little the control he had over the helm was slipping away, and he suspected that by the arrival of the dawn – due around nine a.m. ship's time – he would be utterly redundant because the computers, still in the grip of Macavity's malware or the turncoat Sato's meddling, would have reassumed command and control as the power was fully restored – unless Harry had managed to hack them by then.

Leaning on the increasingly useless helm, he felt the way *Sayonara* pushed through the ocean, and from that judged the strength of the gale behind her and the way it was beginning to moderate. He considered going out on to the bridge wing but decided to leave that adventure for an hour's time. It would be more instructive and enjoyable at dawn. *Sayonara*'s increasingly easy rolling, with the occasional half-hearted yaw told him all he needed to know about the sea. As the wind would be pushing them forward, so the waves would be pushing them westward. And, although the waves were still moving at the dictates of the powerful depression, they were now running in from Japan, whose north island, he guestimated, must lie little more than two hundred miles to *Sayonara*'s lee. So they did not quite attain the size and power of the huge deep-water rollers that had come towering in from the heart of the North Pacific earlier.

At eight-fifteen, as though by magic, the GPS came alive. Richard crossed to it at once, but found himself staring at it with simple incredulity. *Sayonara*'s current position, apparently, was forty-one degrees north, one hundred and forty-eight degrees east. According to Richard's reckoning, that put her five hundred miles south-east of Sapporo on the west coast of Hokkaido or three hundred and fifty miles south-east of Kushiro on the east coast and far further east and south of the position he had thought she must be in. According to these figures, *Sayonara* was five hundred and twenty miles north-east of the NIPEX facility, which was very surprising and not a little creepy.

Because, even after the damage and distraction caused by the typhoon, it meant they were bang on time and bang on target, twenty-five hours' sailing time from the NIPEX facility. *The age of miracles is not yet past*, he thought, shaking his head in simple wonderment.

'Penny for them,' came a flat, almost Afrikaans voice. Richard started, turned and found himself confronting a level pair of opal blue eyes which were crinkled at the corners with an ever-so-slightly self-satisfied smile. 'Jesus, Pitman, you almost gave me a heart attack! It's like living in a Raymond Chandler novel – every time I turn round, someone with a gun comes into the room! What are you doing on the bridge?'

'Talking to you. And from the state of everyone else on board, if we are in a Chandler novel, it'd be *The Big Sleep*. This is more like a dormitory than a ship. But I got a couple of messages.' She paused, registering that Richard was well from the helm. 'Shouldn't you be driving this thing? As you seem to be the only person apart from Harry, Ivan and me who's actually awake?'

'I'm redundant. Story of the twenty-first century – the computers have taken over.'

'Hmmm,' said the Pitman sceptically. 'That's part of the first message. Harry says don't trust what the computers are telling you.'

'Does that include the GPS?' he asked, immediately suspicious.

'Yup.' The Pitman nodded.

'But I thought it was nearly impossible to screw with the GPS. Don't you need this special red control box? Don't you have to reposition the satellites?'

'That's the way you do it in James Bond movies,' said the Pitman. 'In the real world – well, in *Harry's* world – you just screw with the computer that interprets the signal. Or the one that relays the information to the screen. In my world, of course, you just buy a GPS blocker off the internet and no one knows where you are or what you're doing – speed-wise, even.'

'So Harry's message is that the ship thinks it's in one place but actually it's in another.'

'That's it. Given that you're cool with the idea that *the ship thinks . . .*'

'But anyone observing the ship, like the automatic tracking satellites that read the black box info, for instance, will know she's in the wrong place,' he said. 'So what's the use of fooling the ship?'

'I guess they'll see *Sayonara*'s not where it's supposed to be – no matter where it *thinks* it is. But I guess the question is *will they do anything about it*? I'd say it depends how far off-target the ship is pushed by the inaccurate readings. What sort of deviation is going to ring alarm bells on shore?'

'That depends . . .' said Richard. Then he straightened. 'Shit!'

'What?'

'The storm. No one will be surprised if *Sayonara*'s a little off course or ahead of schedule if she's just come through a typhoon.'

'OK,' said the Pitman, exploring – and extending – Richard's reasoning. 'So, the ship thinks its bang on target and is programmed to proceed accordingly. But we know the GPS that's telling it where it is has been compromised.'

'She's actually a good deal further along the course than she thinks . . .'

'OK. We go with that. Everyone is happy to see the ship because it's ridden out the storm. No one's worried if it's a bit ahead of where it should be. How far ahead? Twenty kilometres? When do alarm bells start ringing?'

'If NIPEX still can't get control of the ship when the master unlock codes click in for docking when she's fifty miles out because whatever Macavity's done and Sato's made worse is still keeping them out and Harry hasn't been able to counter it, then they'll start ringing pretty quickly – in twenty-four hours' time, in fact. Because instead of pulling up at the LNG unloading facility, she'll sail straight into Kujukuri's floating city. I was beginning to assess this when I was locked up down in engineering. But if they can take control of her at NIPEX, there'll be no alarm bells at all because they'll just override the computers, chopper out a skeleton crew and a ship's pilot if necessary, and bring her in safe and sound. They'll just do it at four-thirty a.m. instead of six a.m. Japan time. And that won't matter at all.'

'So that's Harry's mission, then,' said the Pitman simply. 'To make sure, no matter what else is going on, that these guys at

NIPEX can get control of the ship twenty-four hours from now. Send out a pilot if they want or dock her by remote if they want. Whatever.'

'That's it,' said Richard, surprised, somehow, that it should all come down to something as straightforward as that. He paused, thinking through what he and the Pitman had just discussed. And it seemed to him to hold water. It all *did*, in fact, come down to something as simple as ensuring the men at NIPEX could take control of *Sayonara* in exactly twenty-four hours from now, no matter how far ahead of schedule or how badly out of position she actually was, as long as she was still within the control parameters.

'But why bother?' asked the Pitman suddenly. 'Why go to all this trouble to make the ship think it's in one place when it's really in another? I mean, shit, even if this is some kind of Mafia insurance scam like Ivan says his father and your London Centre people suspect, then it hardly seems likely that it all turns on this boat being a couple of hours ahead of where she thinks she ought to be.'

'The prime directive,' said Richard. 'It's buried so deep in the programming that not even these guys can get at it. No one can. If *Sayonara* gets within fifty miles of her destination and is more than a few hundred yards off position, she's programmed to shut down, send out a distress call and wait for someone to come aboard and put her safely and securely where she's supposed to be. She's a bit like a super tanker, remember. She may behave well enough in the right hands and under the right circumstances, but she takes a hell of a long time to stop. Even longer to turn round. So, if there's any danger, then she shuts down. Prime directive. We thought it was foolproof.'

'Cool. Like Isaac Asimov's laws of robotics.'

'We took every precaution we could think of. Well, that Rikki Sato could think of. I mean, look at how far advanced the Japanese robotics industry is. What was the name of the voice-controlled robot they sent to the International Space Station in 2013? Kirobo?' He paused for a moment, then added: 'But you have an important mission too, Pitman. You have to make sure that if and when *Sayonara* does dock at NIPEX tomorrow morning, that there's nothing on board designed to go *bang* at an inappropriate moment. I mean, these guys have gone to a hell of a lot of trouble to do whatever they're doing. If we're talking *surprisingly simple*, what could be simpler than fooling around with the programmes to distract us from the fact that there's a socking great bomb somewhere on board? Remember, Kolchak said there was a whole network of bombs attached to the signal blocker up above our heads. Why shouldn't there be something even bigger somewhere on board that we don't know about? Perhaps you'd better check on that. Now, what was the second part of the message?'

'Oh. Right. That was from Ivan. As we're sure we're dealing with the 'Ndrangheta, he's got a list of people on board who have contacts with Italy. I mean, he threw the net pretty wide. Even counted this guy Aleks Zaitsev, just because he's skied there a lot.'

'Do you have the list?'

'No. He needs to talk it through with you. I mean, fair enough, Doctor Sato's daughter is in Italy and someone might well be able to pressure him through her. But does he count Zaitsev because he's skied there? Or this other guy because he served with NATO in Naples, or the cocksmith who's got an Italian firecracker girlfriend? I mean, where does he draw the line?'

'He doesn't draw the line anywhere. Steve Penn has Italian blood, I'll swear. Not to mention Domenico Giancarlo DiVito . . .' He massaged the crusted lump on the back of his skull thoughtfully. 'If anyone on board even likes Italian food, I want to know.'

'Well, you can start with me then. I'd live on pizza and pasta given the chance. But I'll pass on the message.' The Pitman became just another shadow, moving silently to the back of the bridge.

'If you lived on pizza and pasta you'd be the size of a house in no time,' whispered Richard.

'Don't you believe it,' she breathed back as she oozed out of the door. 'I have a lot of nervous energy. And I lead a *very* active life.'

By the time the Pitman left the bridge it was coming up to nine a.m. on *Sayonara*, and dawn in the outside world. Richard returned to the helm. He tested the telegraph again but the engines continued doing their own thing. Or rather, the computer progamme's own thing. He swung the helm hard over to port. And *Sayonara* continued on her pre-programmed course without deviation or hesitation, wherever that course may now lead them to. 'OK, computers,' he said. 'You have the ship. I'm going out on the bridge wing for a breath of fresh air. As if I didn't get enough when the windows came in.' He strode past the pilot's chair – which now looked a little the worse for wear having been blasted with shattered glass and hosed down with a considerable volume of the North Pacific Ocean. He opened the bridge-wing door, surprised at how stiff and unwieldy it was, and stepped out into the truncated tube-train carriage of the covered section. On his right was the doorway leading on to the external companionway, up which they had carried the wounded Kolchak uncounted hours ago. Straight ahead, at the far end of the covered section, was the door out on to the open area where the equipment necessary for docking was – if humans were doing the ship handling. There was a secondary heading readout, a slave telegraph for the engines and a gyrocompass. But Richard was planning to use none of these because they were all rendered redundant by the fact that the computers were back in control. Instead, he was going to take the binoculars from their pouch on the wall beside the bulkhead door that led outside and watch the dawn coming up.

But as soon as he stepped off the command bridge, Richard was aware that something was out of kilter, literally. For the bridge wing was at a slope now, where it had been level and square when they carried the wounded soldier out here. He found himself looking up a slight slope, aware that the deck on his left was slightly uphill from the deck on his right. He remembered the strange noises during the typhoon and the moment Macavity had leaped out of the pilot's chair to appear at his side while he still held the helm. The wing had been hit by a wave big enough to warp it. He remembered reading about how the first Queen Elizabeth had been pounded by a rogue in the North Atlantic when she was working as a troop carrier during World War Two. The impact had been so colossal that it had torn the whole superstructure back by two clear feet.

Without further thought, he jumped up and down on the spot. Everything seemed solid enough. So he continued with his excursion as planned. With all his attention focused on the far door he walked forward, compensating for the slope so he could keep in a straight line. His attention was fixed on the door, and it wavered only for the second it took for him to flip up the top of the binoculars' pouch and pull them out. Then he twisted the handles on the outer bridge-wing door, swung it wide and stepped out into the morning.

Richard had been paying no attention to the gathering brightness, nor the widening vistas in the windows of the covered bridge wing on purpose. Like a child, saving all the best-looking presents to be opened last at Christmas, he had been anticipating this moment. After the darkness of the prison cell followed by the dimness of the typhoon and then the total obscurity of the stormy night, he had planned that he should be overwhelmed by the enormity of the dawn. And so he was, even more so than he had anticipated.

The sky above him seemed unimaginably vast. From the horizon away on his left a veil of thin cloud rose up to the very top of the dome. Then it stopped and there was dark blue curving down from the deeps of space towards the invisible Japanese coast away on his right. The cloud stopped in a straight line. Richard turned slowly, through one hundred and eighty degrees, using his eyes alone at first, then his binoculars. It was as though the sky had been painted in two different colours. And the straight line which was the edge of the cloud led directly along *Sayonara*'s path, as though the computers guiding her had somehow arranged for the whole world – the entire universe – to help guide her home. The wind gusted steadily from behind him as he faced forward again, pulling the binoculars away so that he could appreciate the enormity of the phenomenon. The northerly wind blew gustily but persistently, as though trying to push him – as well as his command – forward along that predetermined line. It smelt of freshness, of ozone, of new paint and metal. It carried, within its rumbling gusts, the sound of distant gulls at their morning feed.

And the ocean seemed to catch colour from the strange sky. On Richard's right, from where the waves were running in, the water was deep blue, the troughs between the tall rollers as dark as the deeps between the stars. Their faces, though, were pale, almost steely, taking their colour from the clouds on his left towards which they were running. But as they passed the ship, their backs caught blue from the sky on his right, dragging flashes of periwinkle, lapis, sapphire and ultramarine into the pale grey expanse of the eastern ocean dominated by the cloud cover. For a moment the waters around the gently rolling vessel looked like a huge blue opal. Distractingly like the Pitman's pale, opaque blue eyes.

But then, away on the eastern horizon, at the very point where the grey clouds closed down on the curve of the sea, a bright green light appeared. It was the moment Richard had come out here to enjoy. The sun was rising, past the eastern curve of the earth. Shining through the thickness of the North Pacific Ocean and igniting the whole of the watery eastern horizon in shades of gold and emerald, as though there was some huge, almost nuclear explosion being detonated in slow motion far beneath the distant waves.

It was dawn, thought Richard, uplifted alike by the beauty of the moment and the promise of the new day, completely oblivious to the fact that the image of the rising sun came all too close to the possible fate of this vessel as he had just been discussing it with the Pitman. He was far too focused on the fact that it was eleven a.m. on board. Seven a.m. in Japan. Seventy-seven hours since the first alarm went off.

Twenty-three hours to go.

23 Hours to Impact

Austrian Airlines flight OS51 completed its short finals and approached Narita airport more than half an hour ahead of schedule. The sun was lost behind a high overcast away to the right over the North Pacific, but it was strong enough to give a strange, pearly luminescence to the oddly two-toned sky. From this angle, it was possible to see

that the wall of cloud that ran straight across the crest of the
heavens from north to south was edged with tall battlements of
cumulus. And that, above their rounded, almost woolly tops,
the sky was clear and already a strikingly dark blue. The land
and sea beneath this odd arrangement were an unsettling mixture
of light and shadow which caused many of the passengers to
crane their necks as they looked out of the windows, simply
awestruck by the view. Robin Mariner did not look out of the
window at her right shoulder to gawp at the atmospheric anomaly
or the spectacular lighting effects that resulted from it. She did
not turn her golden head to admire the burgeoning floating city
of Kujukuri in the bay beneath the starboard wing. She didn't
even glance at the brightly lit Bashnev/Sevmash floating nuclear
facility *Zemlya*, though her company had long been associated
with it and actually owned and crewed the two tugs *Erebus*
and *Terror* that were secured to either side of it. *Zemlya* needed
Erebus and *Terror* to move her, for the huge facility was simply
a nuclear power station that had been built on a barge. It could
– and did – give out thousands of kilowatts of heat and energy,
but was unable to move itself. In that way, the power station
was a perfect symbol of the symbiotic relationship between the
British shipping company and the Russian energy giant. Without
the Heritage Mariner tugs the Bashnev/Sevmash power station
was, effectively, powerless. But such thoughts were far beyond
Robin's capability at the moment. In her head it was still eight
hours earlier – ten p.m. London time – but in her slowly
wakening body it was far too early for her to be facing a new
day. The whole experience was disorientating at best. Distressing
at worst. And downright irritating in the absence of her morning
cup of fragrant English Breakfast tea.

   The flight from Vienna had taken eleven hours, and Robin
had toyed with the idea of doing some work to distract herself
from her worries about her bloody husband and his bloody ship.
But then she had decided that the best refuge lay in what she
needed most in any case – sleep. If she slept during the flight,
she would arrive in Tokyo bright-eyed, bushy tailed and raring
to go. Ready to face whatever crisis loomed and overcome
whatever disaster Richard had got himself mixed up in now. Or
that was the theory, at least. But then, as Robin was making

her plans, the chef came around with menus and she was at once distracted by the thought of food, for she had eaten nothing since the previous evening. Even the tea at her breakfast meeting seemed incredibly far in the past. Her most recent gastronomic memory was of talking herself out of buying those wonderful strudels in Vienna International. Fool that she was, how she regretted her self-discipline now. So, when the crew had taken orders for the meal, Robin found that hers was a surprisingly lengthy one. Although in her head it was only half past two, she treated the late lunch as though it was a full dinner, hoping to fool her subconscious into believing that after dinner time came bed time.

Her meal made her feel full but not in the least bit sleepy, in spite of the wine that went with it. In her head it was still early evening – her subconscious had not been fooled at all – and in Richard's absence her body had become used to keeping student hours. So in the end she had taken a couple of Zoliclone tablets and they had simply poleaxed her, in spite of the fact that her seat was not the most comfortable she had ever sat in and the legroom felt a little cramped, especially as her slim ankles were wedged between her laptop case and her handbag. Now, eight hours later, she was regretting the combination of dinner, wine and sleeping pills, even though it had meant the equivalent of a full night's deep and dreamless unconsciousness. The promise of being bright-eyed and bushy tailed seemed a long way off. Never a morning person, she blinked sleepily awake as the flight attendant leaned across the silent Japanese couple in the middle and aisle seats to her left and shook her gently by the shoulder. The plane was lining up for the landing. It was too late to visit the lavatory – and her mood was further darkened by her pressing need to do so.

An irritatingly ebullient pilot came on to the tannoy, reminding them that he was Captain Ernst Mach, and announcing in jolly Germanic tones that they would be landing more than half an hour ahead of schedule at seven a.m. Japan Standard Time. The weather in Tokyo was clear and sunny, he informed them cheerily. It was currently twenty-five degrees Celsius, though thirty-one degrees was predicted. The humidity was a sticky seventy-six per cent and there was a light, northerly wind blowing at

approximately eleven miles per hour. The unbearable Captain
Mach said more but Robin was too busy setting her watch to
Tokyo time as a distraction from the demands of her bladder.
She pulled her handbag up from beside her ankles, put it in her
lap and pulled out her compact. She flipped up the mirror section,
studied her face and hair and gave a groan that made the young
Japanese couple beside her glance over in silent concern. 'Oh
you bloody, *bloody* man,' she snarled. 'This is all *your* flaming
fault!'

Robin came out of International Arrivals like a Valkyrie
heading for a battlefield. Anastasia was waiting for her, and it
was fortunate that the pair of them were old friends, but nothing
fazed the Russian, so she would probably have handled the wild
woman who was unexpectedly confrontational without too much
trouble. 'Lavatory!' was Robin's first word, for the facilities in
the baggage collection area had been out of order. Anastasia
obligingly led the way, making no comment at all about the
state of Robin's travelling outfit, make-up or coiffure. She stood
guard over Robin's luggage trolley for the better part of fifteen
minutes before a very much more cheerful and presentable
woman emerged to greet her friend with her second word so
far: 'Tea.'

Unfortunately the only café nearby, *Ikkyu*, did not sell English
Breakfast tea, so Robin contented herself with a cup of coffee
that turned out to be very pleasant indeed. Fortunately so, for
the smell of noodles in fish stock was not the sort of thing
Robin liked to expose herself to at breakfast time, and the young
Japanese couple from her flight were partaking of the restaurant's
famous Kansai-style soba noodle breakfast. But as the caffeine
hit her system, the day began to take on a much more positive
aspect. 'What's the news?' she asked at last.

'*Sayonara* seems to have come through the typhoon all right,'
Anastasia answered. 'There appears to be a bit of a conflict
between the last GPS report we've had from the ship itself and
the position as reported by the Japanese coastguards, but apart
from that things are looking more positive.'

'So I've come rushing out here for nothing?' Robin's expression darkened.

'Not quite,' soothed Anastasia swiftly. 'The NIPEX board

has called a meeting for midday local time in their new Choshi headquarters, and both Bashnev/Sevmash and Heritage Mariner have been invited. I thought I was going to have to go alone. But now I don't.'

'OK,' said Robin. 'So we need to discuss what that's all about, and plan how we're going to play things. I'm booked out at the Radisson. Where are you?'

'The Radisson,' answered Anastasia. 'It's high end, Western-friendly and does not do Japanese scale micro-accommodation. Moreover, it's convenient for the airport. But it's twenty-five miles or so from Choshi.'

'OK,' said Robin, finishing her coffee. 'Radisson first, Choshi in due course. Cunning plans on the hoof as we move. Let's go. Shuttle or taxi?'

'You kidding me?' Anastasia's brown eyes were wide with outrage. Her hands made an elegant gesture that emphasized the breathtaking little Chanel two-piece business suit under her Peter Jensen black lace coat, all accentuated by a white quilted Chanel shoulder bag that matched her white-piped black kid stiletto pumps that had Christian Louboutin written all over them. 'I'm not some penny-conscious British businesswoman worried about tax returns and expenses. I'm a *biznissman*! I do not *shuttle* anywhere. Come on. I have a limo waiting. And a guy who'll take care of all this baggage!'

A uniformed chauffeur was waiting patiently at the nearest meeting point and he relieved Robin of her trolley before leading them out into the car park, where a gleaming black Toyota Century limousine sat looking a lot like a Rolls Royce waiting to transport the queen. And, thought Robin, glancing enviously at her stunning companion, that was just as it should be. It was a fifteen-minute ride to the Radisson in a blissfully air-conditioned silence that smelt of fine leather and wood polish, then the chauffeur handed Robin's cases over to a bell boy who accompanied her to the airy white marble reception and helped her check in while Anastasia made sure that the driver and his limousine would be ready to run them over to Choshi at eleven. The women and the bell boy rode up in the capacious lift together to Robin's top-floor suite. 'Now this is more like it,' said Robin as they followed the bell boy into her accommodation. She had been booked into a junior suite with business-class upgrade. The room was huge for a Japanese hotel, with more than fifty square metres of airy space. As they came past the bathroom, the little entrance corridor opened to reveal a big double bed, a free-standing mahogany wardrobe, armchairs, a coffee table groaning with complimentary fruit and flowers and a work area with a desk, lamp, chair and laptop port. The decor was a quiet and tasteful mixture of browns and creams. Robin felt herself relaxing as she took a deep breath and let the atmosphere soak in. 'I'd stick with coffee,' said Anastasia. 'There's a Nespresso machine over here.'

'Tea,' said Robin forcefully. 'Is there a restaurant we can go to while they unpack my cases?'

'The California,' answered Anastasia. 'I could do with something to eat myself. A little American *obed*. Let's go.'

Robin pondered the oxymoron that coupled the concept *American* with the uniquely Russian meal *obed* on the way down in the lift. But when they arrived at the California restaurant, she understood what Anastasia was talking about. In the face of a bewildering selection of cold meats and fish, salads, cheeses and noodles chilled or steaming, they both settled for what the menu called 'The American Breakfast', which Robin would frankly have called a Full English in any other context. Bacon, eggs, sausages, grilled tomatoes, sautéed mushrooms, toast and – blessedly – tea. Twinings Traditional English in a teabag with a little label on the end of the dunking thread. As far as Robin was concerned, it was as welcome as anything even Fortnum and Mason could have served back home at 181 Piccadilly. 'Now,' she said as she finished her third reviving cup and looked at her friend across the meagre remains of two American breakfasts, 'what's all this about a meeting of the NIPEX board in . . .' She checked her watch. '. . . just over three hours' time?'

'Three hours?' said Anastasia. 'But it's an hour in the car! You have only two hours to change and get ready! How on earth are you going to manage?'

The answer to that was *by the skin of her teeth*. But even as the chauffeur came up the steps from the hotel's porte cochère to find Anastasia waiting impatiently in Reception, so the lift door opened and her English equivalent arrived. The black pencil dress with the ruffle collar was by Alexander McQueen, as was the wave-panel short dress coat in household cavalry red that she wore over it, open, with its tails flapping in the wind of her passage. It might be hot and humid but, like Anastasia, Robin was dressed to impress. The stiletto pumps marching determinedly across the marble were black to match the dress, as was the Heroine tote shoulder bag that was just big enough to take her laptop as well as all the necessities she had transferred from her travelling bag. And if her freshly coiffed hair was not quite dry – if the coat was still a little warm from its steam-pressing, nothing could detract from the simple impact Robin made as she strode across Reception.

'Right,' barked Captain (Mrs) Mariner, her quarterdeck voice carrying to every ear in the place – and at least some in the eight-sided temple at the far end of the garden. Even Anastasia jumped. 'Time for the *off*.'

20 Hours to Impact

Angela van der Piet is an unusual person, though she doesn't think of herself as such. Nothing frightens her. Nothing and no one. Or so she tells herself. And she needs to keep reminding herself of this fact on a regular basis at the moment because her subconscious keeps on screaming to her that she is buried in an airless grave and slowly suffocating to death. Her subconscious knows what it is screaming about, too, for during her days as one of the few female frontline operatives in the KCT, the Dutch equivalent of the British Royal Marine Commandoes, she was buried alive at least once. And lucky to survive the experience. Since as well, during her days as a mercenary, she has been in tight situations, in tiny, airless places, both ashore and on board ship, with the feeling that she has been entombed and forgotten, like a long-lost Egyptian mummy. But she is not, in fact, buried. It just feels like it. Or it would do so, except that her apparent tomb keeps rolling from side to side and occasionally giving a disconcerting swoop to port that almost brings her stomach up into her throat. And she is moving.

The Pitman is worming her way along a cramped and light-less duct below the bottom deck where the lowest sheaf of pipes joins the undersides of the Moss tanks to each other, a matter of centimetres above *Sayonara*'s bilges mere metres above her keel. The system is an exact replica of the pipework joining the five huge spherical tanks up above the whaleback in the vast-ness of the cool, clean air which is restricted by nothing but the horizon. The contrast, thinks the Pitman bitterly, could hardly be greater. This is the fifth tank she has checked, starting with tank number five immediately in front of – and far below – the bridge. Tank number one, nearest to the ship's bulbous bow, has been the most difficult to get to. But maybe that is just because she is getting tired and bored. A lesser person would have given up long ago, probably at the moment when her radio snagged and she lost contact with Ivan and Harry. A lesser person would never have survived as long as the Pitman has – and proposes to continue doing, into a lengthy, fulfilled, contented and wealthy retirement. If her plans and dreams come true. And if she stays lucky.

There is room for a maintenance engineer to crawl along here with a torch and some equipment. But the average engineer is likely to be a slight-framed Japanese man, not a strapping Dutch woman more than two metres tall with shoulders as wide as a rugby prop forward's. He is likely to be dressed in overalls and carrying a small case of carefully selected tools, not clad in a back camos and battle top, with a bulky bulletproof vest festooned with webbing, hung with a malfunctioning radio, ammunition clips, Glock nine-millimetre handguns and Fairbairn-Sykes fighting knives. Above all, perhaps, the engineer would be holding a sensible torch. He would not be using the beam from the detachable Surefire G2 Nitrolon bulletproof flashlight mounted beneath the barrel of a compact but cumber-some short-barrelled rifle to brighten his way.

But all of a sudden, the Pitman finds herself reckoning that the fear and discomfort have been worthwhile after all. She has just found one of the bombs that Richard asked her to check for. The only one so far, in fact. It is ominously huge and very fucking dangerous. She freezes, breathing deeply and steadily, disregarding everything except what she can see. And that would frighten anybody. As far as the Pitman can make out, the massive bomb is a very professional-looking piece of work. As part of her *Vaktechnische opleiding Speciale Operaties* training after she was awarded her green beret, she went through a demolition course and some basic bomb-disposal work. Since then, in the army and as a mercenary, she has handled C4 and Semtex plastic explosives. The peculiar faint putty smell that can usually only be discerned in close proximity to C4 in confined spaces or when being confronted with extremely large quantities is the clue. Especially in the absence of the distinctive Tolulene paint-thinner odour of Semtex. Or of recent, tagged Semtex at any rate. All three circumstances that identify that C4 rather than Semtex seem to be in play at once here and now. The distinction is important in that Semtex is more powerful than C4. But in quantities like this it hardly matters.

The vast underside of the spherical tank seems to be enclosed in a broad ring of explosive stretching beyond the range of the Pitman's vision. It is impossible for her to see the whole of the tank bottom from where she is. The huge downward swell of the tank, which she can almost feel with its massively crushing weight above her, comes to a point where the pipework reaches down to run back along the duct she has just checked. It is supported by stays like spider's legs that hold the tank and the pipe securely above the deck which separates them from the ship's bilges. The nearest section of the area is open so that she has a view of perhaps a quarter of the entire base before the huge pipes plunge down and bend towards the stern and the next spider's leg blocks her view. And all around the section she can see from here is a double ring of big grey plastic bricks linked together with bright wires. All of her experience with C4 tells her that those wires will end in a detonator. And that the detonator will either be controlled by a timer, a remote signal or an impact trigger. Or one of the above backed up by another. Given the placing of the explosives on the first tank, an impact trigger seems the most likely primary detonator. And, she reckons coldly, an impact trigger would probably be the best idea if Macavity and his men want to ensure the destruction but make it look like an accident resulting from some kind of collision.

What was it Richard was saying about the incorrectly set GPS taking *Sayonara* into the middle of the floating city? That would be very messy indeed. This amount of C4 would make a big enough bang itself. But the C4, of course, is only designed to be the detonator of a far larger explosion when the cargo of an LNG tanker goes up, like the high-explosive trigger that sets off a nuclear bomb. She taps her throat microphone again. 'Ivan,' she whispers. 'Ivan, can you hear me? Harry?' There is no reply – not even the faint hissing of an open channel in her ear. With a mental shrug – the only kind she can actually manage – the Pitman starts to worm her way forward once again, her mind returning to the immediate problem. An impact trigger would mean that the main detonator is likely to be on the front of the bomb. So the wires – and there will almost certainly be wires – should lead from the bomb's main detonator to the trigger somewhere on the bows. After five more minutes of effort, she has a clear view of the foremost curve. The circle of explosives does in fact seem to come to some kind of point there, like the noon mark on a clock face. There is an extra element sticking out. There are, as she suspected there would be, wires stretching forward. The bright beam of her Surefire flashlight allows her to follow the line of bright wire across the deck and up the far wall.

The Pitman lies half on her back for a moment, her opal eyes fixed on the upward track of the wires and her mind far removed from her current position, even when the hull gives one of its occasional swoops to port and the sound of a wave crashes like thunder rolling along the tall steel hull behind and far above her, where the surface of the ocean is. She is thinking about the big, bulbous bow that begins on the far side of the wall where the wires are, and how far under water it is. She has, ghost-like, unsuspected, been observing Macavity and his men since soon after she came aboard. She has seen the way they are holding Richard's men hostage – suspiciously easily. She is not surprised that Richard wants Ivan to check for Italian connections because she suspects that Dom DiVito is not the only member of the Heritage Mariner team who could be playing for the opposition. Aleks Zaitsev and Macavity are thick as thieves. Steve Penn shuttles between them in a free and friendly manner. Even some of Ivan's other soldiers are getting a pretty easy ride. And was Rikki Sato the only technician who seemed to be playing a double game? But no matter who has been where, and doing what – and why – she has seen no one with anything that looks even faintly like diving equipment. So, unless the impact trigger was put in place before the ship was launched, Macavity and his men cannot make use of the submarine section of the bow. Therefore, she decides, the trigger must be above the surface. Up on *Sayonara*'s cutwater or forecastle head.

But then again, she thinks as she worms her way back to the nearest trapdoor that will release her out of the ducting and on to the deck, unless the impact trigger is very small or very well disguised, it is likely to be all too visible to anyone who gets a good look at *Sayonara*. And, no matter what is actually planned to happen during the next twenty hours or so, various people are certainly going to get a very good look at her. Logically, therefore, the impact trigger would be disguised or hidden. But then it occurs to the Pitman that, just as she hasn't seen anyone with any diving gear, she hasn't seen anyone with any heavy-duty cutting gear either. There is probably welding gear on board, together with the other emergency equipment such as that required to fix the bridge windows, she thinks. But heavy-duty cutting gear – that's something else again. On the dockside at Mitsubishi Heavy Industries shipbuilding yards – yes. On board *Sayonara* – probably not. So, how could Macavity and his men get the impact trigger on to the outside of the forecastle head without cutting through the bow plates?

Just as there are companionways leading from one deck to another within the bridge house and halfway along the hull, so there are at the bows. These, unlike the ducting, are brightly lit. Brightly enough to show the wire the Pitman is following as it continues to mount from the keel towards the upper decks, sometimes half-hidden among the wiring on the forward-facing wall of the companionway, beside the labels announcing the numbers of the decks, and sometimes on the wall at the far

forward end of the corridors the companionways lead to. By
the time the Pitman has oozed like a shadow through the brightness following the wire up to Engineering Deck C, she has
worked out the most likely answer to her own question. They
must have put it through the hawse hole and concealed it behind
the anchor. And proof seems to be offered by the fact that the
wire has vanished by the time she reaches Deck C. Wherever
it has gone, it went on Engineering Deck D. There is, she knows,
an anchor on each side of the forecastle head. A moment's more
thought, however, makes her certain that the impact trigger will
be behind the starboard anchor. *Sayonara* will be coming south
out of the North Pacific when she arrives at the NIPEX facility
in Choshi. So the starboard side will be nearest to the coast of
Japan, to the facility, to whatever is the target.

As part of her preparations for this assignment she had gone
through the details of the ship's design in the finest detail
Richard's laptop and Harry's hacking into the Mitsubishi
computer records could provide, as well as everything she
could discover online about ships – how to supply, maintain
and handle them. She knows every deck, compartment, nut and
bolt of *Sayonara*. She knows that the hawse holes – if that is
the correct term for whatever lets the anchor chains out and
in – open from the chain lockers themselves. There are sizeable
windlasses on the forecastle head on either side of the helideck
that will raise and lower the massive anchors themselves, and
the chain rises and falls through chain-pipes from the deck.
But the chains are kept in chain lockers and *Sayonara* is so
designed that the hawse holes are right at the top of these.
When *Sayonara* is at sea, the anchors hang secured in place
– carefully secured if the wild gyrations during the typhoon
have not set anything off, which in itself would seem to suggest
a perfect place to hide an impact trigger which could appear
to be just another piece of the ironwork holding the anchor
securely in place. The entrance to each of the chain lockers is
on Engineering Deck D, one deck down, and the Pitman is
retracing her steps when she freezes. The bow section has been
quiet for hours. Deserted, apart from her. But now she senses
that someone else is approaching. She holds her breath, focusing
all her senses on trying to hear who might be nearing, and

where from. Almost silent footsteps advance but up on the
deck she has just left. Swiftly and silently, she slides on down
until she has reached the door into the chain locker. She had
planned to pause and try to fix her radio now she has more
space, but the unexpected footsteps have changed her priorities.
She opens the handle, thankful that this, like everything on
board, is new, well-greased and silent. She steps through,
climbing on to a ladder secured to the wall immediately inside
the door, easing the heavy metal access closed behind her.
There is a handle on the inside – a twin to the outer one. She
half-closes it, hoping that no one will notice anything from
outside. And then she turns.

There is some light in the locker, coming in from the hawse
hole in the starboard bow. But she flicks on her flashlight as
well. She looks around, breathing in the strange atmosphere
of new stainless steel overlaid with the timeless smell of the
sea. A smell that comes from below and all around her – not
just through the hawse hole on the vagrant breeze. The locker
is not large; it's little more than four metres across. As she is
standing one rung up from the top of a great coil of chain she
has no real notion of how deep the chain locker is but it rises
little more than a metre above her as she straightens to full
height. The bright yellow beam of the Surefire flashlight
searches the walls and finds the wire almost at once. And it
follows a clear line, carefully secured to walls and the deck
head, over towards the brightness of the great square hole
beneath which the anchor is secured. Glad of her Bates GLX
Ultralite boots but wishing she had the extra security of her
steel-toed Doc Martens, she steps down and begins to cross
the slight hillock of anchor chain, her mind focused on
following the vivid thread of wire. The massive hill of metal
is unexpectedly hard to walk on. The links are like rocks on
the seashore, round, unstable and slippery. On her second step
she nearly falls. Her third step brings her close to the big square
hole in the forecastle head, with its roller more than a metre
wide at the bottom to ease the passage of the chain. The chain
itself reaches out to where the anchor is secured against the
flare of the forecastle head. The last few links, as big as rugby
balls with a cross-section halfway down their length, are lying

across the roller, bearing no weight because of the way the anchor is secured. She takes another, shorter step, craning to see the top of the anchor on the outside of the hull. A huge bolt secured through a massive metal ring shines brightly in the morning sunlight. The anchor itself hangs below – nearly two metres of it, ending in a flat wedge that stands out like a little platform. Under the water, this will dig into the sea bed and hold the vessel steady. And, somewhere behind that little ledge or behind the two metres of the shank or the cross-piece above it, there is the impact trigger that will set off Macavity's bomb. If only she can just get a good look at it.

But then disaster strikes. *Sayonara* gives another roll, which ends in the sideways twist that almost made her sick earlier. The motion is enough to make the chain move in sympathy. It stirs like a sleepy serpent; the hillock on which she is standing imitates the wave *Sayonara* has just crossed. The Pitman is thrown forward. She loses her grip on her rifle and only its shoulder strap saves it from flying through the hawse hole. The Pitman follows it, however. She slithers helplessly forward. Her head and shoulders slide out across the roller, which moves in turn. She just has the presence of mind – and the simple naked luck – to grab on to that final link of the chain. Then she is outside, hanging on for dear life, her feet scrabbling to find purchase on the flat ledge of the anchor secured below her.

The momentum of her disastrous tumble swings her right round until her back is to the flare of the forecastle head, nearly dislocating both wrist and shoulder in the process. Her rifle bangs against black metal at her side. She has a single horrified glance across the vastness of the ocean that begins so terrifyingly close below her feet. All movement stops. Her heart thunders in her ears. The wind buffets across her face. The waves hiss and roar against the foot of the ship's sharp bow, rolling off the bulbous torpedo shape like surf off a reef.

And the door into the chain locker slams open behind her. A rough voice with an accent frighteningly similar to her own calls, 'Who's in there?'

18 Hours to Impact

Macavity relieved Richard immediately after dawn. He put another helmsman beside the helm and set another of his men to stand watch while the computers were in command. Then he returned the almost comatose Richard to the cell in engineering from where he had been brought up the better part of twelve hours earlier to bring the ship safely through the typhoon. As the pair of them went down from the command bridge to the lower engineering decks, Richard saw none of the men he had brought aboard with him and assumed they were still in captivity too, unless they were in the makeshift clinic or had switched sides. Or, like Rikki Sato, seemingly, both. But the truth was he was far too tired to think straight. As soon as Macavity pushed him in through the door he used the latrine in the corner and, finding a sleeping bag on the floor – a pleasant surprise – he slept like a dead man for the next seven hours.

Macavity woke him at four in the afternoon, ship's time, and Richard realized immediately that something was seriously wrong. 'Out!' ordered the South African, and Richard obeyed warily, his eyes narrow, his gaze shooting everywhere. Unlike Robin, he had the ability to spring awake firing on all cylinders, and it looked as though this ability was likely to serve him well in the immediate future, though he took his time in obeying Macavity's peremptory command, letting his mind clear just that little bit more as he assessed the new situation and checked his naked left wrist, looking for the time. Nearly all the men he had brought aboard were assembled in a line down the corridor leading towards the engine room with almost all of Macavity's command standing opposite them, guns on show. It was like a scene out of a war film: *Colditz* or *The Great Escape*. Richard glanced down the line on his left. Aleks Zaitsev was there. Konstantin Roskov, his right-hand man, stood at his shoulder. Then it was a straggle of Russians and Japanese. Of course, Master Sergeant Vasily Kolchak was with Rikki Sato and the others in the makeshift clinic with a couple of Macavity's men keeping an eye on them, no doubt. And there were at least two more pirates up on the bridge as well, Richard remembered, which explained why the two commands were of almost equal size, especially given that Richard's men had suffered fatalities so far – Yoichi Hatta and the unfortunate Boris Brodski.

But the problem for Richard was that he felt he could not trust these men. Ryzanoff was there, as were Theo Gerdt and Pavel Kosloff. The latter two had close associations to Italy, like Aleks and Sato – and who else? Then, last but not least, there was Ivan Karitov, the unit chef. Richard wryly wondered whether he specialized in the sort of Italian cuisine that would commend him to the Pitman while his suspicions were roused even further. *Paranoia's setting in with a vengeance*, he thought. The other faces in the line of soldiers were familiar but Richard hadn't had much to do with them personally. Engineers Murukami and Esaki were there with the rest of the computer men and the shipbuilders. And the last few relative strangers must be the NIPEX LNG men. Then, of course, there were Dom DiVito and Steve Penn – Steve now also high on Richard's list of men he suspected of playing a double game. He felt the back of his head automatically. His paranoia was well grounded on a painful swelling there. But it was not Richard who was first to express his disquiet.

'*Right*,' said Macavity. 'Now that we're all here, will someone please tell me just what in hell's name's going on?'

Richard simply gaped at the angry South African. His hand dropped to his side. 'What on earth are you talking about?' he demanded, his face blank with genuine astonishment an instant before suspicion of the truth stabbed through him.

'There's someone else on board!' snapped Macavity. 'I'm almost certain of it. And if there's someone else on board then one of you people knows all about it.'

'Have you seen anyone?' demanded Richard as his mind raced. 'Anyone other than the people here or in the medical room or on the bridge?'

'No. But . . .' Macavity wasn't giving much ground in spite of the negative. His eyes were narrow and, although Richard would never know it, his mind was filled with the disquieting suspicion that he had come within a whisker of discovering a stowaway in the starboard chain locker.

Richard followed up at once. 'Then how can you be sure? Has any of your men seen anyone?'

'No.' Grudgingly now, a little less certain.

'So it's just a feeling. Nothing concrete . . .' Richard tried to sound dismissive without being challenging. He wanted to undermine Macavity's confidence and allay his suspicions without making matters worse. Ivan, Harry and the Pitman represented the only edge he had. They were his only real chance of working out exactly what Macavity was up to, who on board was helping him and of countering their plans. Without his Rolex or his Galaxy Richard had no notion of the time, and so wasn't sure how long they had to outwit the pirates, but without Plan B they were dead in the water.

He rounded on the men beside him. 'Aleks,' he demanded forcefully – calculatedly – 'have you or any of your men seen anyone else on board?'

'Well, you said you were going to bring Harry Newbold and the Pitman . . .' answered Aleks sharply. Several of his men nodded, frowning.

Richard heard a sharp intake of breath from behind him. He could almost feel Macavity's icy gaze stabbing between his shoulder blades. His heart was thudding. *I've got to play this hand very carefully indeed*, he thought. 'Right,' he agreed, keeping his voice steady and reasonable by a sheer effort of will. 'But did they ever come aboard? Did you see them arrive? Have you seen them at all during the last few days? Did any of you see anyone other than the people here at any time since we arrived?'

'Well . . .' Aleks frowned.

Richard thanked God that Ivan, Harry and the Pitman had been so careful and stayed completely invisible. 'Except for the people we already know about?' he persisted. 'Any strangers?'

'No,' Aleks shook his head, eyes downcast.

'And has anyone noticed anything unusual? Anything that's moved unexpectedly, except for things that have been tossed about in the storm? Has anything been open when you thought it had been closed? Have you heard anything? Suspected anything?' Richard swung round, raising his right arm to include the whole line. 'Dom? Steve?' Both shook their heads.

Richard turned right round to face Macavity once again. 'You see?' He shrugged. 'We're a few men on a huge vessel. We're all tired and strung out, not to mention lucky to be alive after that typhoon. It's easy to get a bit paranoid under ordinary circumstances, let alone under these—'

'Right,' snarled Macavity, quickly shutting Richard down, 'what we're going to do is this. We're going to split you into teams. And there'll be a couple of my guys with each team – armed and with orders to shoot at the first sign of trouble. We're all armed with hollow-point bullets – manstoppers that won't go through to do any damage to the gas tanks.' He tapped his chest meaningfully. 'They'll go in the front but they won't come out the back. Just make a horrible mess inside. And, all together, we're going to search this vessel from the sharp end to the blunt end; from the top to the bottom. Mariner, Zaitsev, DiVito and Penn, you're with me and Mr Verrazzano here. And let me just repeat: any trouble from any of you and we'll shoot you dead where you stand.'

NIPEX's new building was a modest skyscraper on the water-front in the Ohashicho district of Choshi. It towered beside the city offices, in the middle of what in Blackpool would have been the promenade overlooking the port, the river mouth and the brand-new LNG facilities out beyond the point. Although the building itself faced northwards, the boardroom on the top floor had panoramic windows on three sides that commanded views stretching from Moromochi in the west across the Tone River to Kashmarosai on the isthmus of the far bank and then out across the ocean beyond to the space-age NIPEX installation dead ahead, and to the bustling city of Kujukuri across the bay down in the east. A horizon the better part of twenty miles distant, Robin thought.

As the board members of the huge Japanese energy company assembled, Robin and Anastasia were courteously shown the view by the company's chief executive, Mr Ikeda Hiroshi. 'The view is one of the benefits of this poor building,' he explained. 'Here we are forty-five metres above the ground. We can in consequence see more than thirty kilometres in every direction. You observe the aeroplane making its approach low over the ocean to the north-east of us. It is heading into Narita, and if we were to go to the observation platform at the rear of this floor, we would be able to observe it landing. By the same token, theoretically in sixteen-and-a-half hours' time on the horizon beneath that very aeroplane, thirty kilometres north across the water, we should be able to see *Sayonara* making her final approach to our LNG facility. But therein lies the problem we are gathered here to discuss, I'm afraid.'

They all assembled round the boardroom table and Mr Hiroshi made the necessary introductions. The names of the board members were all relatively familiar to Robin, but there were a couple of extra men there. One was in the uniform of a NIPEX engineer and the other was in the uniform of the Japanese coastguard service. These were the men she looked at most particularly as she sat on Mr Hiroshi's right and Anastasia sat on his left, beside the young man recording the conversation for the company minutes. Mr Hiroshi then brought the meeting to order. 'Our purpose in meeting today is to discuss the *Sayonara*,' he said quietly in flawless English. 'We are pleased to welcome Captain Mrs Mariner from Heritage Mariner who co-owns the vessel with us and who can represent Greenbaum International, who will soon complete the sale of the cargo to us. And Miss Anastasia Asov who represents Bashnev/Sevmash, who also have a stake in *Sayonara* and who is of course currently working with us to supply the power needed to complete the floating city of Kujukuri in the bay to the east and south of us. In courtesy to our guests we will conduct this meeting in English. I hope that is acceptable to everybody.' There were nods of agreement from around the table. 'That is agreeable to you, Engineer Watanabe? Captain Endo?' Again, both men nodded. 'Very well then, let us proceed.'

Engineer Watanabe rose and gave a tiny bow. 'The board may not be aware of my duties. I am the engineer in charge of the team whose duty it is to communicate with *Sayonara*, to override her on-board systems under certain circumstances, and to take remote control of her on Mr Hiroshi's direction. Now, you will be aware that communication with *Sayonara* has been partial. Incomplete. Intermittent. No more, in fact than the standard information from her black box recorder and occasional bursts of further information which seem to suggest something akin to a series of accidents. We have found this worrying, of course, for many reasons – most immediately because we need to rely on constant, unbroken and accurate communication with more than just the black box recorder when the ship docks tomorrow. Also because this means that whoever has gone aboard for whatever reason has interfered with the computer programmes on which we also rely, and Captain Mr Mariner and his A Team have not been able as yet to resume regular service. We ourselves have been unable to override the computers and take control of the vessel as we would like to do, even having used the master control codes. We cannot, therefore, guarantee to have control over her tomorrow morning when she approaches the terminal. We most strongly recommend that all on-board computer controls except the basic propulsion and ship-handling controls – engine and helm – be shut down, if such a thing can be guaranteed, and a crew with an experienced pilot be sent out to her as soon as she comes to the eighty kilometre mark. Unless we have control, that is.'

'It would seem sensible to send out an experienced crew and pilot whether you have control of her at that point or not,' suggested Mr Hiroshi. 'There is a European saying, is there not? *Better safe than sorry.*'

'Indeed, sir. That would be the wisest course. But it brings us to the next difficulty, which is this. Although our intermittent communications with the computers have closed down once again, we are in possession of the latest GPS position that the vessel's black box recorded. It was sent to us an hour ago. At that time, according to the ship's information, she was at forty degrees north latitude and one hundred and forty-four point four degrees east longitude. That is precisely where she is programmed to be, despite the fact that she has suffered some damage and been forced into some necessary deviation from her route by the recent typhoon.'

'This might seem to be a very positive thing,' observed Mr Hiroshi. 'If she can have returned so rapidly to her course.'

'But, with respect, sir, we at the coastguard do not believe she has,' interrupted Captain Endo. He did not stand up or bow, but he commanded the complete attention of the board. 'At about the same time as Engineer Watanabe received his information as to *Sayonara*'s location, our vessel the *Hida* observed her. And at that time, she was at thirty-nine point five degrees north latitude and one hundred and forty-four point one degrees east longitude.'

'That does not sound like very much difference,' said Mr Hiroshi.

'It's forty kilometres or twenty-five miles,' said Robin. 'What are the implications of that?'

'Well, there's a time implication, of course,' said Captain Endo. 'It means she is well over one hour closer to the facility than Engineer Watanabe thought she was. So when Mr Hiroshi observed that she might be coming over the horizon in just over sixteen hours, she might in fact be there in fifteen, which in turn has implications governing when we need to alert any pilots or crew you might want to send out to her.'

'It also means,' added Watanabe, 'that there will be some uncertainty about what her position will be when she reaches the point at which the computers have been programmed to allow us to take over her control. How close will we need to let her come before we are forced to take more drastic action if that point never arises?' He looked at Mr Hiroshi for an answer, but the chief executive frowned and failed to meet his eye.

'And, of course, if I may interject a thought here, gentlemen,' added Robin, 'it raises the question of whether *Sayonara* will stop at your facility out there as programmed. Or whether she might sail on those extra kilometres right into the middle of the floating city.'

'No, she won't,' said Anastasia suddenly, her gaze intense. 'If she doesn't stop, then just before she reaches Kujukuri she's going to run straight into my nuclear power station, *Zemlya*.'

12 Hours to Impact

Surrounded by the five men on board he trusted least, under the threat of two AR 15 short-barrelled rifles whose load he already knew all about, Richard led the way down the length of the ship. His path was by no means straight, but he knew the vessel well enough by now to follow it unhesitatingly. This was not the weather deck. He was walking swiftly along the corridors and through the work spaces that made up the second engineering deck, Engineering Deck C. Fortunately, the area Richard had been held in and which they set out from was forward of the engine space itself, or an already long and fairly complicated trek would have been a good deal longer – and more complicated. But, watchful though Richard was, he never felt any temptation to try to slip into a side corridor or go dashing up or down a companionway. The others crowded around him. And, if Macavity and his sidekick stayed aloof, Aleks, Dom and Steve were always close at hand. Macavity had decided to start at the bow, and Richard knew intuitively that this was where the pirate had come across whatever aroused his suspicions. But of all the locations he might have guessed at, the starboard chain locker seemed the least likely.

They arrived at the chain-locker door at the end of the final corridor on the deck he had been following and assembled there because they could go no further. Richard noticed the way Macavity eyed the apparently unremarkable entrance before he began to speak. 'We're going to search this deck,' said the South African. 'Every nook and cranny. And we'll also take a look at the deck below – and perhaps the one below that if I think it's necessary. But the other teams will also be working above and below us, so take care and move slow. If anyone gets shot I want it to be done on purpose.' Even as he spoke, Richard could hear another team beginning to assemble on Engineering Deck B, immediately above them. Above that team there was only the open forecastle head, the helideck between the anchor winches and the forepeak. In all probability there would be another team at the vertical front of the whaleback containing the five huge LNG tanks, also starting as far forward as possible and working methodically back towards the bridge.

Richard had gone through the logistics of all this himself more times than he liked to think. It had been the basis of many of his discussions with Aleks, whose reluctance to vary from the predictable, methodical approach now looked more sinister than ever. Was he in with Macavity? But, from what Macavity was suggesting, he, like Richard, was also going to favour the occasional unlooked-for departure from the predictable search pattern – the unexpected foray down on to the decks below where his ghostly enemies might be lurking. Richard hoped that the three of them had removed themselves and every trace of their presence to a place Macavity would never think to search, and would be content to wait there until the danger of discovery – or worse – was past. 'We start here,' rasped Macavity. 'In the chain locker. Open up, Captain Mariner.' Richard opened the handles and swung the metal door wide, marvelling at how silently it moved on its brand-new, well-greased hinges. Then he held it, feeling its weight shifting in his grip as *Sayonara* continued to ride uneasily over the moder-ating westerly set of the sea. Macavity slung his rifle over his shoulder and stepped up, swinging in and round to stand for a moment on the nearest rung of the ladder just inside the door. Then he stepped down on to the chain and motioned for Dom to follow him. Richard, of course, was calculating the odds of surviving any attempt to slam the door and go for Verrazzano's gun. Had he felt for an instant he could rely on Steve and Aleks to back him up he might have given it more careful thought, but as it was he dismissed the idea out of hand. It served to keep his attention largely focused outside the chain locker, however, so he never really took as detailed a look inside as he otherwise might have done. He simply registered that Macavity prowled suspiciously if a little unsteadily over the pile of chain as *Sayonara*'s head dipped and the chain stirred. He watched him going almost as far as the hawse hole and pausing there, leaning on his rifle to steady himself as he looked down at the anchor secured against the flare of the forecastle.

If there was anything that attracted Richard's gaze into the locker itself, it was the unthinking way that Macavity seemed to trust Dom. Several times he had his back to the Canadian. Once – at that moment when he leaned against his gun and craned over to look out – a simple push might have been enough to eject him through the hole above the anchor, but Dom was ready to help rather than hinder the strange exploration, and both Aleks and Steve showed every sign of having similar thoughts. After a further five minutes, Macavity seemed satisfied and he turned, gesturing to Dom to climb out first. Richard, still holding the door, reached out and helped both men down. Then he slammed the door and closed the handles. But at no time did he look closely or carefully into the iron-smelling little room, so he never saw the wires the Pitman had been following when Macavity had nearly caught up with her less than six hours earlier and sown the seeds of his disquiet.

Macavity's little commando next checked out the port-side chain locker. The technique and result were exactly the same. Then the six of them worked their way back along the length of the vessel. Every now and then, just as Aleks had, Macavity would check with one or other of his men on the shortwave radio. They had brought some radio equipment aboard with them, Richard realized, but they were also using that which they had confiscated from Aleks – probably at about the same time as they had purloined his Rolex and Galaxy. He soon gave up trying to double guess Macavity, or to predict where he would send the other teams or tell his own team to go. The ordered search pattern that seemed to be in place as they all set out soon broke down and Richard saw that Macavity was hoping to catch whoever he suspected of hiding on board unawares. Time passed, but as Richard had spent all of the search so far below decks and without his watch, he had little idea of how much. And no real idea at all of what the time actually was either here on board or outside in the real world.

The next adventure worth his full attention came when Macavity suddenly ordered Verrazzano to lead them down a deck, then another. They were between tanks two and three, immediately below the pulpit where Boris had died and fallen overboard. Up on the covered A Deck, immediately inside the

pulpit itself, the corpse of Yoichi Hatta lay at rest. Engineering
Deck D seemed empty, though Richard thought he could hear
distant voices. The corridors were wider here, for the tanks
were curving inwards at a steeper angle than the sides. Macavity
led them back towards the bows, unexpectedly retracing the
steps they had taken one deck up. Then he led them between
the tanks, from the port side back to the starboard. A curt signal
and Verrazzano was leading them down another narrow companionway to the lowest deck of all, Engineering Deck E – a scant
two and a half metres above the bilges. The sides of the ship
curved in much more acutely here. The passageways were
cramped and claustrophobic. Richard knew that the only real
purpose for anyone to come down this far was to access the
ducting within which the pipework joining the bottoms of the
tanks followed the central line of the keel. He had never been
down here himself, and he was struck by Macavity's cunning.
It must indeed be a tempting place for anyone to hide.

He knelt. The deck was not solid here, but fine-mesh grating
in long sections, capable of being lifted to allow access to the
ducting. And the ducting, like everything else on board, was on
a giant scale. It stood more than two metres square, but the
central section of it was filled with a sheaf of pipes. There was
enough room for a slim engineer with nerves of steel to follow
the metal-sided passageway from tank to tank. He could hardly
bring himself to imagine Ivan, Harry or the Pitman down there.
He straightened and stepped back, only to be replaced at once
by Dom DiVito. The wiry Canadian began to lift the steel mesh
grating section next along the corridor floor. But Macavity spat,
'No! Leave it!' And the six of them turned away and went back
up into the light and air of the upper decks.

It took nearly four hours to search the ship. Then, when they
all assembled in the engine room, it took another two hours to
search the engine and ancillary equipment spaces as well. By
the time they had finished, everyone on board felt that the vessel
had been thoroughly inspected. And they'd found no sign of
anyone else. At last, Macavity announced that he was satisfied.
He assembled them all back at the starting point and locked
Richard and his men away once again. But this time he left the
lights on. And it was not long before Richard understood why.

Section by section, in the teams assigned to the ship's search, he allowed the prisoners out to be fed and watered. Ivan Karitov was in charge of the makeshift galley but there was little left by the time Richard, Dom and the others arrived except the noodles and fish sauce that the Japanese engineers and programmers had brought aboard with them. But then, to be fair, once Richard tucked in to his ramen with miso, he suddenly remembered how much he liked Japanese cuisine, and how much he had been happy to pay for just such fare as this at restaurants like *Shinatatsu Ramen Mentatsu Shichininshu* in Tokyo. Then, full at last, and with his mind more at ease about Ivan, Harry and the Pitman, he allowed himself to be locked up again. He used the latrine, stretched out on the sleeping bag and decided that this was as good a time as any to think things through carefully from start to finish – or at least his most recent experiences, and to really get on top of things.

He was asleep within five minutes. So deeply that he did not even register when the lights went out. When the engines stopped, some uncounted time later still, however, he woke up at once, stood up, felt his way to the door and started hammering on it as loudly as he could.

6 Hours to Impact

'Twelve hours?' repeated Anastasia. She looked at Robin, horrified.

'Twelve hours to close it all down safely according to procedures, to disconnect it and to prepare it to move,' emphasized Dr Gennadi Obukhov, director of the nuclear power station *Zemlya*, not best pleased at being called from his bed at midnight. 'And according to protocol, we need to consult the men in charge of the Kujukuri construction project before we even start. It is their power we would be removing, after all.' Anastasia, Robin and the director were sitting in his office on board the nuclear power facility. The NIPEX chopper which had brought the women here sat on the helideck under the yellow security lights, waiting to whisk them away again once they had solved the little local difficulty of removing the power station from *Sayonara*'s possible path of destruction. It would take them to the Radisson if they had any sense – and to their beds. But what had seemed a relatively simple matter was proving to be anything but.

'Removing Kujukuri Construction's power would be better than removing half their city by blasting it to smithereens – and contaminating the rest with radioactive fallout,' snarled Anastasia.

'Just so,' answered the director frostily, and not a little pompously. Director Obukhov had been put in place by Anastasia's late father and did not take kindly to being bossed around by importunate women. 'But remember, Miss Asov, the procedures are also there to avoid just such eventualities, whether there is the danger of a collision or not. Look at Fukushima . . .'

'Fukushima was abiding by its procedures!' snapped Anastasia. 'They just didn't include losing power to the cooling system. And, before you bring it up, Chernobyl was testing its procedures when the wheels came off. Look, Doctor Obukhov, how short can you cut procedures and still get ready to move safely?'

'I would have to consult my engineers,' the director huffed.

'Kindly do so.' Anastasia dismissed the man. He rose stiffly and went off to do her bidding. She turned to her companion. 'Robin, how soon could your tugs *Erebus* and *Terror* be ready to move *Zemlya*?'

'Within the hour, as long as we weren't moving her too far, though the tugs' crews won't relish being dragged out of their bunks either. If you want her moved any great distance we'd have to refuel. That could take some time.'

'It sounds as though you'll have plenty of time if Obukhov gets his way.'

'But in theory we won't have to move too far. Just enough to make sure *Sayonara* doesn't collide with us if Richard can't regain control in time.'

'No. You'll have to move further than that,' said Anastasia. 'Right out of the blast radius that might occur if she collides with anything and explodes. And we don't know if the 'Ndrangheta might leave a present on board . . .'

'Damn!' swore Robin. 'You're right. I didn't think of that. I do hope Richard has! Do we have any idea how wide the blast radius is likely to be?'

'There must be someone at NIPEX who has some idea,' said Anastasia.

'That Engineer Watanabe seemed to have his wits about him. He'll know if anyone will,' Robin suggested. 'And he said at the end of the meeting, before that impossible bloody dinner, that he would be on the night shift tonight.'

'Can we get on to him without waking up Mr Hiroshi?' wondered Anastasia.

'I think so. My laptop is set up for contact with our London office and they have a link to NIPEX control. Give me ten minutes to get through and check, then I should be able to Skype him.'

As Robin was looking into this, Director Obukhov returned. 'My chief engineer says we might be able to cut the normal shutdown time in half. But six hours is the fastest we can manage things. And we can only handle that if the Kujukuri Construction people are on the ball. We can insert the control rods within the first hour, in a precise manner. As you mentioned Chernobyl, you will remember that it was the attempt to push the control rods into the core too rapidly that jammed them, shattered them and started the most serious phase of the disaster in Reactor Number Four – the phase that blew the roof off. Then, after *Zemlya*'s control rods are safely in place, we will have to allow some time for the residual heat to dissipate. We use the North Pacific as our cooler pool, of course, so we're one step ahead of Fukushima there. But we must use ocean water under very strict conditions. Then, if we are going to move any distance at all, we will have to disengage from the power grid, which means that tenders must come out and take the cables from us because we cannot just drop electric power lines into the ocean. When all of these matters have been attended to, the tugs can start to move us. How far do you envisage moving *Zemlya*? And for how long? I will need to begin negotiations with Kujukuri Construction's night manager. And you may need to consider alerting your lawyers as to the possibility of a lawsuit – and your accounts department as to

the likelihood of claims for considerable damages.' He looked
at his watch. 'Though I doubt you will be able to contact anyone.
It is after seven in Moscow – the vodka hour. And that means
it's *tea-time* in London.' He rolled his eyes.

While Director Obukhov was delivering himself of the speech
that was likely to end his employment with Bashnev Oil and
Power if they were all still alive in twelve hours' time, Robin
was making Skype contact with Engineer Watanabe. The intense
young man's face almost filled the screen, but there was room
enough to make out Captain Endo behind him, deep in conversation with someone just out of shot. The NIPEX facility was
clearly buzzing, in spite of the hour. As succinctly as possible,
Robin explained what they needed to know about the possibility
that the nuclear power station might collide with *Sayonara* or
be caught in the blast even if she moved out of the LNG tanker's
way.

Watanabe frowned. 'We have done much work on the problem
of LNG leaks and their explosive potential, examining everything from accidental discharge to a full-blown terrorist attack,
such as that planned in the Yemen in August 2013. Up until
quite recently the general belief was that a gas cloud that is
basically freezing methane would spread around any leaking
container. It would remain at ground level or sea level until it
began to warm up, then it would lift and disperse, if it had not
ignited. The wider the cloud spread, the less the chance there
would be of a fatal explosion. This is because an explosion – as
opposed to a fire – requires combustion at an extremely fast
pace, usually in some kind of container. The potential energy
must be released extremely rapidly or there is no blast. But in
the situation of a leak and a fire, this is unlikely to occur.
Certainly the famous comparison between a cargo of LNG and
fifty-five atom bombs has been generally discredited because
although the potential is comparable, the different physical laws
involved in the nature of each explosion are very different.' He
frowned and leaned forward, his broad face filling the whole
of Robin's screen. 'Certainly, the possible blast area arising
from any collision involving *Sayonara* would depend on how
many tanks were ruptured, how the gas cloud spread – which
would be affected by the wind, of course – and the speed at

which the gas cloud catches fire. As I said, the received wisdom until recently was that the methane within the gas cloud would burn quite slowly and certainly not explosively, so there would be relatively little blast damage. However, in China on the tenth of October, 2012, a road tanker carrying LNG crashed. A cloud spread just as we expected but then it did explode. It exploded with great force, far more powerfully than we had believed possible. Several people died. There was a great deal of destruction to cars, lorries and nearby busses. The tanker was still burning twenty-four hours later. Since that incident, we have been forced to reassess what LNG might do if it ignites.'

'So, what are you telling me?' asked Robin.

'That if *Sayonara* explodes with much of the LNG still in place, there may well be a great deal of blast. There will quite possibly be a great deal of blast as well as high temperatures if a significant amount of the LNG escapes from one of the tanks. If there is a wind, the gas will spread downwind and the effects of the explosion will be greatest in that direction. At the very least I would recommend that *Zemlya* should be moved two kilometres away from *Sayonara*'s likely course. If there is a wind, between three and five—'

Watanabe was interrupted by someone calling his name. He sat back and looked round. Coastguard Captain Endo was speaking rapidly and gesturing excitedly. After a moment, Watanabe swung back into close-up. His voice was breathless and his expression elated. *Sayonara* has been in contact,' he said. 'She is short of the agreed point but she has stopped. We will send aboard engineers, coastguards, armed police, a crew and a pilot to bring her in!'

'Do we still need to move *Zemlya*?' asked Robin.

'No!' said Watanabe. But then he paused. His usual thoughtful expression returned. 'But perhaps you had better stay on board and continue the preparations,' he suggested. 'Until we have *Sayonara* securely in dock, with her cargo and everyone on board her safely ashore.'

'It's all right, Richard,' came the Pitman's voice from outside the door. 'Hang on a minute and give your knuckles a rest. I'll have you out in a second.'

'Pitman!' In the darkness Richard didn't need to close his eyes to have a clear mental picture of what Macavity's hollow-point bullets would do to her. But he closed them anyway. 'Watch out! They'll shoot you on sight.'

'No, they won't.' The Pitman opened the door and Richard opened his eyes. The light brought tears to them. That and the brightness behind her made her hair shine like a halo. 'They've gone,' she informed him cheerfully. 'Taken the lifeboat and vanished overboard. All of the pirates, by the look of things, and some of the guys you brought aboard as well. The turncoats, probably. But they've left some people behind, living and dead. All the living are locked up. I just need to check with you who else to let out, that's all.'

'We'll decide that in a minute. What's the matter with the engines?'

'They've shut down.' The Pitman shrugged. 'Harry says the computer sent a file out on the protected channel we can't access, the one the black box has apparently been using, presumably to NIPEX and Heritage Mariner. Then the engines stopped. She thinks the main programme has switched back on and we're sitting here waiting for a skeleton crew and a pilot. It's as though whatever the pirates did to override the computer system was effectively wiped out when the bridge flooded. But she can't confirm anything with NIPEX at the moment because whatever they have on board blocking our main communication with the outside world is still in place.'

'My God,' said Richard, stepping out of his prison cell. 'Stopped and waiting for the pilot. Just like that.' He looked around the artificial brightness of the engineering deck. 'Where are we? What's the time?'

'Four a.m. ship's time. Midnight in Japan.'

'Six hours out. But she was supposed to call for the pilot four hours out – if the NIPEX people couldn't get control of her.'

'Was that by time, position, or what?'

'I don't have any real idea about that. Where's Ivan? There might be some details on my laptop.'

'Ivan's in the sick bay. Or maybe we should start calling it the mortuary. The guy with the massive shoulder wound's dead.

Kolchak, was it? And so is Rikki Sato, by the look of things. If he was really working for them, then I guess that's why they've left him. Anyway, there are a few other guys in there who look to be at death's door. But neither Ivan nor I are much good at first aid, so it's a case of "wait and hope", I guess.'

Richard was torn. He was first aid trained to accident and emergency level, and he kept his qualifications up to date. But there were the engines to worry about. He had to check the men still in the makeshift cells and decide who could be trusted and who could not, balanced against who could be most helpful and who would be least. He wanted to talk things through further with the Pitman, particularly about the jamming device on top of the bridge house that Kolchak had given his life to find. As the Pitman had also done a bomb disposal course, could she disarm the booby traps that were supposed to be protecting it? He was bursting to talk to Harry about what had actually been done to the computer programmes by Macavity and his men and whether Rikki Sato as chief programmer was involved as he acutely suspected; even the apparently unthinking warning Alex had given the programmer about Harry Newbold being part of Plan B back in the hangar at Yelizovo airport suddenly gained a sinister undertone, especially as that revelation had also served as a heads-up to Dom DiVito. And he wanted to go through the records on his precious laptop with Ivan. But there were people apparently dying. And, with the main control programmes apparently kicking in, that fact reordered all of his priorities. He went to the mess.

There were half-a-dozen occupants of the makeshift sick bay, not counting Ivan. They were all crowded in on the floor, most of them lying on sleeping bags. The huge Russian was seated on a plastic chair in the corner, Richard's laptop on the edge of the one remaining table – which was piled with unused medical equipment, bandages and medicines. 'Ivan,' said Richard as he entered, 'can you take a look at whether *Sayonara* was supposed to alert NIPEX she was ready for the pilot by time or position?'

'I'll check,' rumbled Ivan. 'Nice to see you back in command, by the way.'

'As opposed to the pirates, eh?'

'I was thinking more of the Pitman.'

The only medical supplies were the field packs Richard's team had brought aboard, and these were very basic. The late Master Sergeant Vasily Kolchak had been relieved of his painkiller drip, which had been pushed into the arm of one of the Japanese men wounded when the bridge windows had come in. Kolchak's pressure bandage was still on his shoulder because there was no other use to which it could be put. Rikki Sato's drip had also been pulled from his arm and inserted into another more lively limb. Kolchak was grey and beginning to leak at both ends. Richard thought he should double-check Rikki, though, as nobody else seemed in immediate danger of dying in spite of what the Pitman had told him. And it seemed to Richard's wise eyes that the vein from which the needle had been pulled had started to ooze enough bright blood to arouse his suspicions. The Japanese computer engineer was badly cut up. He was covered in blood and as still as a corpse. It was easy to see why anyone glancing at him would assume he was dead. But Richard had been trained to make doubly sure. He folded the coverings down, remembering what Dom had said about the engineer's guts being held in with duct tape. But the Canadian had been exaggerating. With infinite care, Richard rolled the apparent corpse on to its side and folded it into the recovery position. The body was cold, but not stiff, which again gave him hope. He replaced the blankets. Then he opened Rikki's mouth and checked his airways. A wad of snot and half-dried blood came free as he moved the engineer's tongue, and Richard felt that there was just the suspicion of a breath there too. He rolled Rikki back and started a gentle CPR, trying to ensure that air was going into the engineer's lungs without running the risk of pushing any shards of windscreen glass deeper into his thoracic cavity or of bursting the stomach wound open. After a few moments, Rikki stirred. His eyes fluttered. Richard sat back and watched the computer man's chest begin to rise and fall as he breathed unaided.

Richard covered Rikki in as many warm sleeping bags as he could find, and was just retrieving the drip when Ivan said, 'It's by position. *Sayonara*'s supposed to go into external control mode when she reaches thirty-six point four north latitude, one four one point four east longitude. Four hours out.'

Richard frowned. 'That should make the ship's time oh two hundred. Japan time twenty-two hundred, four hours behind. But the Pitman just said it was two hours later than that.'

'So *Sayonara*'s signed in late?'

Richard interrupted him. 'She's either signed in late, or she's signed in on time but she's much further south than the on-board computers think she is.'

4 Hours to Impact

Once Richard was sure Rikki Sato was breathing, he checked on the others. Then he went to find Harry. She was not in the back-up control room where he had last seen her, and it didn't take a lot of insight to work out that she would be on the bridge where the main computer access was. Ivan tagged along, and as they went he continued their conversation. 'So, what happens next?'

'The world and his wife descends on us. I'd half expect the Japanese navy! Well, that's pushing it perhaps; coastguard more likely. An armed emergency response unit of some sort. And then NIPEX men and, if it was me, I'd send out a full skeleton crew and the best damn pilot I could get.'

'But you know what's been happening on the ship, remember.'

'And there are things I still want to know!' Richard interrupted. 'Rikki Sato can give me some answers when he comes round, but . . .' And on that thought, Richard stopped. 'Can you contact the Pitman?' he asked.

'Sure. Her radio went off line a while back but she's fixed it now.'

He called the Pitman, who was still deciding whether she should release anyone else. As he made contact, Richard explained what he wanted. 'Hey, Angela,' Ivan called. 'Richard needs someone who can look after the guys in the sick bay.' Both Karitov the chef and Murukami, Sato's second in command, claimed some basic first aid experience, so Richard told the Pitman to release them. Then he and Ivan went on up to the bridge. 'Is there anything we should do to get ready for our visitors?' asked Ivan as they climbed the rickety companionway.

'I don't know what you brought aboard,' said Richard. 'But I'd ditch or hide anything that's going to make the authorities feel like shooting you.'

'That's not going to be too hard for me to do,' laughed Ivan. 'But the Pitman may be another kettle of fish.'

'What's up with my Pitman?' asked Harry, overhearing the end of the conversation as Richard and Ivan crossed the bridge towards her.

'Nothing,' said Ivan. 'We're just expecting a few more Japanese than there were at Pearl Harbor and we don't want her to frighten them. Or piss them off.'

'If you don't want to piss them off, Ivan,' said Richard, 'I'd try to be a bit more politically correct. In the meantime, Harry, how's the computer?'

'Closed down. Offline. Waiting for someone to take control and bring *Sayonara* home. No buried programmes or protocols that I can find. It all looks clean up here. Have you talked to Rikki Sato?' Richard shook his head. 'Well, I don't get it. He should have been able to get this all under control. It was expertly hacked all right, but not *that* badly.'

'He was probably working for the opposition,' explained Ivan. 'His daughter's studying in Calabria. They could have pressured him through her. Made him just pretend to be trying to fix things while actually making them worse.'

'The Italian connection,' added Richard. 'But still no communication, nothing incoming?' Harry shook her head. 'Well, that's our next order of business. I know where the signal blocker is. Kolchak said it was wired to explode if anyone fiddled with it. But it's maybe time to ask our Angela to have a look. These guys told us a lot of lies. Maybe that was one of them.' It was at this moment that Richard noticed something completely unexpected. 'Well, I'll be damned,' he said happily. 'Would you look at that? Macavity's left me my Galaxy and my Rolex!' He crossed to the helm and picked the watch and the smartphone

up from the shelf beside the engine room telegraph. He checked
the time and slipped the steel case into its accustomed place
on his left wrist. Having glanced at his watch, he automatically
checked the ship's chronometer above the clearview windows.
'Oh one hundred,' he observed. 'If they got that message at
NIPEX an hour ago, we can expect some company soon. All
the deck lights are on as usual, so they won't have any problem
putting choppers down on the helipad.'

'Unless they're going to rappel down on to the upper deck,'
added Ivan. 'Special forces stuff. I mean, when we came aboard
they'd just discovered the bodies in Rat Island Pass – and
Folgate-Lothbury face down in the Thames. They might want
to take extra care.'

'What?' said Richard, stunned. 'They found *what*?'

Ivan began to explain what he had heard in the hours before
coming aboard, but Richard interrupted him almost immediately.
'Sounds like they might want to send an armed response just
in case,' he said. 'They have to assume there's a chance
Macavity and his men killed the people they found in Rat Island
Pass and they have no way of knowing they've gone over the
side now. Tell Angela to get up top and take a look at the signal
jammer as fast as she can. We really want to talk these people
down if they're coming aboard like gangbusters. Christ! So,
Ivan, tell me more. What about Folgate-Lothbury?'

By the time the Pitman came through the bridge on her way
to the top deck, Ivan had brought Richard up to speed with
what little he knew about the events of the last couple of days.
Trying to work out how Robin would be reacting to the death
of their chief insurer, while weighing the implications of the
deaths on Hawadax Island and the 'Ndrangheta revelations,
Richard followed her upwards, pausing only to pull the binoculars from their holster beside the door. 'It's in that structure that
looks as though it should contain the mechanism for the lift
they never installed,' he explained three minutes later as they
crossed the deck above the command bridge.

'Computers don't need elevators,' she observed thoughtfully.
'But this thing looks like a pepper pot, Richard.'

'Long story involving poor old Kolchak. He was the one who
told us Macavity's men warned him that the signal jammer was

wired to explode if anyone fiddled with it.' While the Pitman began her examination, Richard strode to the forward edge of the upper weather deck and put the binoculars to his eyes. He started searching the southern horizon first to establish how soon they could expect a fleet of choppers to come swarming above them. But, as soon as he had established that there were three distant helicopters making a determined beeline towards them, he began to look more generally at the nearby sky, and the sea beneath it.

The typhoon was now long past and *Sayonara* was sitting in what was usually a busy shipping lane where vessels approached the Japanese mainland from all over the North Pacific. She was riding over a swell that was moderating and swinging southwards. There was a gentle north-easterly wind blowing. The sky was clear and there was a low, fat moon. The air was crystal, as it often is after great storms. The binoculars brought everything close in such detail it was like looking through a microscope. The horizon to port was ringed with the running lights of ships of all sizes, designs and purposes. Richard made out their shapes and types but *Sayonara* was the only LNG transporter.

Then something else caught his eye. Closer than any of the other vessels was a white gin palace. She was a big tri-level, the better part of forty metres long with an impressive sonar and communications array. She had a sun-shade over her command bridge like the peak of a cap and a rakish cover over her flying bridge. She was clearly an ocean-going vessel, though it was unusual to see millionaires' playthings this far out at sea. What attracted Richard's fleeting attention was the fact that, instead of the usual six- or eight-seater RIB, she was towing a substantial lifeboat. But even as Richard registered the yacht's existence, before he even had time to look for her name or focus on the boat she was towing, his attention was jerked away.

'I thought you said this thing was wired,' said the Pitman.

'That's what Kolchak told us.' Richard lowered the glasses and crossed to stand beside her. 'It was what Macavity's men told him.'

'Well, unless I'm missing something pretty vital, someone *was* telling lies. It's not wired as far as I can see.'

'Why am I not surprised? Can we switch it off, then?'

'Switch it off, pull it out, chuck it over the side if we want.'

'OK. Good. Let's switch it off. And I'll get to a radio as fast as I can.'

The jammer didn't explode when the Pitman switched it off, but Richard's Galaxy nearly did. It came to life, screaming at him that he had more missed messages than he could easily count. He was still looking at the screen in simple wonderment when the Pitman called out to him. 'Incoming. Twelve o'clock high, as they say.'

The succeeding hours rolled into a dazzle of action, during which Richard felt increasingly out of control. This was inevitable, and he knew it. There was no place for him in the routines of the various teams that came aboard. On the other hand, he was constantly being asked to do things, to answer questions, to explain what had happened. He felt out of place, out of the loop. Still, he hardly had time to check the missed messages on his Galaxy. And yet, he managed to use the time to get a clearer idea of precisely what had been going on and what might still be going on. Particularly now that Macavity and his men, turncoats and all, had simply left *Sayonara* seemingly little the worse for wear after all.

The armed response unit of the Japanese coastguard demanded his attention first. Their commanding officer, a lieutenant, was already on the radio, calling from the lead chopper when Richard and the Pitman arrived on the bridge. He was ordering Ivan, who had answered first, to prepare the vessel to be boarded and to be aware that lethal force could and would be used if there was any sign of resistance. 'I'd better go down to the sick bay,' said the Pitman. 'Get rid of some of the hardware and pretend to be playing doctors and nurses.' She glanced round the bridge and vanished. Harry looked after her for a moment and then turned back to the computers. Richard took over the microphone and assured the lieutenant that there was no current terrorist threat – that his crew, although armed, would offer no resistance, and that there were wounded on board in need of medical attention, though they were currently under the care of a first aid nurse and her helpers. He was curtly ordered to meet the team on the top of the bridge house, so he ran back up into the buffeting brightness below the coastguard helicopter and stood back obediently as the lieutenant and his seven-man team rappelled on to the deck just as Ivan had predicted they would. Then he walked forward as the chopper soared away and the coastguard team fell in around their leader, bristling with Howa Type 89 assault rifles and the ubiquitous Heckler and Koch MP-5 submachine guns.

As they ran down on to the command bridge, Richard explained what had gone on during the last few hours. The lieutenant listened with stony-faced courtesy, directing his men with silent hand gestures into a series of routines that clearly took little account of what he was being told. When they reached the command bridge, he held his hand for silence and crossed to the radio. He changed the frequency and exchanged a few brief words with someone who was on another helicopter, judging by the background noise. Then he looked up at Richard once again. 'Coastguard Captain Endo is coming out on the NIPEX helicopter with a team led by Engineer Watanabe,' he said in English. 'They will land on the helipad in twenty minutes. You and I will meet them there, Captain Mariner. Then we expect an experienced crew and ship's pilot who is expert in these waters to be aboard within the hour. They will take control of the vessel and sail her to the NIPEX facility. We are due to dock there in a little less than three hours' time.' He glanced at his watch. 'That will be oh four hundred Japan Standard Time. Only two hours ahead of schedule. Most impressive.'

'Three hours from now?' said Richard. 'That's pushing it. According to the latest information we have, *Sayonara* is at thirty-six point four north, one four one east. Four hours away from port.'

'That is incorrect,' said the lieutenant brusquely. 'We were requested to double-check her position on our arrival. There has been some dispute. We are at thirty-six north, one four one east precisely. Two hours out.'

Richard suddenly wanted very much to talk to Rikki Sato, for the computer man was the only one who might be able to explain the anomaly – and, perhaps, the reason for it. But his request to do so was flatly denied. 'I have dispatched my medical team to assess the well-being of your wounded. I do not want them or their patients to be disturbed. You may perhaps communicate with Doctor Sato later if he is strong enough. In the meantime, we have things well in hand. But we are on a tight schedule. We have to be at the chopper landing point in fifteen minutes. Lead the way, please.'

'Mind if I tag along?' asked Ivan.

'Very well,' said the lieutenant. 'Miss Newbold, will you wait here with my watch-keepers or would you rather join the other lady below?'

'I'll come down,' said Harry. And Richard reckoned that was a wise move. The combination of brusqueness and condescension the special security team had shown so far was likely to lead to confrontation if they tried it on the Pitman. Harry's diplomatic skills might be challenged, by the looks of things.

Richard found his own skills of self-control being exercised fifteen minutes later, almost immediately after Engineer Watanabe followed Captain Endo on to the forecastle. While the coastguard officers went into a very private conference and Watanabe's engineers disembarked from the chopper behind him, the NIPEX engineer strode forward, hand held out. 'Ah, Captain Mariner,' he said with a smile. 'I believe Captain Mrs Mariner would wish me to extend to you her greetings. She has been very concerned for your welfare.'

'Mrs Mariner?' Said Richard. 'Has she been in contact with NIPEX?'

'She had been with us in person, Captain. She attended the board meeting yesterday, fourteen hours ago. She is now on board *Zemlya*.'

'*Zemlya?* What in hell's name . . .'

Watanabe cut him off. 'She and Miss Asov went aboard at midnight. Their plan was to move her out of the path *Sayonara* would most likely take if she failed to stop at our NIPEX facility. I advised them that they should stay on board and continue to do so. Just in case.'

'Let me get this straight,' grated Richard. 'You thought there was a chance that a fully-laden LNG carrier would collide with a nuclear power station, so you sent my wife and Miss Asov aboard the nuclear power station?'

'Perhaps, therefore,' said Watanabe with an unexpected grin, 'we should try *very hard* to make sure this fully-laden LNG carrier does not collide with that nuclear power station.'

Within the hour a skeleton crew arrived, with a pilot called Captain Ito, who was so august he might have been an emperor in a previous life. Without recourse to Rikki Sato's expertise but in conference with computer engineers Esaki and Murukami, Engineer Watanabe ensured that the computers did not interfere when Captain Ito called for full power and the helmsman from the skeleton crew moved the engine room telegraph to Slow Ahead. Getting the engines ready had been Watanabe's first order of business and they responded powerfully to the pilot's instructions. Captain Ito called out speeds and headings. The helmsman echoed them. The engines delivered them.

Richard stood narrow-eyed on the bridge where he had had so many recent adventures and observed the majestic progress *Sayonara* made across the last forty miles of her voyage from the Greenbaum International LNG facility in Anchorage, Alaska, to the NIPEX LNG facility in Choshi, Japan. The final two hours of what should have been a one-hundred-hour voyage. And the fact that it had been a ninety-eight-hour voyage continued to nag at him, especially as he was almost certain that when she reached her final destination at thirty-five point seven north, one hundred and forty point nine east, her computers – in spite of everything – would still be telling her that she was forty miles north as well as two hours early, so still had a way to go before her voyage was complete. A way blocked by a nuclear power station which had Robin and Anastasia on board.

2 Hours to Impact

*S*ayonara came into the NIPEX facility at four a.m. Japan Standard Time with the ship's chronometer reading oh eight hundred hours. The pilot was in complete command of the bridge. His helmsman was quietly repeating his orders to reverse engines and, finally, stop engines. Had the docking manoeuvre been in any way complex, the pilot might well have been out on the starboard bridge wing using the ancillary docking equipment there. But this was a floating facility with a deep-water berth specifically designed for this one ship. And it was lit up like a fairground. The weather had moderated to an almost dead calm. There were no other vessels nearby except for those whose job was to help her to position alongside. A child could have berthed her.

So Captain Ito remained at his ease in the pilot's chair. Coastguard Captain Endo stood beside him. The lieutenant stood beside the captains. Engineer Murukami was in charge of watching the computers – a thankless task for they were behaving perfectly. NIPEX Engineer Watanabe was in the engine control room with ship's engineer Esaki waiting for the final 'finished with engines' signal, which would be his cue to meet his team in the cargo control room and oversee the process of unloading the tanks. The facilities on the noon-bright NIPEX dock were all ready to begin unloading the cargo. There was an air of quiet satisfaction on board. And on the bridge, a palpable feeling that someone had been making a lot of fuss over nothing.

Richard was out on the starboard bridge wing, where Captain Ito would have been if he had felt a little less confident, still certain that there was something they had all missed. He was right out on the uncovered section, surrounded by the redundant docking controls. Ivan was immediately inside the covered section with Richard's laptop open across his massive thighs and his father's portable hard drive attached to a port in the side. Harry and the Pitman sat opposite. All of them were notably disarmed. And, on the screen of Richard's Galaxy, Robin made up the last of the team except for occasional reference to Anastasia who was sharing the control bridge of *Zemlya*, which was still sitting, unmoving, two hours' sailing time to the south.

'Right,' said Richard. 'Let's go through this.' He held the Galaxy near his face so that Robin could hear and see him. 'The 'Ndrangheta. Both Robin and I have also heard of them, though this is the first time we have actually come across them *mano a mano*, so to speak. Its base is in Calabria and it more or less runs the port of Gioia Tauro. It is import/export brand leader for cocaine coming in from South America and going on across Europe and the north. Because of increasing public awareness and Italian government pressure, a *capo* of one of the most powerful 'Ndrangheta clans is planning to expand his business overseas. He is already moving his influence through Europe and across the old Soviet Union, using Italian ex-pat communities in the same way as the Triads are said to use Chinese ones. This man Francisco Lazzaro was able to infiltrate Sayonara's insurance syndicate because he supplied desperately needed funds just at the moment Tristan's Italian wife walked out on their marriage and their business – and took her family fortune with her. Lazzaro has apparently decided to finance this expansion by over-insuring *Sayonara* and sending a team of mercenaries aboard to ensure that she and her cargo are lost; something that will net him and his people one hundred and twenty-five million dollars of pure profit – if he can pull it off. But that's not all. According to the FSB, extrapolating the word of one of their spies, since unfortunately deceased, the loss of *Sayonara* will lead directly to the 'Ndrangheta being able to take over Bashnev/Sevmash and use their legitimate shipping and distribution systems for the transport of cocaine, which means that *Sayonara* must not only sink but she must do so in a way that damages Bashnev.' He stopped. As there were still no interruptions, he focused his intense blue gaze on Robin's face, which filled the screen of his Galaxy. 'Which brings us to *Zemlya*. It seems logical that Lazzaro plans to use *Zemlya* to sink *Sayonara*, thus destroying at least one and prob-ably both vessels. Bashnev shares will crash on the stock market and Lazzaro will buy the company for a song. He might even plan to do the same to Heritage Mariner if our shares are hit. But that means the two vessels must collide.' He stopped again, thinking. The vantage point of the bridge wing showed him how close *Sayonara* was to docking, and how little time he had left to complete his thoughts.

'But how is he planning to ensure a collision? Both of these vessels are so carefully watched, and fenced round with so many cut-outs and fail safes. A collision such as they plan is even more difficult to arrange than crashing one plane into another – and on purpose, in a post-9/11 world. And we're still not sure how they have planned to pull it off. But it has obvi-ously involved an intricate set-up. Members of the A Team have been targeted as double agents. Pressure has been brought on those with any contact with Italy, most obviously Rikki Sato. How did Lazzaro get the names of the Japanese team members? Perhaps through Rikki. But how did he get the Risk Incorporated names?'

Ivan looked up. 'My bad,' he said gruffly. 'I let Aleks pick his own team.'

Richard nodded. 'So that confirms it. Aleks must have been one of Lazzaro's men as well. But don't give yourself a hard time. Remember, Dom DiVito and Steve Penn were feeding him information too, by the look of things. They knew everything Greenbaum International knew about the cargo and, via Greenbaum's contacts with us, everything Heritage Mariner knew about the ship and the crew, and the A Team. But not about me choosing to lead them. Nor about Harry and the Pitman until it was too late for them to interfere. And in any case, Tristan Folgate-Lothbury was feeding them everything we told Lloyd's and our insurance syndicate about, probably in all innocence, just passing on whatever he was asked to the man who appeared to be his saviour and guardian angel. Which was, of course, *everything*.' He looked down at the bustle on the deck below as Captain Ito's men came out, preparing to throw the mooring lines on to the dock. And the dock was bustling with men waiting to receive them. Time was running out now.

'So the not so angelic Lazzaro suggests to Tristan that he try one more security test,' Richard continued. 'But he substitutes his own team for Tristan's. The exchange happens on Hawadax Island and the old team end up floating in Rat Island Pass and frightening the life out of the local fishermen. He can make the suggestion of the final security test as I say because he has agreed to back Tristan financially after the Folgate-Lothbury marriage hits the rocks and his ex-wife cuts off access to her father's fortune, perhaps at Lazzaro's suggestion – more Calabrians.' He paused. 'Now, where was I? Ah, yes. There is some kind of confrontation on Hawadax Island and Tristan's team end up in Rat Island Pass. In much the same way, he ends up in the Thames. Macavity and his men come aboard. Tristan has warned Lazzaro that the A Team will respond, and so Lazzaro makes it part of his plan that certain members of the A Team, whose details are fed to him by Alex, are bribed, blackmailed or whatever. Or there are already mafiosi in place, like these guys at Duisberg Reinsurance in Vancouver.'

'OK,' the Pitman interrupted. 'They come aboard, but what do they do? They piss about with dud grenades and signal blockers that are not attached to bombs after all . . .'

'They keep us occupied,' said Richard. 'But they do so in a way that does not endanger the ship. They can't risk a shoot-out like the one on Hawadax Island because they haven't got complete control of the A Team, which is well armed and up for a fight, and although their bullets won't penetrate the tanks, ours will when we start shooting back. They muck about with the programmes, make enough changes to spook us and get the already compromised A Team out, secure in the knowledge that the man who wrote the computer programmes, the man who will therefore be in charge of undoing the damage, is completely under their control. So, up to the point that Harry became involved, the plan was for Rikki to make things worse, not better. Which also explains why Aleks was so keen to proceed so slowly and so calculatedly by the book. Then the storm shut everything down and Harry managed to sneak some sort of control into the system after all, which has brought us to this point. To safe haven. Except . . .' Richard watched the first lines snake towards the dock. The NIPEX men there caught hold of the light lines, crossed to winches and fothered them on, ready to pull the heavy mooring lines ashore. *Sayonara* was all-but docked.

'Except?' demanded Robin, her voice seemingly as distant as he, in fact, was, nearly forty miles further south on board *Zemlya*.

'Except that we're missing something,' said Richard. 'Something vital.'

On the command bridge, Captain Ito gave his final order to the helmsman – the last words of a pilot's job well done. The tugs were snugging *Sayonara* safely against the fenders of her berth. The voyage was over. There was nothing to do but to get those on board onshore and start to unload the cargo. 'Finished with engines,' ordered Captain Ito. The helmsman put the engine room telegraph levers into their final position.

And then the opposite of what should have happened,

happened. *Sayonara*'s computers came alive. Her helm froze at Dead Ahead, her engines came up to the top of the green and the vessel surged forward out of the dock, tearing her mooring lines off the shoreside winches as she gathered pace, heading inexorably, unstoppably, south towards *Zemlya*.

Impact

S uddenly the starboard bridge wing was very crowded. Captain Ito appeared beside Richard. 'Have you done this?' he shouted. Captain Endo and the special ops lieutenant were at his shoulder, both looking confused and angry. *Sayonara*'s last mooring line snapped with a sound between a gunshot and a whip-crack. The bridge radio became a babble of questions from the shore. Richard held his hands up. 'Nothing to do with me.'

'Richard! What's going on?' demanded a distant voice. Richard cautiously lowered his Galaxy. 'Looks like you and Anastasia had better get ready for company,' he told Robin. '*Sayonara*'s on her way south again and no one on board seems to have any idea what's happening.'

'Bloody hell!' she answered. 'You'd better find out and stop it. In the meantime, Anastasia and I will try to move this thing out of your way.'

'To hear is to obey,' said Richard. He turned back to Captain Ito, who had swung round to watch the vanishing facility with unbelieving eyes. But it was not the pilot he needed to speak to most urgently. 'Lieutenant, I really need to talk to Doctor Sato. Whatever programme has just taken over, he either put it in place or has a good idea of who did. And what it's designed to do.'

The lieutenant hesitated. 'We have two hours,' Richard emphasized. 'The programmes have been fooled into believing that the final GPS position *Sayonara* has been heading for is forty miles south of here. And that's where she's going now, at full speed. In just less than one hundred and twenty minutes, the computers will have delivered her safely to her destination. But there's no dock there, just a nuclear power station. A power station that we probably won't be able to close down, uncouple and move out of the way in time.'

The lieutenant opened his mouth to speak, but he was prevented from doing so by his personal radio. 'Can anyone hear me?' came Engineer Watanabe's unmistakable voice, loud enough for all to hear and, like the pilot's, lacking its usual reserve. 'What *hakuchi* ordered Full Ahead Both? What *baka*'s at the helm?'

'It's the computers,' answered the lieutenant. 'Captain Mariner is on his way down to see if he can override them.'

'Harry,' said Richard, already stepping through on to the covered bridge wing. 'I'll need you. Lieutenant, tell Mr Watanabe I want Mr Murukami through in the sick bay as soon as possible. And then could you find some way of contacting the Japanese Embassy in Rome. Find Yukio Sato, postgrad student of Applied Economics at the University of Cosenza. Ivan has her address.'

'It won't be easy, but I'll try. However, I must ask, what's the point of doing this?'

'She's Rikki Sato's daughter. I'm pretty certain that the men who arranged this are threatening her but I need her father's full and immediate cooperation. That's our best chance.' He looked around. 'The rest of you can go back on the bridge and I suggest that someone starts talking to the people onshore; beyond that, it doesn't really matter where you are if the computers are conning the ship.'

'Conning,' said Harry as they ran down the rickety companionway. 'Now there's a good word. We've all been conned, not just *Sayonara*!'

'You can say that again,' agreed Richard. 'You see what they've done? Having Macavity and co. vanish, leaving the ship ready to be brought home, then allowing Captain Ito to pilot her in, took the heat right out of the situation. Everyone relaxed. I bet that not even the Japanese navy could get a ship to us in less than two hours now. Not at four a.m. There's no ship nearby with enough power to stop *Sayonara* or even to get a line aboard and tug her off course. I don't see how they could disable her, though if they had a submarine handy they could try and blow the propellers off. I'd guess even Mitsubishi would have trouble scaring up a team of engineers capable of coming aboard and killing the engines at this time of night. The only alternative to crippling her that I can see is to blow her up, which would make one hell of a bang. And which they can't do while we're on board, I hope. But two hours isn't enough time to get us off – unless we all go over the side. And, of course, Macavity took the only lifeboat when he jumped ship. You've got to admit, it's pretty sodding neat. They get their men off safely, make the authorities relax, apparently put us back in control while disguising the fact that their plan is still very much alive. For Lazzaro and co. it's a win, win, win situation!'

'But we can't just let *Sayonara* collide with a nuclear power station!'

'That's what I'm saying, Harriet. I'm damned if I can see how they can stop her. Not in less than two hours.'

'So it's down to us, then.'

'Looks like it, one way or another. Do or die.'

Murukami met them in the sick bay as ordered and the three of them crouched round Rikki's bed while the lieutenant's men stood suspiciously in the background. The chief computer engineer responded only groggily to Richard's urgent hand on his shoulder and blinked owlishly. He tried to sit up but flinched as his wounds tore and he fell back, suddenly pale. He eased his twisted neck, clearly in even more discomfort but more focused, as though the pain had kicked his brain into gear. 'Where are my glasses?' he slurred. Murukami passed them to him, then slipped an arm round his shoulders and supported him into a sitting position. 'What happened?' asked Rikki. 'Last thing I remember I was on the bridge.'

'The windows came in. You were badly cut up and washed headfirst down the companionway. We were told you had fatal lacerations and probably a broken neck. You were left for dead,' Richard explained.

'Captain Mariner has saved your life, Rikki,' emphasized Murukami. 'Now he needs your help to save the rest of us.'

'But Yukio . . .' A look of fear spread across his face.

'I've been in radio contact with the authorities already,' said Richard. 'We have people gearing up to get her off the campus at Cosenza and out of Calabria by morning.' Rikki looked at Richard, his mouth hanging open with surprise as he tried to get his head round what Richard had learned, deduced and done.

'Captain Mariner is telling the truth,' emphasized Murukami. 'You don't need to protect Yukio any more. He's taken care of that. But you can help us. And if you don't, then we'll all die. Was that your plan, Rikki? To die for Yukio?'

'And to let the rest of us die as well?' probed Harry. 'You selfish fuc—' Richard's hand came gently down on her shoulder and she stopped speaking.

'Yukio is safe. You don't need to die. Nobody needs to die,' Richard insisted. 'Help us break into the programme. Give us back control of *Sayonara*.'

'I can't,' said Rikki. 'It's all too deeply embedded. It's not just a question of hacking and reprogramming.' He looked earnestly at Harry. 'You'd need to actually replace complete sections of the computer itself.'

'What do you mean?' she demanded.

'Well . . .' The language got very technical all of a sudden, especially when Murukami joined in, but Richard was enough of a techie to follow the main gist of what Rikki was explaining. As with the deceptively simple trick of setting a trigger on the 'finished with engines' setting of the engine room telegraph, Rikki had approached the problem of taking control of *Sayonara*'s computers with a combination of malware programmes and physical changes.

Like many commercial computer systems, *Sayonara*'s was an amalgam of superfast multicore processors, massive hard drives and banks of state-of-the-art RAM boards where random access memory could run incredibly quickly. But at the heart of the system were the motherboards. As far as Richard was concerned, these individual components hardly seemed to exist as physical entities. He experienced them as a set of electronic interactions. He did not even consider the programmes themselves and it certainly never occurred to him to try to estimate the billions of calculations that were carried out in nanoseconds to access the incoming signal from Robin's phone and to bring her picture on the screen of his Galaxy as her words were transmitted through the speaker, or which sections of the motherboard were involved. He took them for granted and only worried when something caused the computers to misbehave. But he still thought about such interference as electronic, like the attacks of hackers who constantly assaulted the computer systems of corporations, companies and countries worldwide.

The discussion between the three engineers turned on the interrelationship of the processors, the drives and the RAM boards as they were organized through the motherboard of each computer system on board. And it was the motherboards that soon emerged as the cause of the trouble. Rikki had put extra chips in these boards that interfered with the information passing from one place to another. Not programmed, not only hacked after all. He had actually added extra sections to the boards themselves – daughter boards, they were called – and he had slipped them in here and there. Not only had he added boards but, devious as ever, he had put all of the contaminated boards into the back-up control areas, knowing that the systems on the bridge were likely to be the ones that people checked on first. It had been a simple matter to reverse the protocols so that the back-up systems down here took all the vital decisions. And it had proved very effective at first, for not even Murukami had noticed anything amiss when they focused on checking the systems up on the bridge. It was only when Harry started interfering with the systems down here after the whole lot fused that she had managed to restore a measure more of control than Macavity had planned, though finally her work had been of little benefit, for it had been overridden at the moment the pilot had signalled 'Finished with Engines'.

'So,' said Harry, 'what happens if we just take out the infected boards?'

'The same as what happened when the bridge flooded and the system fused. The back-ups come online and they will still guide *Sayonara* to her destination.'

'Can we replace them one by one with uninfected boards?' she persisted. 'With virgin daughter boards?'

'That might restore some control. But it would only be the beginning. We would need to add new drives to overcome the original programmes.'

'Could we get them flown out?' demanded Richard.

'Not in time to replace them. Not in ninety minutes. If we had some here, now, we might stand a chance, but . . .'

'Wait,' whispered Harry. 'OK. I have a range of SSD's with me – the drives we need to add. But the daughter boards are something else. Except that I have a detailed design for a standard daughter board on my laptop. And I mean *detailed*.' She clicked what she was talking about up on to the screen. There was one of these in each of *Sayonara*'s control systems, all facilitating the passage of orders. All, according to Rikki, like translators at an international conference mistranslating one language to another, causing calculated confusion and confrontation.

'That's of no help to us,' answered Murukami, looking at Harry's laptop screen. 'A design on your laptop, no matter how detailed, is useless.'

'Not in this case,' said Harry. 'I also have a 3D printer with a copper granule feed. I could print a gun and shoot you with it. I can sure as hell print a daughter board, with all the wiring in place. In fact, I can print board after board and have SSDs to put on them!' She looked at the three of them, glowing with elation. 'Oh, come on, guys, isn't anyone going to say, *By heaven, Harry, it might just work?*'

Richard ran back to the bridge and updated the men there, focusing most of what he was saying on Ivan and the Pitman, both of whom went below at once to see if there was anything they could do to move matters along faster for Harry. Then he walked out on to the bridge wing, pulled out his Galaxy and contacted Robin. As briefly and clearly as possible, he explained what the problem was and what Harry was trying to do about it. 'I think you'd better keep working on moving *Zemlya* out of the way, though,' he concluded. 'Harry's plan looks like a long shot to me.'

'Can we think outside the box a bit?' she asked. 'I could get one of the tugs to come and meet you, maybe pull you offline . . .'

'I thought of that. But you need both to stand any chance of moving *Zemlya*, and there's no guarantee that either or both of the tugs could get here, send cables aboard and pull us off line in time. Meanwhile, you'd be stuck at the bull's eye in the target *Sayonara*'s heading for.'

'Could you drop one of the anchors? Try to drag her offline?'

'I thought of that too but there's no bottom. It's too deep for the anchor chains we have on board. Even if there was some way of joining both chains together, we don't have time. I'm relying on Harry. What about you?'

'The tugs are ready. The control rods are down and the core is cooling. But there's a problem: we can't get anyone out here to disconnect us from the grid. If we just drop them and run it could be disastrous and *could*'s the problem. These people will only act on stone-cold certainty. Could, might and maybe just don't motivate them. If we can't cut loose, we'll have to go the other way; push in towards the land, get really friendly with the nearest city folk and hope you can squeeze past on our seaward side. It's possible, but it'll be close.'

'How close?'

'Somewhere between a nose and a whisker.'

'OK. Let's look at this *cup half full*. If you move a couple of metres and we swing offline a degree or two, there should be clear water between us in just over an hour's time.'

Richard went back to work. He prowled the forecastle head, trying to work out whether he could in fact drop the port anchor in the hope that it would catch on the sea bed and slew *Sayonara*'s head round to the seaward side. But of course, even if that proved possible, he would have to make sure he dropped it at the last minute so *Sayonara*'s treacherous programmes could not pull her back on line. Turning these thoughts over, he walked out to the forecastle head and looked forward. Right on the rim of the horizon dead ahead he saw the brightness of Kujukuri, telling him that *Zemlya* was still supplying power to the floating city. And that she was still dead ahead, just under an hour distant.

In a frenzy of impatience, he ran back up on to the bridge. Macavity had taken all of the kit he and Richard had brought aboard, but he'd talked a radio out of the lieutenant and discovered that Ivan had done the same, so he was able to keep abreast of Harry's attempt to replace all of Rikki's polluted mother boards with virgin daughters and SSDs. Meanwhile, he assembled a kind of council of war to discuss options once again. There was no use shorting out the computer again, even supposing they could. There was little point in checking the helm or the engine room telegraph – though they did so every five minutes. Watanabe took the Mitsubishi engineers down to the engine room with the lieutenant as communications officer. But although they knew how to go about switching off the engines, their knowledge all revolved round using the engine room telegraph to 'stop engines' and eventually to 'finish with engines' which had already proved to be so fatal. It occurred to Richard that they could open the sea cocks and hope that *Sayonara* would settle beneath the ocean before she collided with *Zemlya*. But the sea cocks, like all the other controls, proved to be firmly in the power of the computers. And there was some question in Richard's mind – and then in Watanabe's and Endo's, not to mention the men at NIPEX – of whether *Sayonara* would sink or, buoyed up by her five great tanks, simply proceed half submerged to her doom.

In the end, it all turned on Harry and Robin. As the last twenty minutes ticked up on *Sayonara*'s chronometer, so Harry came through on Richard's radio. 'I think we have partial control,' she said. 'We've been concentrating on the engine and navigation systems which will give you control over the helm. It's too late to piss about with anything else. You'll just have to turn the helm as hard to port as you can and hold it there. You'll have partial rudder control, but you won't be able to play around with the propellers like you did when you turned her in the typhoon. It's the best we can do at this stage. Good luck.'

Richard took the helm himself and did as Harry advised, swinging it over to port with all his strength. He could see the gathering brightness of Kujukuri's floating city and, for the first time, found that he could distinguish the lights of *Zemlya* where she sat fifteen minutes dead ahead. He placed the Galaxy on the control surface beside him, near the useless engine room telegraph. He dialled Robin's cellphone and left the channel open as the machines tried to make contact. Teeth gritted, eyes narrow, he glanced up at the heading monitor above him. One degree to port, it showed. Two. The helm would move no further. His arms ached. His shoulder joints tore. He thought his back would break as he strained against the recalcitrant wheel. His forehead was abruptly slick with sweat. His breath came short and ragged.

Suddenly Robin was there. Her face filled the screen. 'I'm delivering my end of the bargain,' he grated. 'Two degrees to port and ten minutes out. How are you doing at your end?'

'Both tugs at full throttle,' she answered. 'We're pushing in towards the shore. I have no idea how far. We'll be hard up against the first section of Kujukuri any minute, then things'll slow. Not even *Erebus* and *Terror* will be able to push a floating city ashore. Though God knows, they're trying hard enough.'

'Right,' said Richard. 'Ask *Erebus* to try even harder. It's only for a few minutes and if we survive I'll pay to have her motors fixed myself.'

Richard broke contact then and concentrated. Sweat was running into his eyes but he disregarded it. *Zemlya*'s rear wall suddenly seemed very near – and very tall. He could see *Erebus* on the near side, straining to pull the power station out of his way, smoke belching as her captain obligingly burned her motors out, adding as much extra thrust as he could. And *Zemlya* was answering, swinging round to an increasing angle across his starboard quarter, inch by inch. He felt *Sayonara* continuing to pull to port. But there was no doubt in his mind that they were going to crash. 'Stand by for collision,' he called. 'Captain Ito, sound the ship's alarm.'

Alarms began to sound right throughout the ship, but Richard hardly heard them. He was rapt in the finest calculations of velocity and angle, vector and impact, as though he were playing billiards with balls of unimaginable scale, and with a cue over which he had very limited control. *Zemlya*'s rear wall, a steel cliff reaching five decks straight up out of the sea, was coming round to an angle of maybe twenty degrees away from *Sayonara*'s course. And *Sayonara* herself was bearing further and further away. But it was all too little, too late. He closed his eyes.

The LNG tanker, moving at twenty-two knots, impacted with the nuclear power station, her starboard forequarter smashing against the wall that towered four more decks above it, as high as the ship's command bridge. The flare of the forecastle head buckled, screaming and juddering. The starboard anchor tore off and took several metres of chain with it before the force of the collision snapped the steel links and let the ruin fall. The whole starboard quarter of the forecastle head buckled and tore. The deck rose in waves that reared and froze. The starboard anchor winch broke free and rolled across the corrugated helipad until the port winch brought it up short. But the impact on the forecastle head soaked up the energy of the collision before it could do any serious damage to Moss tank number one. *Sayonara*'s head bounced off *Zemlya*'s back and the whole ship juddered round to port, pausing only to tear off the starboard bridge wing before she was clear. Then the engines stopped.

The loss of the starboard anchor tripped Macavity's carefully hidden impact trigger. Electrical impulses raced along the copper wires towards the detonator the Pitman found when she was exploring beneath the forward tank. Down the forward wall behind the bulbous bow they went like lightning along the wire, across the deck and down. Down to the open area beneath the massive downswell of the tank. And here they shorted, sparked and died. Because the detonator, like the bomb, had gone.

Richard stood, held erect only by his iron grip in the helm, looking over the rest of the bridge watch who were rolling like skittles across the deck, as his brain slowly registered that there would be no explosion resulting from the collision after all. Sometime during the collision his Galaxy had gone skittering across the engine room telegraph and he had caught it automatically without realizing. Suddenly it began to ring. The screen went blank. He hit reply, thinking it must be Robin. But no. 'Hello,' he said. 'Hello. Is there anybody there?' There was nothing on the screen or in the sudden massive silence around the ship. Except, perhaps, a distant flicker and a rumble as though thunder was threatening away to the east. Then Robin came through at last. 'You bloody man,' she said. 'Just look what your big rough boat has done to Anastasia's poor little power station!'

Richard was gasping as though he had just run a marathon. 'Look what her big rough power station's done to my poor little boat,' he croaked.

And she smiled, her eyes full of tears, her joyous expression filling the whole screen, and then some. 'Hello, sailor,' she said. 'Welcome home.'

The ocean-going gin palace that Richard had noticed earlier is called *Volante*. She sleeps ten passengers in palatial splendour, has berths for eight crew and she is Francisco Lazzaro's pride and joy. Since the typhoon, which *Volante* rode out safely in Sendai harbour, Lazzaro himself has captained her out to shadow *Sayonara* with only a two-man skeleton crew to help. The 'Ndrangheta chieftain has revelled in the challenge of watch-keeping and helming his pride and joy for two days and nights, in eight-hour rotations with the others. And it was Lazzaro, in fact, who was at the helm when *Sayonara*'s lifeboat came alongside and the pirates Richard simply knew as Macavity's men came aboard. Then, of course, Lazzaro had been happy to hand over command to the lieutenant from the South African navy. From being all-but deserted, *Volante* had become overfull, so crowded that even the wounded had to double bunk. Thus their kit remains in the twenty-four-seater lifeboat which remains secured to *Volante*'s stern. Because, Macavity has explained to his employer, if *Volante* is to shadow *Sayonara* to her final cataclysmic meeting with *Zemlya*, she will have to stay far out to sea, where a lifeboat this size might be the difference between life and death for so many men on board.

At the moment *Sayonara* and *Zemlya* come together, to the very second as plotted on Macavity's MTM military chrono-meter, he and Lazzaro are on *Volante*'s bridge, watching the western horizon for the blinding flash and mushroom cloud that will tell them their plans have come to fruition; that they are one hundred and twenty-five million dollars richer. That Bashnev/Sevmash and Heritage Mariner are theirs for the taking. That they are all made men. They already hold wide, flat glasses of Niccolo Rizziconi's Dom Perignon brought all the way from Moscow for the occasion, ready to toast their fortunes made. But something keeps the glasses from their lips. Darkness at the point where *Sayonara* and *Zemlya* have met. Darkness and silence.

But the second of convergence passes. And the next second. And the next. Lazzaro swings round to face his South African henchman. 'Something's wrong,' he snarls. Near-priceless champagne slops out of his glass like icy, golden tears.

The lieutenant blenches, despite his special forces training. When things go wrong in Lazzaro's world, people begin to meet lengthy and ugly deaths. That is why he put the insurance of the huge C4 device beneath tank number one. That is why he put in place a back-up in case the impact trigger behind the anchor failed. Ultimately, that is why he gave Richard Mariner his Galaxy back. 'Just a moment,' he says. 'The game's not over yet.' He takes out his cellphone. 'I can trigger it with this.'

'But they can trace the call, you fool,' snarls Lazzaro. 'Since Al-Qaeda started using cellphones as detonators, the companies log calls and alert the CIA and the NSA. It is one of the things that Snowden revealed before he vanished into Russia. They'll know it was you. And, through you, me!'

'I thought of that,' Macavity swears. 'This phone will contact Richard Mariner's Galaxy. When it does, it will switch on a programme I inserted myself. When he calls back, *he* will trigger my bomb beneath tank number one.' He speed-dials Richard's number and hears the Galaxy respond. 'Now!' he says. '*Kabloom!*'

And Richard indeed replies. The signal from the Galaxy streaks at the speed of light to the detonator beside the C4 explosive. But while Macavity, Richard and the teams under the pirates' guns were searching the chain lockers and the rest of *Sayonara* back to the engine spaces and beyond, the Pitman, Harry and Ivan were hidden in the one place Macavity dared not look – beneath his secret bomb. They used that time to disarm, dismantle and move it. And, under the Pitman's careful guidance, pack it aboard the lifeboat they knew they would use for their escape, filling the bilge beneath the removable decking with all of the C4. And the Pitman, being a fan of retribution, has replaced the cellphone detonator she found, purposely leaving it on.

So that the instant Richard replies, the detonator explodes, setting off the huge bomb. But not on board *Sayonara*: in her lifeboat, immediately below *Volante*'s stern. The lifeboat erupts into a ball of fire that towers a hundred feet in an instant, so powerful that it almost attains a mushroom shape. The blast tears *Volante* apart even before the flames can consume her. The explosion is so sudden that no one on board even realizes they are dying before they are dead. Even the speed-of-light communications of the cellphones is overcome. As Macavity, Lazzaro, *Volante* and all on board are blasted out of existence, Richard is still saying, 'Hello? Hello? Is anybody there?'

But no one is. Except, after an instant, Robin.

240 Hours After Impact

Little Rat Cay lies one hundred and twenty-five miles south-east of Nassau. On the northern side of the cay there is a white sand beach protected by Rat Cay proper, which sits little more than three hundred metres north-east across a deep-water channel called Rat Cay Pass. Behind the beach stand a couple of mahogany-walled huts which look like shanties roughly fashioned from the cascarilla and strong-back elder scrub that clothes the low hillock of the cay. The shanties are strengthened with timber from the coconut and banana palms that fringe the beach and roofed with their leaves. But the appearance is deceptive. Inside, the huts are havens of modern convenience, floored and walled with red cedar; fitted with stainless steel, marble and tile. Cookers are fuelled by gas canisters, as are the water heaters for basins and showers. Refrigerators, televisions, lights and the huge fans that turn lazily above massive, down-stuffed beds are powered by generators puffing discreetly in the brush; generators which also support the solar-powered distillation units that supply fresh water when the rainwater butts run low. The tallest and straightest by far among the palm trees is a disguised aerial, which receives and transmits as necessary, radio, TV, cellphone signals and wifi. The huts have wide verandas of Caribbean pine and candlewood and supporting hammocks woven from sisal; they look out over the flat white sand and the deep blue pass to the low green heave of Rat Cay.

At this time of year, the sun comes up out of the sea beyond

Blow Hole Cay on the horizon far to the east and sets behind
Brigantine Cay equally far away to the west. The sun set a
couple of hours ago in an orgy of red and gold and there is
a full moon rising above Alligator Beach on Cat Island, a hundred
kilometres distant due north across the calm, clear Caribbean.
The evening breeze smells of sea and tamarind, woodsmoke
and seafood. In the scrub behind the huts, frogs and cicadas
have begun to sing, beetles to stir and scuttle. The sky beyond
the bay is bright enough to show – jet black against opal and
ultramarine – flocks of birds returning to roost and columns of
bats whirling out to hunt above Rat Cay. Its gathering silvery
brightness is just beginning to outline the little Beechcraft
Bonanza A36 float plane that the Pitman piloted down here this
morning, where it bobs in the shallows of the bay.

Harry and the Pitman have made no use of the hobs or cookers
yet, though they've made much of the fridges and the showers.
They dived this afternoon, after unloading and unpacking. The
Pitman caught two lobsters and a grouper. These she has killed
and roasted in a fire pit on the beach, and she and Harry have
just consumed them with roast plantain from the palms and an
avocado salad purchased in the South Beach shopping centre
on their way to pick up the Beechcraft at Nassau airport this
morning. Harry has also sipped her way through a good deal
of Californian Murphy-Goode Sauvignon Fumé Blanc and is
on the tipsy side of utter relaxation. As the Pitman makes sure
the fire pit is safe, burying the lobster shells and fish bones in
preference to using garbage disposal or dishwasher, Harry
swings at ease in her hammock with her laptop lying across
her naked thighs. With access to any news service in the world,
she has settled on her hometown website, the *Boston Globe*.
She is lazily trawling through the Boston, American and World
News sections when she sees a familiar name and clicks on the
link. 'Hey, Angela, look at this. It says, *Heritage Mariner stock
rises on back of successful delivery of gas to Japan.*'

'Oh, yeah?' answers the Pitman. 'I thought there was going
to be a big investigation. It was a pretty near-miss after all.'

'Apparently not. I'll scroll down. Here it is.' Harry begins to
read, her tone lazy, throaty and low. '"The Japanese minister
for environment and power announced today that there is no

need to investigate the reported collision between the LNG gas transporter *Sayonara* and the floating nuclear power facility *Zemlya* any further. 'The impact was minor and caused no damage except to the vessels involved and that was slight,' Minister Takahashi said. 'Now that *Sayonara*'s cargo is safely in the NIPEX facility, the power supply to the floating city of Kujukuri has already been switched over to gas. *Zemlya* is on her way to her next assignment in the Kamchatka region of Russia, with the thanks of the entire Japanese nation for a job well done.' It is reported that *Sayonara* will resume her work after some refitting and extensive work on her on-board computers. In the meantime, she will proceed with a human crew. The owners of the two vessels, Heritage Mariner and Bashnev/Sevmash, have both seen their stock rise on exchanges worldwide since the announcement. Shares in both companies are trading at twice last week's price and seem set to rise further. The Mariner family, who are known to own a great deal of their own company stock, will have seen their personal wealth reach unprecedented heights, London analysts say. Madame Anastasia Asov, Chief Executive of Bashnev Oil and Power, announced in Moscow that this is a new dawn for her company. The Bashnev's second floating power station, *Zemlya II*, is due for launch later this year and there is already a waiting list for her services. Two more are on the way. Miss Asov is pictured making the official announcement en route to a reception at the Mariinski Theatre with her associates, Mr Ivan Yagula and Mr Felix Makarov. She is wearing the legendary dress designed by British designer Debbie Wingham. The black and red *abaya*-style outfit features a design in red diamonds and has an estimated value of eighteen million dollars.'"

'Hunh,' says the Pitman. 'Give me a good piece of hardware any day. Talking of which . . .'

'Wait,' Harry interrupts. 'There's another piece. "Canadian Authorities confirm that they have closed down a major organized crime ring centred around the Duisberg Reinsurance Company of Vancouver. A spokesman for the Combined Forces Special Enforcement Unit Integrated Gang Task Force of the Royal Canadian Mounted Police stated that Duisberg Reinsurance was a local expression of a worldwide threat. He told our reporter that the IGTF was in contact with authorities in Italy, Great Britain, Holland, Belgium and right across the old Soviet Union. Duisberg Reinsurance was a cover for Mafia-style dealings by the Calabrian 'Ndrangheta, he said. An upsurge in criminality, particularly in drug-smuggling, has centred round a man called Francisco Alberto Lazzaro, for whom an international arrest warrant has been issued. But, as is common under these circumstances, Lazzaro has dropped out of sight and is believed to be hiding somewhere in Calabria, though he was last seen on board his ocean-cruiser *Volante* which has also been reported missing in the North West Pacific, off the east coast of Japan.'''

'Do tell!' The Pitman chokes on a laugh. 'I'll bet he was with Macavity and the others when they got the surprise of their lives. The *final* surprise of their lives. Now come over here, lover. I have a new SBR I want you to see. It's got a custom-cut barrel with a stabilized inner, a Noveske rail and a Magpul CTR Stock. Come here and I'll show you how to field strip it.'''

'Oh put that stuff away and come over here, Angela,' says Harry, her voice still throaty as she closes her laptop and puts it aside. 'It's about time you stopped messing about with your boys' toys and started to field-strip *me*!'